DEDICATION

This book is dedicated to my mum, my sister Vanessa–my greatest supporter–and my long-suffering partner, Patrick. Thanks for putting up with me and for all the help you gave me.

CHAPTER 1

Legs freshly shaved, hair newly set, Maureen waited for Alan to come. Splashing out on *Company* magazine, she had followed the beauty tips exact instructions and plucked and sculptured her eyebrows. Despite the fortune spent on the trip into town to Boots, it had been worth it. She had even bought an all-over body mask. Naked, freezing and covered in the drying mud, she had stood like a statue for twenty minutes in her bathroom, scared she would get a mess on the carpet.

She spread the chequered blanket across the edge of the cornfield. The ground was hard, and bits of stubbly corn poked through the weave. It still felt perfect. Sandwiches had been lovingly made, and the crusts cut off. She had agonised over the choice of wine and had settled on Mateus Rosé. It lay chilling in the boot of her Mini. Stuffing the fridge's small ice compartment, she'd been determined it would be the right temperature. Having no ice bucket, she had improvised by rinsing out an old bucket from work. Even Mr Abraham, her regular cleaning job employer, had paid her early. The envelope of cash was still in her glove compartment, forgotten with the excitement.

He would be here soon. She lay down like a child under the oak tree. The corn, stretching for miles, offered seclusion. This was their special place. Everything was still, and insects crept up the stems of the corn. She watched them intently and enjoyed the heat on her body.

She sensed him long before she saw him. Then he was standing above her, his light-yellow jumper tied around his shoulders. He loosened it and then folded it neatly on the blanket.

"It's Lacoste." Alan prided himself on his looks and told her, "You have to buy quality."

Grey flecks had begun to speckle his hair, but it was still thick and flopped fashionably across his face. Sitting gingerly on the blanket, he was careful not to get dirt on his expensive Ralph Lauren beige trousers. He had bought them in Cambridge and had baulked at the exorbitant price tag.

Before he even greeted her, he tried to kiss her. His hands were in her hair, and he roughly pushed his hand inside her shirt and tugged at her bra strap.

"Alan, wait! I've got sandwiches…." She could hardly talk as he frantically pulled at her clothes. "And a bottle of wine."

"Later," he insisted.

"I've made a picnic. Please, I want to talk."

"Only got an hour before my next appointment."

"But we planned the whole afternoon. Alan, please."

As if to appease her, he cooed, "You look beautiful."

In her anticipation, she had imagined him appreciating the effort she had made on her appearance. She doubted he had even really noticed. He continued to paw at her while removing his clothes.

"Oh, you look so good."

Suddenly they became aware of raised voices coming closer. "Jesus Christ. Maureen, who is that?" Alan lay flat on the ground and pulled Maureen down. Straining above the corn, she tried to see who was making such a racket. "Get down!"

"Get off. I'm trying to see."

Above the line of the corn, she could make out two figures striding with purpose up the narrow lane. She recognised one of them. Everyone knew Tina Green; she was notorious in Trotham. Maureen had been intimidated by her on more than one occasion. She was one of the rough local bikers who hung around the bus shelter drinking cider and shouting at cars.

The other girl was much slighter than Tina. She wore light-blue dungarees, which billowed at the waist and white espadrilles. It was her hair that was most striking. Shaved at the back and long on top, it looked almost angular. Maureen immediately thought of the models in her magazine she had been poring over all week. Whoever that girl was, she was not local.

Alan continued to hold her down, and she pushed his clawing hands away.

"Trying to see."

"Maureen, for Christ's sake!"

The girls were quite close now, and Maureen could see and hear them well. Tina was shouting.

"Wait," Alan commanded.

"Get off." Maureen continued to try and loosen his grip.

The slight girl spun around and pushed her tormentor with such force that Tina fell. Her hands broke her fall, and Maureen could tell it was the unexpectedness of the push which had shocked her.

The smaller girl furiously continued to stride away. Picking the grit out of her palms, Tina got to her feet and ran after her. She continued walking. Grabbing her shoulder, Tina shouted, "Wait! What the fuck is up with you?"

"Why are you following me? You called me a stuck-up bitch yesterday."

Maureen's blue Mini was parked on the grass verge just ahead of them. It was a bright blue and contrasted with the brilliant yellow of the cornfield. The younger girl seemed to fix on it and quickened her step towards it.

"They've seen us!" Alan's voice was a panicked rasp.

He had scoped out their spot several times, checking visibility from all angles. Surely no one could see them. Sweat rolled down his back as they crouched and listened. Clenching Maureen's arm to the point she was in pain, he commanded her not to move.

"Get off, Alan! She's going towards my car. What are they doing?"

The smaller girl reached the Mini, and Maureen could see the anger on her face. She realised she had left the keys in the ignition, and worse still, the window was open. The girl furiously snatched the keys and raised her arm to hurl them into the field.

"Jesus. She's got my car keys." Maureen went to get up, but Alan pulled her down. She just managed to see Tina prise the keys from the other girl's hand and shout, "Get in!" Pushing the younger girl, she gestured to the passenger seat and repeated, "Get in."

Maureen broke free of Alan and charged through the corn towards her car. Pushing her way through a gap in the hedge, she winced as the branches cut and pulled at her bare arms. She came out the other side about twenty feet from the car.

"What are you doing? Give me my keys." The two girls looked at one another, shocked. Maureen realised she was virtually naked from the top. Her bra flapped around her shoulders, and twigs littered her hair. "I'll get the police on you, Tina Green."

Tina smirked, all the time keeping eye contact. Within seconds she was revving the engine and jolted away. It sped past Maureen, who tried to grab the door handle but only managed to slam her hand hard against the metal. She saw the face of the driver tense with concentration. Her passenger looked thunderous, staring straight ahead. Maureen watched her car hurtle past as it sped down the narrow lanes further away.

Making her way back, she started to cry. She painfully pushed her way back through the hedge and cried out as the branches tore and scratched her skin. Alan was furious.

"Jesus Christ! Don't tell me you parked near here. What possessed you?"

"Yes, but…."

"For God's sake. Don't you have any sense?"

"But I had sandwiches and Mateus Rosé. I needed to…."

"What the hell were you thinking? Now they've seen you…look at the state of you. Jesus." Maureen looked at Alan as he hastily put on his clothes. "They might have seen us. You know how careful we need to be. I'm married, for Christ's sake."

"The car…."

"If you report it," he leaned in, "say you lost it miles from here."

"I need to report it. I need my car. Can't work without it."

"You keep my name out of it. Do you understand?"

"I'm sorry," she whispered meekly.

Alan was not listening. He was hurriedly putting on his clothes. Despite leaving his socks on, he cut his foot on a sharp piece of flint.

"Jesus. This is a bloody mess."

Maureen felt sick. The day had been a disaster. How was she going to work without a car? It would be all over the village that she was semi-naked in a cornfield. Worse still had been Alan's reaction. She called after him, but he had already scuttled away.

CHAPTER 2

Mel's neck ached. She had been staring out of the window for nearly two hours, desperate to ignore her father. They had been in the stifling car without talking, and she was determined not to look at him. The countryside flew by in a single colour, flat, dull, field after field. Eventually, the road narrowed to a single lane. Hedgerows framed each side of the car, giving the impression she was in a tunnel. Mel was hot and felt like she could not breathe. She fingered the back of her neck. Her short, shaved hair was strangely comforting.

"Stop sulking, Mellie." She continued to stare out of the window. "It's only for six weeks."

"Only."

"You used to love Pauline...we've been through this."

Mel spun around. "You're always making fun of Aunty Pauline."

"Come on, that's not...."

"You hate her."

"Not true."

"What about the time she campaigned with a bunch of women about the lorry drivers who kept throwing pee out the window in lemonade bottles? They collected over fifty bottles on the A45. She got an award and the story in the local paper."

"Oh, come on."

"You stuck that picture of her clasping the bottle of wee on the fridge. You thought that was hilarious. You called her 'Pissy Pauline'."

The newspaper cutting of Pauline grinning and proudly displaying over fifty bottles of urine collected by the roadside had caused much laughter in their household. Even her mother had found it funny but had gently chastised her husband when Mel had been around.

"You hate her and Clive. You always have."

"That's not fair."

"You call her the Suffolk Dumpling."

"Well, she is short and stocky."

"You laugh at her clothes and think Clive is an idiot."

"Clive. We went to college together; we're just different."

"Yeah, why do you call him 'failure to thrive Clive'?" Mel raised her voice another decibel. "I've heard you."

"I went into the city. He's an academic. Pipe and slippers just wasn't for me."

Mel continued to sulk and thought back to her friends in school. She had been invited to Italy with Jennifer's family, the ultimate test of popularity. Every year 'the lucky' girls were chosen to go to her villa, and this year it was her turn. She had been thrilled. She had cried for two solid hours when she found out she couldn't go. Now she had to spend her summer holiday at her aunt's in the middle of nowhere. When her father broke the news, he had pulled a face and said he would make it up to her—God, how she hated him.

"Why can't you cancel your trip to Singapore? You don't care."

Julian sighed and resigned himself to the hostile atmosphere. He said nothing and lit a cigarette. Mel furiously opened the window and coughed. Her melodramatics were not lost on her father. Even to him, though, the smell of the smoke was almost overwhelming in the small confinement of the car. They continued in silence.

After ten minutes, Julian pulled the car over in Trotham.

"Got to get some fags."

Mel had been oblivious to the surroundings but realised they were in her aunt's village and outside a shop. The Mace local store was the only shop in the village, and a group of leather-clad teenage girls milled around the entrance as Mel climbed out of the car.

"Out of my way, ladies," Julian boomed and pushed his way through the door.

Mel followed behind and found her path blocked by the aggressive greaser girls. They were all in their heavy-metal uniform of jeans and band T-shirts. Mel had just had her hair cut in 'Gavin's', an expensive trendy salon—long on top and shaved at the back. The hairdresser had left enough hair for a single thin plait. The stylist was enthused about how ingenious it was to have the plait not in the middle but at the side. She had agonised over it, but it had proved a great decision. She had gained almost rock-star status among the girls at school. Even Jennifer had approved and told her she was very 'Kajagoogoo'. Mel had felt confident and fashionable. Now she felt ridiculous.

"What's that? A fucking dead rat's tail?" one of the girls hissed as she tugged at her hair. Mel thrust her head down and continued into the store. "Fucking weirdo." She heard the girls laughing.

"Want any sweets, Mellie?" asked her dad.

She picked up a Nutty Bar and a bottle of orange Fanta and threw them at her dad to pay. Grabbing them and not waiting for her father, Mel shoved her way past the intimidating girls and heard one of them mutter, "Stuck up bitch." She kept her head down and sat in the car. She bit all the peanuts off the Nutty Bar and sucked on the fudge.

This was the first time she had been invited to Jennifer's holiday villa, and instead, she was here. It looked like a foreign country. One of the greaser girls stuck two fingers up at her and pulled a face.

"Bet the locals around here have never seen a car like this."

"Yeah, why would they need a car? There's nothing here."

Julian surveyed his daughter; glad the journey was nearly at an end. Lighting a cigarette, he inhaled deeply. He had not been looking forward to this trip. Thank God it would all be over in a couple of hours. He would just have to endure a stodgy meal, stilted conversation, and then he could drive away. Taking a deep breath, he said as cheerfully as he could muster, "We're here. There's the Dumpling and Clive. Didn't take so long, did it?"

Mel could feel the rage build in her chest, making her hot. She glared at her father and followed him up the path to Pauline and Clive's cottage.

They were greeted at the door by Clive and Pauline, who Mel always felt looked like a dinner lady. Pauline stood beaming in her tunic apron over a coloured nylon blouse paired with an elasticated skirt. Her hairstyle, if you could call it that, had never changed—scraped back into a scruffy ponytail. Once black, it now had long strands of grey and white. In contrast, Clive had a slender frame and was dressed, as he always did, in his tweed trousers and long brown cardigan. They were an unlikely pair.

"Come in, come in. Are you too old to give your old aunty a kiss then?" Mel gave her a brief kiss on the cheek and followed her into the house. "Cawd der hell, hint she grown? You're taller than me now, gal."

Mel never really knew what "*Cawd der hell*" meant. It was a strange Suffolk saying, and her aunt used it when she was exclaiming about anything.

Clive stood by the door and shook Julian's hand.

"Looking lovely as ever, Pauline."

The sarcasm enraged Clive. He hated that Julian dismissed his wife, demeaned her clothes and made fun of her accent. He had known him when they had started at Cambridge together. Everything he despised about Cambridge University, Julian had embraced. The sense of entitlement and arrogance. His sister had been impressed by his confidence and swagger, coming as they both did from bookish parents who shunned company. They marvelled at those for whom social situations held no fear, but Clive saw cruelty in Julian that his sister was always blind to.

Once inside, Mel dropped down onto the brown draylon settee. Lace doilies were placed over the arms to protect them. The house was so much smaller than she had remembered. Compared to their modern London apartment, it felt like she had stepped back into another century. Every conceivable corner was stuffed with antiques and cheap China ornaments.

Old, worn, flock wallpaper adorned the walls. Mel did, however, like the ancient inglenook fireplace with the original meat hooks hanging on either side. As a child, Clive would tell her stories of how people would cook on the open flame and showed her the footholds where children would be sent up to clean it. It now housed a heavy grate decorated with a dusty corn dolly.

Julian went out to the car and produced a bottle of Blue Nun. "For the worker," he said, passing the bottle to Pauline.

"Oh, thank ya...do you want me to open it now?" Pauline asked.

"Love to but got to make some phone calls later. Better be on top form." Clive raised his eyebrows. Pauline continued to busy herself with her shepherd's pie. It was a heavy dish, and she slammed it on the table. Julian grinned. "Looks delicious, Pauline."

"Good, well, I hope you like it. Come on, girl. I've made your favourite," Pauline almost sang in her broad Suffolk tongue.

"Not hungry," was the sullen reply.

"Don't be rude, Melanie."

"I've just eaten a Nutty Bar, so I'm not hungry. Perhaps you should have stopped me eating it, but that would involve caring about my welfare, wouldn't it, Dad?"

"That's enough, Mel. If you will excuse us, I need to remind my daughter of some manners." He led her into the lounge. "For Christ's sake, Mel, don't you think I would take you to Singapore if I could? It's hard for me too, you know, with your mum out of sorts. Come on, give your dad a hug."

She reluctantly allowed him to hug her, and they returned to the dining room. She silently sat down on the heavy wooden chairs.

Mel picked at her food while Julian ate his with gusto.

"So delicious, Pauline. You've excelled yourself," said Julian.

"Salt?" offered Clive.

"Oh no, I understand that it's bad for you."

"Whereas smoking is ok, is it Julian?"

The two men glared at each other.

"You are right as ever, Clive. Always the intellect." Julian scanned the room and noticed the budgie cage. "What's the budgie called, Pauline? Is it a new addition to the family?"

"Oh, that's my Diane."

"Diane!" Julian nearly spat his food out. "That's an interesting name for a budgie."

Clive noticed him wink at Mel, but she only returned a stony glare. Clive tuned out of the forced chatter at the table as he became consumed with an intense feeling of hatred for Julian. He had never seen Pauline as Julian had, and it incensed him that he was in their house making fun of her.

Clive had come to Trotham as a tired PhD student trying to find isolation and reconnect with his thesis. Pauline had knocked on his door and somehow bustled her way in. She was trying to get a speaker for the library and had heard he was studying history. The chasm between him standing up and speaking and reality had eluded her. Her enthusiasm and chatter made him instantly like her, and they were soon sharing a pot of tea. After she had gone, she had left a warmth that he couldn't fathom. He was delighted when she popped around to see if he had changed his mind about the talk.

Regular tea invites were replaced by a trip to Grimes Graves, a Neolithic flint mine. She had marvelled at the strange, pocked landscape where ancient miners had dug out the precious flint. It was almost like a moonscape, incongruous against the forest and rolling fields. Clive smiled as he remembered how he tried to impress her with his knowledge.

'Worked between 2200 and 2500 years ago there were over 350 hollows. It was named after the Anglo Saxon God, Grim, and of course, Graves means hollow.' He looked at her. Her love of history wasn't intellectual. She felt it; the people were real to her. Pauline

imagined the scene when the site had been industrial, and she began to talk of a great uncle who, as a child, had scraped a living flint picking. 'But that was just from the fields so the farmers could plough. Knapping earnt more, but many of them died young.' The skilled knapping industry had been massive in East Anglia for many centuries, especially for flints for guns. But the dust from the process had proved deadly to many.

They sat in silence, eating tuna sandwiches and drinking warm cola. Clive had laughed at her tartan sandwich tin but was surprisingly hungry.

'Do you think those ancient miners ate their lunch up here?' Pauline asked, and Clive contemplated the question.

'As no animal bones have been found in the pits, apart from antlers, which were the main digging tools, then probably yes. The miners would have come out to sunlight to eat, but not tuna sandwiches,' he laughed.

'How wonderful to think that all those years ago, about 2000 people sat here, eating, like you and me.' They were both caught up in the enormity of the thought. Clive grasped her hand and felt wonderfully connected to her.

Later that day, they had galloped down the precarious ladders, and she listened to every morsel of information that Clive had. In the following weeks, Clive would spend hours discussing his theories, and she would always listen. He knew she wasn't feigning interest, and as she smiled and encouraged, he became more animated. Trotham hadn't given him the reconnection he needed, Pauline had.

"Clive ...Clive." He suddenly became aware they were calling his name. Pauline smiled. "Reckon you were miles away."

"Sorry, I just remembered something I was meant to do."

"Oh, Clive, always got your head in that thesis. What Anglo Saxon burial site are you working on this month?" said Julian. Clive narrowed his eyes and looked at him.

"Oh, I don't think you would be interested, Julian."

Mel stood up and announced, "Need the loo."

She strode upstairs and slunk into the bathroom, grateful for the reprieve. It looked so much smaller and more dated than she remembered. It still had the picture above the bath of the plump girl with the words *Please remember, don't forget, never leave the bathroom wet.* As a child, she loved the rhyme. There was an old, dusty, blue bottle of Matey. Aunty Pauline had always made sure she had bubble bath, and she would spend hours making bubble clothes. Her mother would always exclaim that she would be a famous clothes designer and wrap her in warm towels. She would then be carried downstairs for hot cocoa and be allowed to stay up late.

Now the bathroom seemed worn and tired. The tiles were coming off the wall and the pink, knitted toilet roll holder, with the doll placed inside the roll, looked grotesque and faded. She threw it back on top of the cistern.

Mel imagined Jennifer's bathroom in her Italian villa—probably marble with a sea view. Thank God none of her friends could see her now. She sat on the toilet, not wanting to move until Pauline knocked on the door.

"You all right, gal?" asked Pauline.

"Yes, fine."

Mel eventually came down the stairs to find Julian busying himself to leave.

"Thanks for the great hospitality. I won't have to eat for a week." He hugged Pauline and shook Clive's hand. "Come on, Mellie, give your old dad a smile."

"Bye, then." Mel felt another surge of fury.

They all watched as he drove away, accelerating and beeping. Clive exchanged looks with Pauline, who grasped Mel's hand.

"Your suitcase is in your room. Perhaps you'd like a bit of time to settle in," Pauline suggested.

Her room felt even more dated. Two beds were crammed into the room with matching pink draylon covers. Mel looked at the blankets. It had been an age since she had slept under them. Everyone now had continental quilts. Again, the room looked so much smaller with the dark heavy wardrobe and dressing table adorned with cuddly toys from her childhood.

Mel picked one up and studied it. It was an orange gonk,

and as she smoothed down its hair, she remembered how she had won it on Felixstowe pier with her mum. Remembering how she had slept with it every night, she placed it gently on her pillow.

Pauline appeared at the door.

"Want some cocoa? Top of the Pops is on."

Mel managed a nod and followed her downstairs. The nylon settee felt familiar, and for half an hour, she watched the telly. John Peel introduced Culture Club, who sang 'Do You Really Want to Hurt Me?'

"That's a chap, is it?" Mel laughed at Clive's reaction as he tried to stifle his confusion.

"He lives around here, you know," said Pauline.

"Who?" asked Mel.

"John Peel." Mel was amazed that Pauline knew his name. "He buys eggs off Doreen's farm."

Mel was delighted that he lived nearby. At night, she would listen to John Peel sessions and memorise the names of the obscure bands. Quite often, she was tired, but she needed to be trendy to impress the girls at school. Mel lay back. She enjoyed the programme and momentarily forgot about being stranded in Suffolk.

"Aunty Pauline, is it ok if I go for a walk? I've been in the car all day."

"Yes, but there hint much to see."

"Understatement of the bloody year," Mel muttered under her breath.

"That's getting a bit dark, so don't be on the drag."

Once outside, the air made her feel slightly better. She wandered up the linear street, walked over the bridge, passed the local pub and up to the old Almshouses, set somewhat back from the road.

The flash of a cigarette caught her eye, and she strained her eyes to make out the figure. It was the rough girl who had aggressively pulled her ponytail outside the shop. She was sitting on the porch staring across the road, but Mel had the feeling she had not noticed her. An older man came out and snatched the cigarette out of her mouth. He puffed on it and then roughly pushed the younger woman inside. The force of his hand caused the girl to trip, and she banged her head on the door. Mel could hear the man laughing.

Something was unsettling about it. Mel turned away and convinced herself it was just a teenager who had been caught smoking and was getting a telling off. Strange that she would do it on the porch. When Mel had stolen cigarettes from her dad, she had walked for a mile before she lit up behind a kebab shop. It had been such an unpleasant experience she had never bothered again. Mel glanced back at the house, but both the girl and the man were inside.

She carried on towards the church and then turned

around. The walk had wasted a good half an hour. A quick cup of cocoa, then she could legitimately ask to go to bed without offending her hosts. She glanced back towards the house where the girl had been sitting. She had gone, but she couldn't get her out of her mind.

CHAPTER 3

Pauline wrapped the striped towel around her wet shoulders. The sun had not quite risen enough to warm the bathroom, and she felt cold. Clive and Mel were still asleep. Keen not to wake them, she tiptoed on the lino floor. She loved the quiet of the morning space to daydream and plan her day. Some of Mel's toiletries, including moisturisers, henna shampoo, and Clearasil spot cream, perched precariously on the bath. She had never bothered with lotions and potions like Alice, Mel's mother, had. Soap and water had always seemed sufficient. Looking at her lined face, she wondered what she might have looked like if she had prioritised her appearance. Her eyes, once a brilliant blue, were now clouded with age and skin tags hung from her neck. She had never shaped her eyebrows, and her chin had begun to sprout uncomfortable hairs. One hair, in particular, spiked out coarsely, and she had named it her 'pig hair'. It was the only one she regularly removed with tweezers.

Julian always made her feel inadequate. She knew that

he laughed at her behind her back. Clive always told her to ignore him, but occasionally, doubt entered her head. Her husband could have done so much better than her. She was, after all, just a local girl who had rarely travelled further than Cambridge, and he had been to university. His family had been unsurprisingly disapproving of their courtship. His mother had called her that 'bloody farm labourer', and Clive had tried to hide it from her, but she had overheard. She was now long dead, but throughout their long marriage, she had appeared fleetingly at weddings and christenings, reduced to a phantom, like a malevolent spirit in the background of their lives. Clive had always put Pauline first.

"If my mother had cared that much about me, she wouldn't have sent me off to public school at the age of five."

Pauline could not imagine the trauma that must have instilled in such a young child. Clive rarely spoke of his schooldays, but she had gleaned enough to know he had hated his enforced exile. His upbringing had been cultured but cold.

She rubbed some Pond's cream onto her hands and chastised herself for not brushing her hair first. Wiping the cream off with some toilet roll, she looked again at the aged face in the mirror.

"Old fool."

Reminding herself that jobs needed doing, the day was running away. She went outside to feed the chickens.

Mel sat in the outside toilet on the old wooden seat. It was attached to the pantry, where three pheasants hung in a row, and a marrow was strung up in a pair of American tan tights, dripping a clear liquid into a bowl. Clive had told her it was an ancient way of making alcohol. The marrow had been stuffed with sugar, fermented and turned into raw alcohol.

"More like paint stripper," joked Clive and winked. He continued to say that's how prehistoric men had first made it, and it was research for his thesis. She hadn't believed him as it was next to the numerous demijohns making all manner of homemade wine using quince, elderflower, and potatoes. Clive had conspiratorially whispered that no one ever drank the wine. Pauline just enjoyed making it, and she would hand it out at various fetes and bazaars.

Mel felt guilty. It was not their fault they were saddled with her. They were doing their best, but she wasn't seven anymore. Pauline meant well, but she had become increasingly irritated by the constant, *'You all right, gal?'*.

Despite the dust and spiders, the outside toilet gave her a bit of peace. She didn't like going to the toilet inside as she felt Clive and Pauline could hear. It was the same at school—she wanted privacy. The walls, like every other space in the house, had various bags hanging off them, which were stuffed with tools, plastic sandwich boxes, and cleaning fluids.

The flaking-paint wooden door had a large gap underneath where it had rotted away and a chicken suddenly stuck its head through. Its scrawny head rotated as it tried to force its body underneath the gap. She shooed it away. Repulsed and slightly shocked, she could hear Pauline outside trying to catch the chickens. They had come from the Saputos' next door.

"Get here, you little...." Her strong, fat hand reached under the door and grabbed the chicken. "Got ya!"

Mel was struck by how capable Pauline was. Her own mother's hands were slender and beautiful, but Pauline's were rough. Her nails were never painted, and the skin was chapped, split and sore. She listened to Pauline talking to Mr Saputo about his chickens.

"That's a bugger, that one. That must get out about four times a week," she said.

Mr Saputo held the chicken close to his chest. He still had a strong Italian accent which intrigued Mel, given they were miles from civilisation.

"I think you need to go in the pot, naughty girl," he teased.

They both laughed, and Mr Saputo apologised and offered her some eggs. Pauline said there was no need, and they joked that the chicken would be renamed Houdini.

Mel stayed in the toilet until everyone had gone. She regretted she hadn't brought the soft toilet roll from inside as there was only the roll of thick tracing paper with '*Government property*' scrawled across it. Only Pauline would have something weird like that, but then again, there were three dead pheasants on the other side of the wall.

Mel suddenly became aware that she could hear raised voices and strained to hear. Surprisingly, it was Clive. He was the most softly spoken person she had ever heard, so it seemed strange. Mel was sure they were talking about her. She quickly pulled up her trousers and slipped into the house. She could hear Clive trying to retain his temper.

"That bastard! That bloody bastard!"

Mel tried to hear more but only managed to catch the odd word. Anxiety flooded her stomach, and she knew they were talking about her dad. She could just make out a few words and tell Clive was agitated. She crept nearer and concealed herself behind the door. Clive's voice, normally so soft and warm, was hard.

"That bastard! Hasn't he done enough?"

"What'd he say? Sure you heard right?"

"Oh, he made himself clear." Mel stood incredibly still. She felt her chest tighten as she silently waited. "He can't stand the strain of the two families, financially or logistically. Mel's the eldest of the kids. Apparently, she needs to live with us until Alice can be a mum to her again."

"That poor girl. She thinks…."

"Singapore, my arse...playing happy families."

"With his other family."

The enormity of what had just been said gripped Mel. She couldn't breathe. Her heart was pounding, and she had to get out. Knocking over the kitchen chair, she ran into the garden, slamming into the wall. Clutching her chest, she ran away from the house as fast as she could.

Clive and Pauline looked at each other, realising they had been overheard. Clive went to rush after Mel, but Pauline grabbed his arm.

"Let the girl go. She needs a bit of time. There hint no talk that will repair that." Clive nodded and held his wife's hand.

Mel ran as fast as she could up the road, only stopping once she had reached the river. She couldn't breathe. The pain in her chest was too great, and she stopped at the grass verge and sat down.

Thoughts rushed around her head. She had to keep moving. Running up the main street, the words she had heard about her father's other family replayed endlessly. She was out of breath and stopped opposite the shop. Tripping on the raised pavement, she fell on a small patch of yellow grass. Slumping down, she rested her head on her knees and stared at the scorched grass. She could hear her breathing returning to normal, but the pain in her chest felt as intense.

A hand brushed her shoulder. Fully expecting to see Pauline, she was shocked when the person leering over her was the girl from the shop.

"What's up with you?" Mel ignored her. "Where's your posh car?" Mel glared at her and told her to go away. "Too good to speak to me, are you?"

Mel spun around and stared at her tormentor. "Just fuck off!"

The words had shocked her, but she was so angry that she was incapable of any other response. The other girl looked slightly taken aback but mainly amused.

"Why you so riled?"

Mel got up and started walking away from her.

"Leave me...."

"Alone." The older girl mocked her. "Why? Are you going to cry?" The girl continued to follow her. Mel began to run. Sweat poured down her neck and to the base of her lower back. Still, she ran, but she could not shake her. "You hint getting away from me."

By now, they were on the outskirts of the village. Mel continued to charge ahead. They had covered some distance when Mel began to tire. She looked behind her, and the dark-haired girl was still in pursuit. Her legs hurt and she felt suddenly exhausted. The other girl was gaining. Anger surged in her chest, a physical pain, and the sensation slightly shocked her. She carried on striding forward, but the older girl caught up and grabbed Mel by the shoulder, pulling her back. Mel was dragged to a violent halt.

"Get off!" she screamed into the girl's face.

As the girl pushed her face up close, Mel could see her black-rimmed eyes and smell the distinct stench of cigarettes. She looked at the girl, and without warning, Mel pushed her. The surprising ferocity of the shove caused her to crash to the ground while Mel stood back and stared. The fall had been painful and unexpected. There was a moment of silence as they comprehended what had happened. The older girl felt the rings on her hand cut painfully into her skin, and a raw graze began to bleed down her arm. She was momentarily stunned while Mel continued to walk away.

"Just leave me alone."

But the other girl picked herself up and continued to follow her. Mel expected at any moment to have a crack on her head, or worse. But she didn't turn around, and she could vaguely hear the roaring behind her and span around.

"Bloody bitch!" While there was violence in her eyes, she did not attempt to follow through with any physical reprisal.

Mel turned and continued to walk, but this seemed to incense the girl who continued to shout expletives at her, but Mel was numb. Her heart, pounding almost audibly, had calmed, and she felt an overriding sense of exhaustion. In a way, she had preferred the anger.

Her mind began to race with questions that she already knew the answer to. So, her father had been having an affair. But worse, he had another family. He wasn't in Singapore at all. It had all been a massive lie. Her eyes were burning, and she had a sharp pain behind her right ear.

By now, the two girls were a good mile outside the

village. They had veered away from the main road and were surrounded by fields. The Anglo-Saxon roads were so ancient that they were below the line of the field, and the corn towered over them on either side. They rounded a corner and saw a brilliant-blue Mini parked up against the verge. There was no one in sight, and it looked strange, contrasting in colour to the corn.

Not sure of what she was about to do, Mel charged up to the car. The driver's window was open, and the keys, on a small, plastic, pink Pierrot keyring, were in the ignition. She reached her hand in and pulled them out. They felt weighty in her hand. She stared at them, amazed at her audacity, and then pulled her arm back to hurl them into the cornfield. But just as she was about to release them, the older girl knocked them from her grasp. To Mel's surprise, she was laughing.

"Got a better idea." The girl opened the door and sat in the driver's seat. Mel stared at her blankly as she patted the seat next to her. "Get in." She opened the door. Mel stared at her blankly. "Get in!"

Mel suddenly saw a woman hurtling through the hedge. She was wildly flaying her arms about and shouting for them to stop. Twigs littered her hair, and she was in a state of undress. The shock momentarily made her unable to move. She looked at the other girl who was laughing. Mel panicked and grabbed the chrome handle. The wild woman was nearly upon them.

Before she could think, she was sitting in the passenger seat. The other girl had started the engine, and they were soon careering down the road. The woman made a desperate bid to open the door, and Mel could hear her palms banging on the roof, but she merely crashed against the side of the car, making them both jump.

"Fucking hell…Maureen Hubbard." The driver grinned at Mel. "Love to know what she was up to." Mel looked at the girl next to her; she was grinning. "Where shall we go?"

CHAPTER 4

Maureen followed Alan. He was now a distant speck, hiding behind trees and scrubs in his eagerness to escape her. Her eyes rested on the picnic blanket which lay crumpled by her feet—all that planning and anticipation, she had never expected it to end like this.

In a daze, she folded the blanket and started to walk. Alan's instructions had been very clear. She was to walk three miles to the next village and get the bus. No one was to know or find out about their liaison. She felt a fool and, in a moment of rage, hurled the blanket into the hedge.

An hour passed, and she continued to trudge on. The sun was fierce, and she could feel it scalding her neck. She had nothing to protect it, and her feet ached. Endless thoughts rushed in her head as she tried to make sense of what had happened.

"Old fool...idiot," she muttered to herself.

She faintly heard a beep and spun around, expecting to see Alan. Her face fell as she realised it was Eric Turner, the local garage owner. He pulled alongside.

"What are you doing all the way out here?" he asked.

She managed some elaborate lie about her varicose veins and having to walk three miles every day. She had read something about it in the expensive magazine she had bought for beauty tips.

"But I could do with a lift." Eric looked at the dishevelled woman. He had always had a soft spot for Maureen and allowed her to jump in.

"You need to put something on that neck, Maureen. You've burnt yourself good." Maureen felt the raw sunburn on her neck and above her cleavage, and she dabbed it with her finger and winced. "Teabags and cucumber, that'll cure it. Me ole mum, she swore by that."

Maureen's mind was racing. While she was aware she was being spoken to, his words seemed muted.

"What?"

"Teabags! Who'd have thought it? Never used it myself, mind, as I always wear a hat."

Maureen's mind raced, and she was only half aware of the inane chatter coming from Eric. Soon they were at her house, and Eric waved her goodbye and sped off.

Thirsty and hot, she made a beeline for the kitchen. The

crusts of the sandwiches she had so lovingly made were strewn across the tabletop. In her haste, she had left the butter out, and the whole place was swarming with ants. Her eyes were drawn to a red ant, and she was instantly repulsed. She couldn't deal with it right now. She snatched the nearest glass from the kitchen counter and filled it with water from the tap. Clutching the glass of water, she walked to her bedroom and collapsed on the bed. Too tired to move or undress, she stared at the Artex swirls on the ceiling.

She was unsure how long she stayed in bed. Each movement sent a searing pain across her neck. The sunburn felt sore, and her head pounded. Sitting up, she caught her appearance in the mirror—an old, middle-aged woman dressed as mutton. Gasping down the last of the water, she tried to move. Convinced there was heat emanating from her front and neck, she splashed on drops of water. The red tide mark was glaring at her and reminded her of when she was a child and had tipped a kettle of hot water over herself. Her mother had run a tap on her leg for a good half an hour. She wanted her mother now. It had been five long years since she had passed, and she missed her terribly. Never having married, she had neither children nor a partner. She berated herself and lay back down.

An hour passed and she eventually got up. Wandering into the hallway, she noticed a package had been stuffed through the front door. It was in a brown paper bag with a note attached. Perhaps it was from Alan—a gift or an apology. Her spirits momentarily rose, and she dashed to retrieve it. Sitting on the settee, she steadied herself and hastily opened the note. *'Thought you might need these. Eric.'*

Inside were two small knobbly cucumbers. She threw them on the floor.

"Damn Alan!"

The cucumbers had rolled under the settee. She almost laughed. She had meant to put cucumbers on her eyes before she met Alan. Trying to block him from her mind, she went back to the kitchen. The ants were still swarming across the surfaces, and she felt powerless. The thought of washing a cup and making tea was too much, so she filled a glass with water and headed back to bed.

CHAPTER 5

Mel sat silently in the car next to the girl who, moments earlier, she had pushed. She turned and looked at her.

"What's your name?" asked Mel.

"Tina," said the girl.

"Mel."

They continued to drive in silence while Tina thrashed the Mini, crunching the gears and over-revving. The ancient Suffolk roads were winding and flanked on each side by hedges. Every bend was blind and wide enough for only one car. Tina manically honked the horn at every corner but did not slow down. She accidentally oversteered, and the edge of the hedge scraped along the side of the car. Several branches flew in, hitting Mel and tangling in her hair. They both laughed in shock. The second time she did it on purpose as they pinballed against the hedges, scraping the paintwork. Faster and faster, they screeched around the winding Suffolk roads. The girls felt exhilarated, the noise of the engine drowning out their laughter. With the ferocity of the swerving, the glove compartment fell open, revealing a Neil Diamond tape, cigarettes, a half-eaten packet of Pacers, and a white envelope. Mel opened it.

"Bloody hell. There must be £15 quid in here."

"Thank you, Maureen. We will have that! Now give me a fag."

Mel fumbled to open the packet, but she made a terrible hash of it as her hands were hot and clammy. In the end, she cut the cellophane with her teeth.

"Come on. I'm gasping." Tina grabbed one and put it in her mouth. "Lighter. Get me a lighter. Matches?" Mel found a yellow lighter and, after three attempts, managed to get a flame. Tina leant over dangerously, taking her eyes off the road. "Bloody hell, I hate menthol."

She continued to drag on it but screwed up her face. Mel opened the Pacers, throwing away the first one as it was covered in dust. Inspecting the green and white stripes of the next, she carefully picked off a fleck, and once she was satisfied, she put it in her mouth. Although she was thirsty, the mint taste only slightly moistened her mouth.

Her anger began to ebb away, and she could feel where her shoulders had been clenching. Her chest still felt constricted, but she was able to breathe. The overwhelming sensation was thirst—her mouth was so dry. She frantically rummaged around for something to drink, and upon finding a bottle of Orangina, she sighed with relief. It may have been opened already, but she did not care. Like the Pacers, it was covered in dust. Holding up the bright orange liquid, she could see the dirty sediment swirling around the base of the bottle. She took a swig. It was warm, and the sugar burnt her throat, making her gag. She suddenly felt tired as the rage of the last hour subsided, leaving her with nothing but exhaustion. Her mind began to think about what she had done.

"Fuck them all," she muttered to herself. Tina looked at her and grinned. "You're a rum one, you know." Tina looked her up and down. "Sandra Cook was the last person to hit me, and she ended up with a broken arm." They drove in silence for a good ten minutes down narrower lanes.

Mel studied Tina properly for the first time. Her nails were bitten but still painted with red nail varnish, although much had worn away. Her fat fingers, adorned with heavy metal rings, some decorated with skulls, clutched the steering wheel. Mel stared at them and combined with the chipped polish, found them slightly grotesque. Tina's hair was brushed into a flick, lacquered hard, and it fell continually into her heavily kohled eyes. She was what Jennifer Hawshore would call a 'greaser'.

Suddenly Tina screeched the car to a halt against the grass verge of the country lane.

"Need a piss." Before Mel could fathom what Tina was doing, she had squatted at the side of the road. Embarrassed, Mel looked away. "That's bloody better," Tina said as she hurriedly pulled up her jeans and gestured to Mel. "Now pass me those fags." Taking a long puff, she exhaled deeply. "Not sure where the hell we are. Let's keep going."

Mel felt numb. She didn't want to go back but had no idea where they were going. She was slightly alarmed by the rather stocky rough girl who was her companion. She had the same build as Aunty Pauline and was what her dad would have called another *'Suffolk dumpling'.* The thought of her father made her body tense, and she felt the ache in her chest.

They came to a crossroads and looked at each other blankly. Tina pulled the car to the right.

"Let's follow the road. Can't remember how we got here anyway." Tina looked at Mel and laughed. "They're not going to miss me, but you're going to give your aunt a right fright."

"Don't care," Mel snapped.

Tina looked at her. "She's all right, you know."

"Mind your own bloody business!" Mel shouted, and the ferocity of her response surprised her. Tina laughed and held up her hands.

"All right, all right. I'll just keep going."

"Do that."

They carried on in silence with the hedgerows whizzing past in a haze. The windows were down, but the temperature in the car continued to rise. Mel despised the endless narrow roads and cornfields interspersed with the odd tree.

"Where are all the houses?"

"You're in the bluudy country now," Tina replied in her strange Suffolk brogue.

They looked straight ahead and maintained their silence. Mel wasn't sure how long they stayed that way, but the scenery continued to rush by and time with it. Finally, they reached a T-junction with an old back and white sign, *Sealtdock 2 ½ miles*. It was the first sign they had seen, and Tina headed for it.

Nearer to the coast, the scenery began to change. Claustrophobic, ancient Saxon roads, which dipped so low you could hardly see the corn over the hedge, were replaced by barren heathland. Swirling dust devils danced quickly across the landscape like spectres. Dust and sand blew onto the road in front of them and covered the windscreen. Purple heather covered large areas of ground and, in between, bracken grew in abundance.

Tina fumbled with the levers until she found the screen wash. The wipers only smeared the sandy grime across the glass, and she struggled to see. Mel felt like she was in another country. Thin tributary rivers crisscrossed the landscape, and she could taste the sea in her mouth. They drove for another fifteen minutes, and, eventually, a wide expanse of the sea came into sight—bright blue, it hardly looked real. Its vastness momentarily took their breath away.

"Cawd der hell," Tina exclaimed.

The road widened, and they found their view blocked by a row of houses, which soon gave way to even larger homes. They caught the occasional glimpse of the sea between the buildings, which momentarily lifted their spirits. Mel enjoyed the contrast to the endless fields of corn. It somehow gave her a lift.

Holidaymakers were getting out of cars laden with suitcases. Various tourist shops lined their route. Tina headed for the seafront and followed the promenade. It was only a small town, but it had numerous shops selling buckets and spades and ice creams. The road soon narrowed, and they began to move away from the centre. The sea flanked the narrow road on one side and mudflats on the other. The sand on their right had been hardened by the sun and then washed by the incoming tide.

"Can't we go back to civilisation?" asked Mel.

"Are you bloody driving?" Tina noticed the fuel dial on the car was on red, and the emergency light was on. "Shit, we've got no petrol."

As Tina was banging the dial, they came across Sealtdock Holiday Park, where an old wooden sign welcomed them in as they drove through the gate. The sign had seen better days and looked like it might fall at any time.

"We might be able to get some petrol," said Tina.

Mel began to worry. Until now, it had been a game, but

now she was stranded with this strange aggressive girl, in the middle of nowhere, and no way of getting back home.

CHAPTER 6

Following the road, they passed the tents and reached the expanse of caravans. There were about twenty of them in various sizes. People busied themselves, hanging up washing and lighting barbecues. Tina managed to pull the car behind the row of caravans before it spluttered to a halt, and they got out.

"That's had it," said Tina. Mel's legs felt stiff, and her jeans stuck to them with sweat. She was desperate for the toilet, and Tina looked at her as if reading her mind. "Dying for a wazz?" They abandoned the car, and Mel followed the signpost for the toilet block.

The concrete toilet block was surprisingly large, with six separate stalls. Several of the doors hung precariously on their hinges, and only a few had workable locks or seats. Water dripped from pipes, the taps were caked with limescale, the floor ran with water, and the whole place stank of ammonia and damp. Mel checked every cubicle, trying to choose the cleanest. She placed the tissue she had in her pocket on the seat before sitting down. In contrast, Tina rushed into the nearest one and had no qualms about the lack of a seat. Mel could hear the gush of urine and felt embarrassed.

"Oh, bursting," Tina said with relief.

Tina slammed the toilet door and made her way over to the grimy sink and, to Mel's surprise, pulled off her T-shirt. She washed her face in cold water and splashed some under her arms. She then took the T-shirt, dried herself and put it back on.

"That'll soon dry," said Tina as she left the toilet block, leaving Mel looking shocked.

Mel soon made her way back to the car and saw Tina was not there. She scanned the site for her and eventually saw her at the far end of the park. Tina was smoking a cigarette and inspecting one of the caravans. It had no one in it and looked like it had been empty for years. She gestured for her to come.

At first, Mel faltered. The caravan in front of her looked like something from a 1950s postcard. Tina tried to peek inside but could not see past the faded, lurid orange curtains. The body of the tiny caravan was black with grime, and the window frames, green with mould, were rimmed with black ingrained dirt.

"Tina, what are you doing?"

Tina prised open the door. It took little effort, and they were both surprised how easily it gave way. The door swung open, and an overpowering, musty smell hit them. Tina grinned at Mel.

"Come on."

"Shit, Tina. You can't just break in."

Tina walked in and looked around. Everything was dusty but had once been loved. There was a little table with two seats on either side, a tiny kitchenette area, and a large pile of *Radio Times.* Mel followed, hoping that no one had seen. At least inside they would be hidden from prying eyes. Tina began to rummage through the drawers and cupboards.

"Little bedroom in here."

"Tina, we can't be in here," said Mel. Caught up in what she had found, Tina ignored her.

"Look, it's got saucepans, cups and cutlery."

There was a half-bottle of Cusson's shampoo, some congealed Shield soap, and something that had once been washing-up liquid. Mel felt incredibly uncomfortable.

"Tina, this is breaking in."

Mel heard a noise and an old man walked into the caravan. Noticing his lined face, she was also distracted by the large set of keys dangling from his waist. Mel froze. When he spoke, his voice was broad Suffolk and hard.

"Hold yew hard. What you girls doing with Mrs Cooper's caravan?"

Mel felt the anxiety sear in her chest. Tina turned around and looked straight at the man.

"I'm her niece. Asked us to clean it, didn't she?" Tina pointed to the cleaning paraphernalia in the back of the Mini. The man had already peered in and seemed convinced by the clothes, buckets, and Vim.

"Yep, she's not been good," he said simply and wandered off. "Oi'll see yer ammorra."

"Tina, bloody hell. I don't even know what he just said."

"He said he'd see us tomorrow. Looks like Mrs Cooper's not coming back."

Inside, the caravan smelt damp. Left exactly since the last occupant had gone, a copy of the *Radio Times* was on the table, and as Mel blew away the dust, it revealed the date 1978. The cover showed a grinning Mike Yarwood dressed in a Father Christmas outfit.

"Looks like no one's been here for about four years," said Mel.

"Reckon we could live here," remarked Tina.

Mel stared at her. Until this moment, it had just been an adventure. She thought her aunt would track her down, and she would be punished and sent to bed. It would be a good story to tell her classmates—her own anecdote when they talked of their overseas adventures.

Tina was opening drawers and exclaiming with each discovery.

"Look, a saucepan, potato peeler, washing-up liquid, blankets." Enthralled, Tina continued her prattle.

Horrified by the smell, Mel only saw the caravan as a filthy hole. It was fun, but she wasn't going to live here. Ashamed, the thought of Aunty Pauline, sick with worry, made her feel guilty. But she was exhausted and would not allow that thought to take hold.

She realised Tina had left the caravan and was rooting around in the car. She was calling for her excitedly.

"Cawd der hell, look at this."

Mel went out to the Mini and looked in the boot.

"Oh my God!"

The boot contained a picnic basket covered in a checked cloth, where underneath revealed a bottle of rosé wine, delicate sandwiches and cakes—all beautifully cut and presented. Tina snatched a packet of crisps and offered one to Mel. Both girls were starving, and now Mel felt exhausted. Tina grabbed the basket, and they placed it on the little table in the caravan to unpack their feast. Tina found two chipped mugs and tried to open the wine, but despite there being knives, forks and a variety of cutlery, there was no bottle opener.

"Mrs Cooper, bluudy woman."

Tina grabbed a knife and pushed down the cork. She then poured two very generous measures, pulling out the broken cork as she went. Mel was not sure of the time but was not used to drinking. The first mouthful made her gag. Tina glared, and Mel didn't want to look weak. She was aware that Tina was more experienced with alcohol. She had only ever been drunk twice; once, at Victoria Montgomery's party, when she was trying to impress Jennifer and at home when she had sneaked a bottle of cider out of the cupboard and drunk it alone. She had been sick on her bed. Her mother had not even noticed. Mel remembered how she had washed the sheets and replaced them, her mother oblivious. A stab of anger interrupted her daydream.

"What's up with you?"

"Nothing," Mel snapped and grabbed her mug, guzzling the rest of the wine. "Give me some more."

"Bloody posh ones! You gotta watch them."

Mel's head began to relax, and soon they began to tuck into the food. The sandwiches were delicious, salmon and cucumber, cheese and pickle with bags of crisps and grapes. The sandwiches were cut into symmetrical triangles and had the crusts taken off. Tina seemed a bit frightened of eating them but took her cue from Mel.

"My mum never made sandwiches like this. I might get a Pot Noodle in my pack lunch box if I was lucky." Mel laughed but realised Tina was serious. The food seemed mountainous, but the girls soon ate most of it.

Mel lay back on the table seat and looked at the caravan. The windows were so filthy that, even with the curtains drawn back, the sun struggled to light the room. It was a shit heap, but it was ok, thought Mel. God only knew how the beds worked in these caravans, but she imagined they came down from the ceiling or something. Tina pulled out another bottle of wine and repeated her ingenious bottle-opening technique when Mel opened a tiny drawer under the table and found a bottle opener. They both laughed.

"Cheers, Mrs Cooper," they chorused.

The wine, combined with the heat, made the girls tired. They stretched out on the seats on either side of the table and slept.

When they woke up, they felt dehydrated. Mel had pain behind her eye, and her stomach was sick. Tina was smoking a cigarette.

"I'm starving. Any food left?" asked Tina. Mel looked at the sandwiches, but the heat had made them curl and stale. Tina picked one up and threw it down. "Reckon that'll kill ya."

Tina opened the crumpled white envelope they had found in the glove compartment and waved it at Mel. "Chips?" she suggested. Mel felt suddenly guilty. It was stealing, but she ignored the thought and followed Tina out.

They walked to the seafront and came across a Victorian pub called The Crown. Mel started to walk past, but Tina gestured for them to go in. The door had two entrances, and they walked into the lounge. Mel assumed it would be better than the public bar. Despite its grand façade, the room was dark and small. There were a few heavy tables and chairs and a worn, stained carpet. A couple of locals sat in silence and stared at them as they made their way in. Mel felt out of place as she had never been to a pub except for when they had Sunday lunch. Tina, oblivious, bounded to the bar.

The landlady dressed a bit like Aunty Pauline, had a cold face and a lazy eye which stared into the distance.

"Abbott," said Tina.

"Pint?" asked the landlady.

"Two."

"Yit."

Mel listened to the exchange. She was underage and was waiting at any time to be told to leave or worse. The landlady, however, merely pulled the pints and plonked them on the bar.

"That'll be one pound forty-three." Tina handed over the money and then placed a pint in front of Mel. It looked enormous.

"Hey, you ever had Abbot afore?" asked Tina. Mel shook her head. "Well, it's grut; that'll get you right pissed."

She picked up the pint and took a long swig. The foam rested on her upper lip, and she wiped it away. Mel tentatively picked up the pint. It felt warm and, while not pleasant, was easy to swallow. Mel realised she was incredibly thirsty, and the liquid went down well. Before long, she had downed her glass, and another drink replaced it. Mel began to feel relaxed. She was slightly dizzy but not out of control.

"Reckon you hint been in a pub afore," Tina surmised. Mel blushed.

"Well, I once got very drunk on Dubonnet and lemonade. I stole a bottle from my mum's drinks cabinet and took it to a party. I didn't realise you had to mix it with loads of lemonade so drank about half a pint virtually neat."

"Didn't that taste bad?"

"Yep, but I thought that was how it was meant to taste. Anyway, someone was sick all over the bathroom, and I had to write a letter of apology to Victoria Montgomery's mother."

"If that weren't you, why did you have to?"

"Cos, I brought the booze… but then other people had cider." Tina looked at Mel.

"Sounds like you got dropped in it."

Mel had never thought of it like that. She had been scapegoated but was so grateful for the invite at the time that she had not even considered anyone else was to blame. She wondered what those girls were doing now. Her line of thought was interrupted by Tina.

"Igor's staring at us." Tina nodded toward the landlady.

"How can you tell?"

Tina laughed, and both girls found themselves giggling. Suddenly she didn't care about the locals' disapproving looks. She drained the other pint and felt the overwhelming need for the toilet. Until she stood up, she did not realise how drunk she was and promptly knocked over a couple of chairs. Walking as carefully as she could, she made her way towards the ladies'. She still managed to walk into a couple of chairs, making a noise that echoed in the empty bar. Once she returned, they left the pub and walked down to the local fish bar.

The sun had lost its heat, but it was not cold. Angie's Fish Bar looked like it was straight out of the 1960s. The neon sign flickered, and several of the letters did not work. The woman behind the counter hardly looked up when they came in.

"No fish left. Only do chips," she promptly told them. Mel was always surprised by the Suffolk lack of charm.

"That's fine," Tina said.

Soon they were holding a big bag of greasy chips smothered with salt and vinegar. Mel was a little taken aback that Tina did not ask if she liked vinegar before telling the woman to put some on but let it go. She was hungry. They sat on the bench outside and, with their wooden forks, devoured the chips. They tasted delicious. Mel realised she had never eaten chips outside. They would occasionally get them as a family but would lay the table and have knives and forks. This was the best way to eat them. Soon only the thin overcooked crispy bits were left, and the girls scraped every morsel before throwing the wrapper in the bin.

They made their way back to the campsite, but Mel had very little recollection of getting there. Tina had decided to take the shortcut and found it hilarious to pull out various tent poles as she went. At one stage, they had to duck behind a tent when the owner stuck their head out. Mel fell over guy ropes numerous times and was relieved when they reached the path. Tina skipped through the campsite, laughing while a few people shouted at them.

"Keep it down!"

Tina had responded by sticking two fingers up at them. They seemed intimidated by the drunken girl in black leather and had meekly put their heads back inside their tents.

"Fuck you," she bellowed.

Mel laughed. She was still quite drunk, and Tina's antics seemed enticingly dangerous. When they got closer to their caravan, Tina gestured for them to be quiet. A line of clothes hung outside, and Tina giggled as she grabbed a shirt.

"Too old," said Tina and rather than leaving it on the

line, she threw it on the ground. There were also two pairs of socks—thick hiking socks with reinforced heels. Mel had seen them in the outdoor shop in London, and they were expensive. Tina quickly grabbed both pairs and stuffed them comically up her T-shirt.

Mel had never stolen anything in her life. It had been ingrained in her from a young age that it was wrong. Witnessing Tina so nonchalantly take clothes off the washing line had shocked her. Tina picked up on Mel's disapproval and laughed.

"Stolen a car, living in someone else's caravan...."

"Shut up. Someone will hear." Mel stumbled to the ground, and they screamed with laughter.

"Need to learn to take your ale."

At last, they reached the caravan and stumbled in. Mel fell onto the makeshift bed and was instantly asleep. Tina looked at Mel, then lit a cigarette dog end from the ashtray and sat on the floor. She also reached for the beer, which was warm and flat, but it soothed her sore throat.

***

It was the middle of the night, and Tina was woken by Mel shaking her arm. When she eventually opened one eye, she saw Mel leaning across, and her face was ashen. For a moment, she thought something was wrong.

"I've started my period."

Tina rolled over. "For Christ's sake."

"I need some...."

"What?"

"Tampax." Tina sat up and looked at Mel. Her face was white. "Tina, what am I going to do?"

Tina reached across her bed, picked up the socks they had stolen the night before and thrust them at Mel, who looked horrified.

"Don't worry. They're hiking socks. Extra-thick."

Mel snatched them off her and scuttled away. Tina lay back down but was unable to sleep. She laughed at Mel's reaction and thought back to her mother. They never had anything in their house. Tina had frequently pilfered socks off her mum's various boyfriends. She laughed when they bemoaned that socks always seemed to get lost in the wash.

CHAPTER 7

At Clive and Pauline's cottage in Trotham, Pauline was distraught.

"It's been hours. She still hint home."

A young policeman sat awkwardly in the chair. He knew he had very little to say that was of use.

"You say you have tried to reach her father?"

"We can't get hold of him." Pauline tried to keep the anxiety out of her voice. Clive grasped her hand. "Where could she be?"

"The officer will find her," said Clive.

"We have filed a missing person report and circulated her image."

Pauline clutched the photograph of Mel in her school uniform. It was at least two years old.

"We'll get a newer one."

"All stations are on alert." Pauline listened to the policeman, but she was not able to take in a lot of what he said. "We'll check with the bus drivers. Try not to worry."

Clive looked at his wife; she was grey. Eventually, the policeman left, and Clive held her close and cooed to her like a child.

"Come on, Pauly. We will find her."

She buried her face in his shoulder and cried. "If anything happens to that child...."

Clive held her hands. "Come on. This isn't my Pauline." She lifted her head and stared at her husband.

"No, you're right. Got to do something. Git me a pen. Let's make a list." Clive quickly obliged, and Pauline barked out her list. "Git an up-to-date photo. Contact Julian somehow. Alice needs to know." Clive looked with admiration at his wife. "Git the village lookin'."

***

When Clive walked into his sitting room, he was astounded by the volume of bodies crammed into the relatively small space. There were the usual faces: Denise Barbara, and Carol—Pauline's 'gang' as he liked to call them. They had worked tirelessly for years to improve the village and had all been involved in the anti-litter campaigns and various other community initiatives.

The identity of the village had changed in recent years. People had begun to buy the old, beamed houses and do them up. The posh, local, private school had meant there had been a rush of couples looking to live nearby. The strong Suffolk accent which had once been ubiquitous was being replaced by bland BBC English. Clive did not have the ancient accent, but he appreciated it and loved how it had not changed for centuries. The new cohort, however, had a pack mentality and certainly would not want their children speaking that way.

People who had lived in their village all their lives also had an inverted snobbery and were not always welcoming to the new residents. Suffolk people often called anyone who was not born and raised in the village a 'furriner'. Unsurprisingly, this came across as rude to anyone new. Clive sighed and lamented that when they had come to help find a missing child, a time of crisis, the two distinct tribes sat away from each other.

"Morning, Clive." Emma Lucas smiled, and Clive managed a polite nod.

He had a visceral dislike of the women perched on the settee. There were three of them: Emma, Clare, and Katie, but Emma was the undisputed leader. Clive called them 'the three witches.' They had moved to the village two years ago and established themselves by busying with the Women's Institute and fundraising for the village hall. Pauline had, at first, naïvely welcomed them with open arms and encouraged them to get involved with all her endeavours. She had spoken highly of their enthusiasm and level of commitment, *'Just what we need, new blood.'* While initially supportive, they started to ignore and organise events without including her. Clive knew how these women operated. There was a similar group at university. The same childish rules of who was 'in' had been carried through to adulthood.

Clive sensed they were looking at his house, judging his furniture and ornaments. More importantly, though, he knew they laughed at Pauline's clothes. They were decked out in the latest polka dot shirts and Monet jewellery. Emma had an oversized blazer with shiny gold buttons and shoulder pads. Her hair was styled like Lady Di's and was always immaculate. Clive, despite the gravity of the situation, found himself distracted by his dislike for them.

Every woman in the room had brought cakes, which seemed very strange to Clive. They were lined up almost on top of each other on the sideboard. No one knew what to say and waited for direction.

"How terrible for you, Pauline," some said.

"We'll do everything we can," said others.

Pauline coughed and gestured for everyone to be quiet. She thanked everyone for coming and stood before them like a general mustering his troops. When the murmuring had settled, Pauline took a moment to compose herself. Clive, for an anxious second, thought she might cry. He knew, however, that his wife was strong, and nothing would stop her from finding Mel.

Pauline finally spoke. “Reckon we need posters, door to door enquires, and every area of ground needs to be searched.” Carol raised her hand.

“Betty’s husband knows Ted, who works on the number ten bus. He’s going to speak to all the drivers.”

“We’ll make a list of things he needs to ask and give him a picture,” added Barbara. “We can call Saxon Radio and put out a request for help.”

Pauline scribed suggestions on one of Clive’s flipcharts. “Doreen, you organised the publicity for the barn dance. Can you remember who you spoke to?” she asked. Doreen nodded.

“Got that all written down, Paul?”

“Posters?” said Clive.

“They need to be out and all over the village,” Pauline agreed.

“All the villages?” asked Carol.

“How many posters do we need?” Clive asked.

“‘Bout fifty? That’s what we had for the harvest supper,” Doreen replied.

Clive interjected. “I’ll get five hundred done at the university. We need a better picture, but I can change that later. Time is of the essence.”

Emma, who had been silent until then, suggested they organise a catch-up meeting to review progress. She beamed when everyone agreed that communication was so important.

"Shall we say tomorrow in the village hall at 6.30 pm?" suggested Emma.

"That'll clash with the Scouts," said Denise.

"I think a lost child trumps a few boys in short trousers," Emma said patronisingly.

"Just meant someone has to cancel it, that's all," Denise muttered.

"Splendid, well, that's settled then."

Pauline thanked everyone again. The women delegated their roles and agreed on a timeline. Clive looked at his wife with admiration. She looked exhausted. While it had allowed them to take some control, the meeting had increased their anxiety.

"Tea?" Clive said. He grasped his wife's hands. She needed to try and relax, and he encouraged her to sit for five minutes. "It's English Breakfast." This was more for his benefit than hers. He knew Pauline would drink any type of tea.

Pauline left the cup untouched. She was restless and paced up and down the lounge. She was rummaging around in the kitchen, trying to find cake tins for the enormous pile of cakes, while Clive sat and drank his tea.

The hot liquid helped quieten his mind. He could hear Pauline crashing around and was not at all surprised when she shouted to him.

"Git your car keys, Clive."

"Ok."

"We have to find Julian. She may have been in touch." Clive knew there was no point in arguing. When Pauline had an idea in her head, it needed instant gratification but there was nothing they could do at this time of night. He promised his wife they would leave first thing in the morning but for now they needed some rest.

Neither of them slept much that night. Bleary eyed, they washed and dressed ready to face the day, hoping Julian would have news and they would find Mel, safe and sound.

They were soon charging along the narrow Suffolk lanes, following Pauline's instructions. It felt good to be busy, and he knew his wife was not the type to sit nervously by the phone.

Pauline had never been to the city of London before. Clive anxiously weaved between the cars and followed Pauline's instructions. She had a map and was poring over it, commanding where to turn.

"If we get lost, park and we'll git a cab," she said.

Despite Clive's fears, they found where Julian worked surprisingly easily. They even managed to park outside, where Pauline produced a small tartan purse with change.

"Always keep this for parking."

The building was imposing and had the name Walton Greaves in large letters above the doorway. Men in well-cut suits scurried in and out, and Clive felt desperately out of place. Pauline, however, bounded up the steps and headed straight to the reception. She demanded to speak to Julian Kemp, explaining that his daughter was missing.

"I'm afraid Mr Kemp is on annual leave." The blonde secretary shot her a disapproving look and puffed herself up, delighted in her self-importance.

"Well, git me his bluudy boss then," Pauline almost shouted.

The secretary directed them to some large leather chairs that were not designed for comfort, and the hard leather against their backs added to their anxiety. Pauline impatiently asked how much longer they would have to wait.

"You have to understand; you don't have an appointment."

Clive spoke up, supporting his wife. "I am sure you can appreciate the desperation of the situation. We must find Julian Kemp."

"As I have explained to this lady. He is on holiday."

"Yes, I know he is on holiday, but surely to God, his superiors can help."

The woman ignored Pauline but did seem to pay more attention to Clive. He did not share her rural accent, and his clothes, while not a suit, were more 'country gentleman'.

"If you could take a seat."

Pauline sat down but found it impossible to relax. Every time someone walked through the reception, she stood up. Eventually, Pauline marched up to the woman and demanded that she call the boss now.

Eventually, a man in a well-cut Jermyn Street suit appeared. He was a similar age to Clive.

"It's ok, Linda. I will see to our guests." He introduced himself as Julian's director and asked them to follow him into a large boardroom where they were asked to sit down.

"Julian's daughter is missing, and we can't get hold of him. Do you know where he is?" asked Clive.

"And who are you?"

"His wife is my sister."

"We hint got no address, no number and that bluudy brick phone, we hint got that number neither." The man was slightly taken aback by her accent, given that Clive was well-spoken. "I don't care about no confidentiality. If you won't give it to us, give it to the police."

In contrast to the receptionist, the man did seem genuinely concerned and keen to help. "I will get the number for his phone, which I can dial now if you like. I will also talk to his colleagues and get them to tell me anything they know."

Clive gave him their number, thanked him and led Pauline out of the office.

"Call us day or night!" said Clive.

He assured them that he would and wished them luck. They were escorted to the door and walked past the secretary.

"Bluudy madam." Pauline glared at her and muttered loud enough for her to hear.

Back in the car, they sank into their seats. Clive looked at his wife; she looked exhausted. She reached beneath her seat and pulled out the same tartan flask she had taken to Grimes Graves and some cheese and pickle sandwiches.

"I hint paying no London prices."

He smiled, and they sat in their car chomping on homemade sandwiches while they watched men in suits hurry past. Pauline felt depleted, and she had hoped that Julian would be there, or at the very least, they could get word to him.

"Clive, I'm so scared for Mel. Do you think we are ever going to find her?"

CHAPTER 8

Mel was awoken by the thunderous footsteps from a seagull parading up and down the roof of the caravan. For a moment, she was not sure where she was. Eventually, the events of the past day came back to her. The seagull now stood on the skylight, and although green with algae, she could make out its enormous, webbed feet. Its presence unsettled her. Her head banged with a searing pain and her mouth felt like tar.

Tina was standing by the door smoking a cigarette. She looked amused.

"Abbott. That'll do that to ya."

She passed her a half-drunk bottle of flat Fanta. Mel was shocked to see that Tina had been organising the caravan. The sandwiches had been tidied up, and the table and kitchenette area scrubbed clean.

"That old boy come over. Wants to know when we're

going to get cleaning." Mel looked panicked, and her mind raced.

"What if he's spoken to Mrs Cooper? He might call the police."

"No, he hint got a clue."

Mel pulled back the curtain, and although a distance away, she could see the caretaker striding towards the caravan.

"He's coming! He's coming!" Tina picked up the Vim, a couple of cloths and threw them at Mel. "Make a start."

Mel began to vigorously rub the window rims, which just produced black smears on the panes. By now, the caretaker was standing watching her work.

"Cawd der hell, reckon you need some water on that. Hey, you got a pail, gal?" he asked. Mel looked incredulous and touched her face.

"Pale? Yes, I am a bit fair not been in the sun much."

Tina smirked and enunciated her words very deliberately. "He's asking you if you got a b-u-c-k-e-t."

"Bluudy furriners."

Tina and the old man laughed at her expense and continued to talk in a language that Mel could not understand. Tina's accent became a lot thicker as she matched his guttural grunts. Mel felt uncomfortable and was grateful when he finally left.

"His name's Norman and he said he's got a couple of old buckets he's going to lend us, and there's a tap just down there."

Tina wandered off and was soon back with a large bucket of water. While cold, it did allow them to raise a lather, and the grime began to lift from the windows and frame. The green algae took more scrubbing, and Mel surprisingly enjoyed the mindless activity. The window was soon gleaming, and she began to clean the door to the caravan, which magically changed colour. Tina was energetically scrubbing the outside of the caravan with a mop, but she was fighting a losing battle.

"That's going to take more than one bucket." Tina stood back and admired their work. "That should keep old Norman happy."

Although situated on the outskirts of the town, the caravan park was next to a sandy beach. Tina and Mel picked their way through the tents, choosing the shortest distance to the road. It was much larger than it had appeared last night, and Mel had little recollection of getting home. She had woken up with a handful of tent pegs that Tina had insisted on taking on their drunken walk home. Some of the tents leaning precariously to one side were probably due to their handiwork the night before.

Mel almost enjoyed the half a mile walk to the main town. The salty air cleansed her lungs, and she began to feel more normal. Large Victorian houses interspersed with hotels and B and Bs stretched along the front. Cars lined the roads, stuffed with suitcases and holidaymakers. Unusually for Suffolk, the road was at a gradient, and they were soon panting for breath. The sun was hot, and they decided to avoid the main street and walk in the shade down a side road.

"Cawd der hell. Look at the size of them houses," said Tina.

"This is where the posh people live."

"You'd know."

The houses were beautiful Georgian buildings with strong pillars and well-maintained gardens. Rather incongruously, one house stood out. The garden was a mass of weeds, and the gate was off its hinges. Stinging nettles, as tall as a person, swayed in the breeze along the path. The house, although once beautiful, looked unloved and dishevelled.

"You might be able to afford that one," joked Tina.

Just as they walked past, the door was flung open, and a large red-faced woman bustled out. A loud cultured voice could be heard from inside the house.

"Now fuck off and don't come back."

The woman, who appeared to be in some sort of uniform, dropped her bag on the ground in her rush to leave.

"Don't worry. I hint coming back. I'm telling my superiors about you," she called back.

"Snitching to the red tops! Now, fuck off!"

The woman hurriedly picked up her possessions, pushed past the girls, got into a brown Mini Moke and dashed away. She looked like she was going to cry.

Tina laughed. "Well, she got bloody told."

"Poor woman," said Mel.

"Reckon she got off lightly. My mum once threw a pan of chip fat over my social worker."

"Goodness."

"Well, suppose it wasn't that bad. The pan wasn't hot."

Mel looked at Tina so matter of fact. She had never met anyone with a social worker before. Her mother, however, had a community psychiatric nurse, but she would never have raised her voice. She was always so compliant and weak.

"You all right, posh?"

Mel nodded. "Yeah, fine."

The girls walked on, past the other millionaires' houses, as they had dubbed them, until they reached the surprisingly busy high street. There was a pub called The Hound, several cafés, a garage and, rather bizarrely, a large pet shop. Mel spotted the 1930 Focus Cinema and an American chain restaurant called Fatty Arbuckle's. The picture of the large greasy burger on the window attracted them. They pressed their faces against the pane and watched the tourist clientele tucking into enormous portions of chips and burgers.

"Cawd der hell, I could just eat that."

"No chance. I think we got about £2 left."

Mel turned again to look at the gluttonous tourists. Her stomach felt acidic, and she needed food. They wandered down to the seafront and looked at the pier. It was surrounded by excitable children ready to play the penny slot machines. Many of them were queuing for ice creams at the bright pink ice cream van.

"Can we have an ice cream?" asked Mel. Tina took out the crumpled white envelope.

"Yep, reckon we are at the seaside."

They joined the line of children and looked at the boy serving them. He was about eighteen with a thick mop of black hair, as it got in his eyes. He wore a stained, white nylon overall that was a little too tight and not entirely buttoned up so you could see his Iron Maiden T-shirt underneath. His black hair was restrained by an equally grubby cap which he raised in greeting when the girls approached. He caught Mel's eye and smiled, and she found herself self-consciously looking away. The boy laughed and joked effortlessly with the children. While he had an unmistakable Suffolk accent, his tone was not as harsh as Tina's. He took time with each child, commenting on their clothes and asking about their holiday.

"And how old are you? Four? I thought you were at least six." The child beamed. Eventually, they reached the end of the queue.

"Yes, what can Eddie get ya?" He had the same sing-song voice as Tina but less gruff.

"What you got?" The window was plastered with pictures of ice creams. Eddie pointed and laughed.

"Well, I hint got no Funny Feet, but I can do you a Screwball or a 99er."

Tina pondered her choices. "I'll have a 99er."

"Make that two, please," added Tina.

"Do you want a flake?"

"Oh, yes, please," Mel gushed. He handed over the ice cream and winked at her.

"Put extra sauce on yours. Reckon you need feeding up."

"Yep, she needs feeding up," said Tina.

"Reckon I hint seen a hairstyle like that round here. You on holiday?"

"Sort of," Mel muttered. He smiled a broad smile.

"Enjoy. See you around," he shouted.

They sat on a nearby bench and ate their ice creams. After a while, the pink van spluttered into life, and they saw it disappear around the corner. Tina looked at Mel and raised both eyebrows.

"Well, he was a good 'un. Reckon I'd like to see more of him." Mel blushed. "Reckon he fancied you."

"No, he didn't."

Tina poked her with her finger. "The ice cream dream." They licked on their ice creams and wandered down to the shore. Tina sat on the beach and immediately threw off her socks. The stones hurt her feet, but she did not seem to notice.

"Come on." She rushed into the sea. "Brrr, it's cold, but come on."

Mel tentatively followed her. The stones cut into her toes until she was at the shoreline. The sand was a welcome relief, and she rolled up her trouser legs and slowly waded in. While the water momentarily froze her legs, the numbness felt delicious. A wave splashed onto her jeans, and Tina playfully scooped handfuls of water over her until she was completely drenched.

"Get off!"

"It's only a bit of water. Got to toughen you up."

They ran out of the sea laughing and lay back on the pebbles. Mel looked at the sea salt splashed on her bare legs, and she ran her finger over the silver sheen, then licked her finger. The salt tasted good. The glimmering residue was almost like a painted-on armour. Lifting the soaked bottom of her jeans, she saw a large white tide mark. How would she get that off? She only had the clothes she stood up in. But as soon as the anxiety came into her head, she let it go. Tina read her thoughts.

"Don't worry about that. Eat your ice cream."

Mel looked down. Her 99er was running onto her hand and dripping onto her jeans.

"Shit!"

Tina laughed. "Just wash them out in the sink; they'll be fine. That'll dry in half an hour."

Her ice cream tasted slightly of seawater, and although melted, it still tasted good. Mel loved the way Tina dismissed every concern: her lack of clothes, the lie to Norman, the fact that they had no food or money. Tina just moved forward. Mel marvelled at her attitude. She was, in contrast, a natural-born worrier. Aunty Pauline always said she would worry that the sky would fall if she let her.

The ice cream had settled their stomachs, and they started to wander back. While they were soaking, it was pleasant relief against the midday sun. They walked slowly past the pet shop and Fatty Arbuckle's, with both girls taking another look in.

"Reckon we will eat in there in a week," Tina said.

"In your dreams."

Wearily they wandered back the way they had come, up the hill and past 'Millionaires' Row'. They suddenly stopped in their tracks when they saw the pink ice cream van parked outside the 'unloved' house. Eddie was knocking at the door. Almost immediately, the door flew open, and an old woman dressed in black embraced him. Her grey hair was stylishly piled on top of her head. She was slightly bent over and walked with a cane and she beckoned him into the house. The girls looked at each other. This was the same woman who had so brutally thrown out the carer they had seen earlier.

"Perhaps he does home delivery," Tina grinned.

Almost as soon as he had gone into the house, he left. A withered hand squeezed his affectionately, and she waved him goodbye. Eddie blew her a theatrical kiss and left. The older woman saw them out of the corner of her eye and threw them an aggressive look. Mel glanced at Tina and was surprised to see her looking away as if intimidated. They hurriedly carried on the long walk to the caravan.

Back at the campsite, Mel realised her legs and pants were still soaking wet and sandy. They passed families walking with their dogs and a Scout troop of what looked like thirteen or fourteen year olds. They were in wetsuits and walked in single file down to the beach. They were completely blocking the path, and rather than wait, Tina walked through the middle of them. Mel meekly followed behind.

"Looks like she's pissed herself," one of the boys

shouted to his friends. He was blond and confident in his looks. The others were in the unfortunate teenage limbo of adolescent growth. Some of them sported fuzzy hair on their upper lip and were plastered in spots.

Tina shoulder-charged him and knocked him to the ground. "Watch where you're going."

The other boys looked down in fear and carried on walking. Tina glared at the blond boy, daring him to challenge her. He picked himself up and joined his friends. Mel, momentarily stunned, felt invisible. Tina strode on ahead, laughing.

Eventually, they reached the caravan. Mel's legs, while sodden, were warm, and she trailed sand across the floor. Fumbling around, she found a worn, frayed towel.

"Aunty Pauline would be proud of this. I'm off to wash out my clothes." There was no washing powder, only a smidgen of washing-up liquid congealed in a plastic bottle. "See you in a bit." Tina just grunted and lit a cigarette.

Once in the shower block, Mel quickly checked no one was around, whipped off her jeans and pants, and wrapped the towel around herself. There were no plugs, and the water was stone cold. The corroded pipes seemed even more filthy than normal, streaked and tarnished with horrible green. She soaked her clothes the best she could and tried to get all the bubbles out. She then ran back, self-consciously, to the caravan where she lay the jeans on the grass and put the knickers on the inside windowsill.

"Hope they bloody dry," she moaned.

"Stop worrying." Tina didn't look up. She was reading a copy of the *Radio Times* from 1979.

Mel suddenly felt very tired and lay down on the flat seat at the side of the table. The sun warmed her bones, and she closed her eyes. She wasn't sure how long she had been asleep but was aware Tina was no longer there. She got up and reached for her underwear. It was dry, thank goodness. The jeans were slightly wet, but she had no choice but to pull them up her legs. She thought about Jennifer and the girls from school sunning themselves on the beach and luxuriating by the pool. She had been wearing the same clothes for an age. Not only that, but they were also damp, and she was sleeping in a dilapidated caravan. It was so tragic; it was almost funny. A surge of anger swept through her, but she did not have the energy to feel it, so she let it go and went out to search for Tina.

Mel wandered down to the sea and paddled for a while. She enjoyed the cooling sensation of the sea on her legs, but this time was careful not to dip her jeans in the water. The sun was not as hot as it had been, and the air felt lighter. She had not thought about her dad or Aunty Pauline for a few hours. She couldn't let those thoughts in. They just needed to be blocked.

Her mind, however, began to race with worry. What if it was true? The thought of *him* with another family was too enormous to comprehend. No, it couldn't be true. She would know. For many years she had witnessed her mum and dad falling apart. He had supported her initially, but her mother had slowly withdrawn and become impossible to reach. She had sat on her bed, imploring her to get up, but she often stayed there for days, little by little, pulling away from her. It made it worse that she had once been so full of laughter and light.

Mel had eventually gone to boarding school—sent away from the problem. She had hated it but secretly felt thankful that the problem had been removed from her. She no longer had to try and coax a reaction from her mother. Her time was taken up with her trials of trying to fit in. She always believed her dad did his best, but he had to work. She was not so sure now. Now she didn't know what to think. The shock of that phone call had hardly settled in. She couldn't go back. It was all too much.

The light was beginning to fade, and Mel ambled back to the caravan. Taken aback, she could hear voices—Tina laughing and a lower voice. She couldn't quite make out what they were saying. The curtains were drawn. Panicked, she hesitated and wasn't sure whether to knock or not.

"Hello."

She smiled as casually as she was able. It was only a second later that she realised the male voice was coming from the 'ice cream dream'. Tina grinned at Mel. The caravan was grey with smoke, and Mel realised that it wasn't tobacco they were smoking. Empty beer cans littered the room.

Eddie passed a lit spliff to Mel. She had never tried one before and, embarrassed, held it up to her lips. She faltered and then inhaled as deeply as she dared. Immediately she started to cough and gag. Her throat burnt, and her lungs screamed. She tried to speak, but Tina and Eddie were in fits of laughter. Tina passed her a beer, and she hastily drank from it.

"Hint had it before?" It wasn't an accusation but a fact. "That always gets you the first time," Eddie said. He had a kind persona, and Mel felt very comfortable. She shook her head. "That were a good try. First time I had it, I was sick on my brother's bike."

"My mum used to leave unsmoked ones in the ashtray," Tina grinned. "So, I had a couple of goes on them when I was a kid." Mel tried not to look shocked.

"How old were you?" she asked.

"Not old. Used to wash it down with White Lightning."

Mel thought about how the girls at her school would have reacted to the situation. While everyone had experimented with alcohol, to her knowledge, no one had smoked.

Eddie expertly laid out three Rizla papers, crumbled in the black resin, rolled it up, licked the end and put in a paper roach. When it was done, he ran his hand along the cone shaft and admired it.

"Help yourself," he gestured to Mel. "I'll give you lessons."

Mel murmured something about sitting this one out and drank out of the warm beer can. The spliff had burnt her mouth, and the cheap beer was a perfect antidote.

"How come you're here?" asked Mel.

"I'll let Tina tell you that," he laughed.

"Caught me nicking a T-shirt. Well, we hint got no clothes, have we?"

"I promised not to tell if she let me come in for a beer."

"We've been here about half an hour. Feeling fairly wasted."

Soon Mel began to enjoy herself. They told Eddie how they had stolen the car, found the money and blagged their way into the caravan. Eddie had seemed quite taken aback.

"Reckon, you're a couple of fugitives. When are you going back?"

The mood suddenly dropped. The girls looked at Eddie. Neither had thought about what they were going to do. Eddie broke the silence.

"So, what did you spend the money on?" he asked.

"Abbot," they said in unison.

"Fags," Tina added, and they all laughed.

Mel began to feel relaxed again. And had another puff. This time she didn't inhale as much. While she still hacked and spluttered, her reaction was not as violent.

"Getting it, gal," said Eddie.

"Yeet, reckon," Tina echoed. She then asked Eddie how he knew the old lady up on the hill. "We saw her kicking out some woman."

"Margaret Wilbraham to you. She's actually a well-known artist. My mum used to clean and cook for her for five years. My mum was more like a housekeeper until she got ill and couldn't manage it no more. Margot has never liked anyone else."

"Does your mum still see her?" Mel asked.

"No. Been dead seven years."

"Sorry," Mel muttered.

Eddie broke a slight silence. "I drop round dope to her."

"Marijuana! Really? She's about eighty," Mel blurted out in surprise.

"Arthritis... reckons that helps with the pain."

"So, who cleans for her now?" Tina asked.

"Well, no one. They never last more than five minutes. She's a nightmare. Place is a tip. Gets drunk and swears at people."

"Sounds like my mum," Tina muttered.

Tina looked eagerly at Mel. "We could do that. We could clean for her."

"Yeah, right." Mel scoffed.

"Reckon we could. We need the money."
Eddie laughed. "Well, I could put in a word for you, but she will shout and scream and probably be drunk."

"Do it," Tina said quickly. Mel looked hesitatingly at Tina but got caught up in the moment.

"What's the worst thing that could happen? She's not going to murder us, is she?"

"There is always a first time."

When the last can was drained, Eddie said he would have to go. He was a little unsteady on his feet as he left. Tina stumbled into the bedroom at the back, which she had decided was her domain. While this irritated Mel, she was impressed with how direct Tina was. If she wanted something, she would go for it. Mel felt exhausted and she collapsed onto one of the seats at the side of the table and was soon asleep.

CHAPTER 9

The next morning Mel woke with a screaming sore throat. Tina, as always, was up.

"You heard what Eddie said. Let's go and see that mad old gal. She needs a cleaner."

The conversation of the night before was a bit of a blur for Mel. She had a vague recollection of Tina's excitement that they could earn money. Mel looked down at her top and wiped the stale ice cream off. She had been wearing the same clothes for a couple of days now and was aware she looked rough.

"Got you a new T-shirt," Tina half-sang. "Now go and wash your pits. You stink."

Mel made her way down to the toilets and did as she was told. The cold water jolted her to life, and she decided they might as well try and earn some money. The new stolen T-shirt, decorated with a hand clutching a razor blade with the words AC/DC emblazoned across it, was a little tight, but she had no choice but to wear it. She looked at herself in the toilet mirror. If the girls from school could see her now…. She rinsed her mouth with the remainder of the toothpaste and made her way back to the caravan.

Making their way through the tents and caravans, they walked along the shore. There was very little breeze, and it was already hot. Hungover, Mel found it difficult to keep up with Tina, who strode purposefully along. When they eventually rounded the corner to Mrs Wilbraham's house, Tina seemed uncharacteristically nervous.

"You do the talking. You're posh," said Tina.
Mel knocked on the door, and after an age, a withered hand pulled it back. Despite being only about five feet, she had the most imposing manner. She was dressed in a black dress that hung from her bony body, and her grey hair was pulled back from her face and clipped dramatically behind. Though not pulled back severely, like Aunty Pauline's, it flowed in curls down her face. She smelt of cigarettes and had a glass of red wine in her hand.

"Yes?" the voice boomed accusingly.

"We noticed you weren't happy with your last cleaner, so we thought we would offer our services," Mel stuttered.

The woman seemed amused and looked them up and down. Tina tried to stare back, but Mel found she was blushing as the woman took an age to reply. Mel interrupted the silence.

"Eddie told us to come."

The woman's eyes slightly softened, and she looked at them, feeling intrigued. Mel realised they did look a motley pair. The older woman glared at Tina and lightly flicked Mel's ponytail.

"You're not from around here," she said to Mel. "I like that."

"No, I'm from London, and I just need to get some money."

"So, you can leave this backwater?"

"Yeah," she managed feebly.

"Well come in then. You can start on the kitchen."

Tina piped up rudely, "What's the pay?"

The woman threw an aggressive look, "We will discuss rates when you have successfully completed your trial." Mel expected Tina to argue, but she meekly followed the woman.

The girls walked through a dark hallway that was adorned with pictures. The furniture was heavy and ornately carved, and Mel could tell it was antique. It was different to her mother's taste, but she could tell it was expensive. Eventually, they were led to a kitchen with a flagstone floor. Large saucepans were hanging from the ceiling, and a half bottle of red wine sat on the side. The kitchen had various large cupboards, a butler sink with enormous taps, and a large Victorian pine table with a couple of dilapidated chairs. Every surface was grimy, and the floor was almost black with dirt.

"This is your first job." The woman dramatically picked up a bottle of liquid cleaning fluid and, holding it with both hands, sprayed the entire contents all over the kitchen surfaces and floors. Tina and Mel looked on, astonished. "Right, there you go. Cloths under there." With that, she left, and Mel and Tina looked at each other and laughed. The bright yellow liquid splashed everywhere and began to drip onto the floor.

"I think we should go. She's obviously a total loon."

Tina grabbed Mel's arm. "We are doing this."

Tina found a grey matted mop that was dried hard. Cold water helped to loosen the tangles as filthy water ran into the sink. Tina pulled her hand through it and teased out the knots.

"Water's bluudy cold but reckon that'll do."

There was no mop bucket to be found, and so she filled up the sink and, after each laboured mop, squeezed it out with her hand. Mel marvelled at how practical she was while her efforts with a filthy cloth just seemed to transfer dirt from one area to another. A stained, frayed curtain hung under the old butler sink, and behind it were ancient cleaning products: silver cleaner, polishes, Jif, and some washing-up liquid. Tina grabbed the Jif powder and threw it at Mel. Tina found an old tea towel, tore it in half and pushed Mel aside.

"Use this for cleaning. This for drying," she demonstrated. "See?"

Mel did her best and found herself scrubbing at a ferocious pace led by the speed of Tina, and soon the surfaces looked clean. They had not tackled the cooker; caked in years of grease and neglect, it struck Mel as being impossible to clean.

"Going to have to use hot water on this one," said Tina as she pulled down an enormous pot and filled it with water. After finding her plastic lighter, she lit the old gas stove. "Give me a lid, or we'll be here all bluudy day." Once the stove was lit, she proceeded to light a cigarette. "Reckon, I need a break." She pushed open the old door and put the mop outside.

After five minutes, she was back rummaging around for more cleaning equipment. She found some Brillo pads and used the hot water to attack the stove. Her hands were soon red and worn, but she didn't pay any attention. Mel picked up a Brillo pad and a cloth and followed Tina's lead. The black water congealed and blocked the sink. Mel looked for an instrument to unblock it, but Tina put her hand in, unclogging a massive mass of hair and filth.

After a while, Mrs Wilbraham returned and inspected the cupboards and floor.

"Well, it could do with a bit of a rub down and polish," she paused for dramatic effect. "But girls, I am impressed." Tina grinned, but her smile was not met with a response.

"So, have we got the job?" Tina asked directly.

The woman faltered, "Yes, but I need someone reliable. I expect my staff to be on time." The girls nodded. "I need people who are trustworthy. Some of the art in here is worth thousands. I can continue your trial. I have bathrooms and other things to clean."

"So, how often do you need us?" Tina pushed.

"Well, the house could do with an overhaul. Come back tomorrow, and you can finish this." She theatrically dragged her finger along the kitchen cupboard. Tina and Mel looked at each other. The house had not been cleaned for a while. "I have a large house, and I have struggled with reliable staff. So, I will need you to come tomorrow, and then we will discuss your appointment, depending on your performance."

Mel wanted to bring up money but felt unable to.

Tina just chimed in, "Can you pay us now?"

The woman put her hand into her dress and pulled out a ten-pound note. Tina snatched it a bit too quickly, making Mel wince, but she was grateful, and soon they were running out of the house, down the road, clutching the money like a trophy.

"Not bad for an afternoon's work," said Tina.
"Tina, you were brilliant. I didn't dare bring up money."

Tina looked amazed. "We did the bluudy work. She can bluudy pay us."

"Her staff! That house hasn't been cleaned for years.

It's a pigsty."

"Yeah, but a very beautiful pigsty."

"Right, let's go and spend this," Tina laughed. "I need fags, cider…."

"Milk, bread, washing powder," Mel interrupted.

They almost skipped to the local Mace store, where they spied a gang of girls outside smoking. They were in the same 'uniform' as Tina, letting everyone know they were bikers. The fact that none of them had bikes always seemed hilarious to Mel. If her dad were here, he would have something funny to say. Mel felt intimidated, but Tina pushed her way through.

"Thick as shit, you are," said the biggest of the girls.

The gang leader was large boned. Her hair was in a typical flick, and she stamped out her cigarette in front of Mel. She brushed the back of Mel's hair.

"Looks like a duck's arse."

Tina pushed her back. "Watch your mouth, bitch. Now get out of my fucking way."

The ringleader was taken aback, and the group of girls moved back to let them pass. Mel recognised the same startled face when she had pushed Tina that very first day. This was the way to deal with bullies, but she never had the strength of character. Mel felt pathetic but also exhilarated by Tina. She was crippled by being polite. Today had felt like a victory, and they would have something to eat tonight.

Tina made a mound of jam sandwiches, and they ate until their stomachs groaned. They had both been exhausted and fell asleep early.

* * *

While Tina had woken up before Mel, she misjudged how late it was. When they finally arrived at the house, they were late, and Mrs Wilbraham stood at the door, scowling.

"Girls, I said ten o'clock." Mel apologised, while Tina just shrugged. "The hallway needs a thorough cleanse. But be mindful of my art."

Mel had not properly looked the day before but was astonished by the array of paintings and sculptures adorning the walls and furniture. She recognised some of the styles as Cubist and touched a beautiful onyx bust.

"Don't pick that up," Mrs Wilbraham bellowed. "But you may dust it lightly." Mel knew enough about art from her mother to realise a lot of the work was original. She couldn't recognise the artists' names, but most of them were signed.

While the girls were busying themselves, finding cloths and dusters, Eddie poked his head around the lounge window. The old woman's face lit up.

"Avon calling," joked Eddie.

"Come in, come in," insisted Mrs Wilbraham.

He sat next to her on the settee. She was very fond of him and stroked his face. He sat in the lounge with her and rolled her four or five joints.

"Don't know when I can next come. My dad's got some jobs."

"That brute. And how is that useless brother of yours? Is he in prison yet?"

Eddie laughed. "Not yet."

Mrs Wilbraham held Eddie's hand. Her voice was uncharacteristically tender.

"You're not like them; you know that. Don't get caught up in their shenanigans."

Eddie held up the five joints like a fan. "Well, Mrs Wilbraham, you are a fine one to talk."

"Just keep safe, Edward." She squeezed his hand again, and Mel glanced over. While Eddie laughed and shrugged off her warning, Mrs Wilbraham seemed serious. "I mean it, Eddie. You keep out of trouble."

Mel caught Eddie looking down. A look of panic flashed across his face. Then he was smiling again, teasing the old woman. Something was wrong, and she wondered what it was.

CHAPTER 10

When the girls finally finished, they wandered outside. The ice cream van, an old 1960s Bedford, was parked on the other side of the road. Up close and in the brilliant sunshine, it was a lot more battered than it first appeared. The bumper had several dents, and while an attempt had been made to paint over them, the pink bodywork did not quite match. Eddie tapped the bumper, which was falling off.

"Did that one driving into a gate." *'Yippee, it's Mr Whippy'* was emblazoned above the front and the hatch. The stickers advertising different ice creams were worn and peeling off. Eddie yanked open the door. "Thought I'd give you the official Sealtdock tour." The girls looked at each other and nodded. "Only got two seats...someone will have to sit in the back."

Tina pushed past Mel and jumped into the passenger seat. Like the rest of the van, it was worn and torn. A packet of Golden Virginia tobacco was on the dashboard, and the rest of the cab was a mess. Cigarette butts littered the floor, and an old greasy newspaper from a bag of chips lay crumpled at her feet. Eddie took Mel around to the back doors. Between the freezers was a small space on the floor where there was an old sleeping bag and a pillow.

"Got to make it comfortable for passengers." Mel climbed into the space and sat down. The countertops were covered in splats of ice cream that had congealed in the sun. "Wouldn't eat those cornets. They've been knocking about for years." With a smile, he closed the door.

Mel leant against the side and tried to get comfortable. The sleeping bag was black with dirt, and she wondered if it had ever been washed. She could hear Tina laughing with Eddie in the front and felt annoyed. Tina always pushed herself forward. She was not burdened by niceties and took what she wanted. She had taken the only bedroom in the caravan, and there had been no discussion about it. Mel was comfortable on the seat, which was her bed, but she was not given a choice. She resolved to raise the subject the next time they were home. 'Home'. She rolled the word around in her mouth, thinking of Pauline.

The van's suspension was very poor, and Mel felt every bump. The packet of cornets fell on her head as they turned a corner, and she held on as she picked crumbs out of her hair. Once out of the town, they sped up. The roads were twisted, and Eddie seemed to drive recklessly. It reminded Mel of the journey away from her aunt's house. She could see the countryside and marshland behind her. It was much more open than the claustrophobic ancient roads around Trotham. The vibrant purple of the heath was so different to any environment she knew. She was mesmerised. At last, the van came to a halt and Eddie and Tina got out. Eddie cranked the old doors open, and they both laughed at the broken cornet in her hair.

They had stopped by a tributary river and could see how it meandered across the landscape as it made its way to the sea. Mel was amazed at how clear the water was. Even the river in Trotham had the occasional crisp packet or beer can floating in it, usually near the bus stop where Tina and her biker friends congregated.

The bank naturally sloped, and they could easily reach the edge of the water. Eddie pulled up his jeans.

"Learnt to swim here."

Mel had learnt on holiday in Spain but was not a strong swimmer. She was always in the bottom group at school and had once been rescued when she had a cramp. Jennifer had found this hilarious and had labelled her a *'natural-born sinker'*. Mel had laughed it off but had avoided the pool and the annual swimming galas, even though you got the afternoon off from lessons. The memory embarrassed her even now. She wondered what Jennifer and her entourage were up to in Italy.

"Can't swim." Tina blurted it out without the slightest hint of embarrassment. "Never went to no swimming pool in my life."

Mel was amazed. "Didn't they have a pool at school?"

"No and was never at school anyway."

Eddie laughed. "Me neither. Well, after my mum died, my dad always had jobs for me to do. I'm a rubbish swimmer too."

By now, Eddie was knee-deep in water. The girls took off their shoes and socks and followed suit. The water, despite the hot day, was extremely cold, but after a while, they became accustomed to it. The bottom was also sandy and felt silky between their toes. Tiny fish darted around them.

"Sticklebacks. Shame you can't eat them," said Eddie.

They all sat on the bank and dangled their toes in the water. Eddie pulled a rolled joint out of his pocket and lay back, nonchalantly puffing on it. He passed it around, and they all lay back listening to the running water.

They sprawled out on the verge, talking for what seemed like an age, when Eddie suddenly sat bolt upright. He could hear the bike long before he saw it. The baffles had been taken out, and it made a terrible din, and soon a cloud of dust accompanied the guttural sound of the motorbike.

"Shit! It's my brother," said Eddie.

The driver drove at full throttle toward them, then dramatically skidded the bike around, throwing debris over the three of them. It was a black Norton with classic gold lettering, and astride it sat Eddie's brother.

"Get home, bah!"

He dismounted the bike and stood before them. The sun partially cast his features into silhouette, but his frame was large and imposing. His jeans seemed impossibly filthy, and he wore a faded denim jacket adorned with sewn-on heavy metal badges. He had a much larger frame than his younger sibling and long auburn hair. His square jaw was accentuated by rough gingery stubble. Like a ferocious Viking warrior, he towered above them, glaring. Snatching the joint out of Eddie's hand, he inhaled it and sat down.

"Who's bin bum sucking this?" When he spoke, his voice was broad Suffolk, and he inspected the end. "Pretty shit, Eddie. Or did you do it?" He looked at Mel.

"Fuck off, Vince, it's fine," Eddie replied. "Give it here."

His brother grabbed his arm to stop him. "I'm keeping this." He rolled it between his forefingers which were black with grease. "Now git the fuck home. Dad's doing his nut." With that, Vince got up, took another long puff on the joint, threw it on the ground, climbed back onto his bike and roared away.

"Sorry, got to go. I'll give you a lift back."

Eddie dropped them off at the local shop, and Tina rushed in and bought a large bottle of White Lightning cider. She waved it triumphantly at Mel.

"This will get us pissed."

It was still early, and they decided to wander down to the shore. They were passed by the same group of schoolboys carrying a canoe on their way back from the beach to the campsite. The teacher strode alongside them, barking orders. They all wore cut off wetsuits of various sizes, and most of them were too small and accentuated their stomachs and crotches. The boys formed a long line, with the stragglers quite a distance behind. They giggled and nudged each other as Tina and Mel passed. Once a safe distance away from their teacher, one of the boys wolf-whistled. Tina carried on walking and, without looking back, stuck two fingers up at them. The gesture was met with much hilarity. Mel laughed and looked at Tina. She, as ever, was amazed by her lack of embarrassment.

Following the well-worn path, they made their way down to the seafront and sat on the sand. It had been a busy day, and it felt good to relax. Tina pulled out a readymade joint and lit it. A couple of holidaymakers stared at her, but she did not seem to care.

"Tina, that's illegal. We could get arrested."

"Who they going to tell?" She shouted loud enough for the couple next to them to hear, who packed up their picnic and moved further down the beach. Mel felt anxious, but Tina was enjoying herself. "Pass me that cider and shut up." Mel did as she was told, and within an hour, they were both on their backs looking at the sky. She wasn't sure how long they lay there listening to the waves while enveloped in the warmth of the alcohol and sun.

The cider, in the heat, had gone straight to their heads and they had dozed off. Although it had gone dark while they slept, neither of them felt cold. With the heat, it was difficult to know the time, but Mel guessed it must be nearly ten o'clock.

Tina skipped through the campsite, laughing. A few people shouted at them.

"Keep it down."

"Children trying to sleep."

Mel laughed and realised she was still quite drunk as Tina wove in and out of the tents. Twice she tripped over guy ropes and once fell on top of a man cleaning his shoes. Tina spun around and told him to watch it. The man responded with a tut, but Tina just told him to fuck off.

They passed a row of different family tents, all locked up for the night. Their occupants had gone into town, and pathetic little locks hung at the tip of the door.

"I could break into them. No trouble," said Tina.

The tents belonging to the schoolboys were obvious. They were all the same beige canvas and arranged in neat rows. The canoes were neatly lined up and chained together. A worn flag hung limply on a flag pool outside, which they assumed was the teacher's tent. They had lit a fire, but it was now just a smouldering mess of kicked earth. Tina dropped down to her knees and began to crawl between the tents. They could hear the boys whispering to each other inside. Tina beckoned to Mel to get closer. Mel grinned as they realised they were talking about them.

"Which one of them...the big one or the little one?"

"Big one, got bigger tits."

Tina sniggered and put the thumbs up to Mel. They covered their mouths and tried desperately not to laugh. The inane chatter continued.

"What's that shop in London where you can buy anything?"

"A camel, chocolates…."

"Even a bottle of cum!"

"Harrods."

They stuffed their T-shirts in their mouths. Tina neatly pulled out two of the tent pegs, and they stealthily crawled away on their stomachs.

Although it was late, Tina wasn't ready for bed. She grinned at Mel and insisted they go back into town.

"It's ten o'clock." Tina pulled a face, and Mel laughed.

They raced down to the road and were nearing the centre of town. The old village hall sat forlornly on the road. It had been built in the sixties and had a gravel car park. Each space had been filled by holidaymakers, despite the signs politely requesting them not to park there. Tina sat on the steps and rolled a cigarette. Mel looked at the door and tried to read the homemade posters. There was to be an art show and a country and western dance. She turned around, but Tina was gone. Walking around the hall, she saw Tina opening one of the side windows. In the heat, someone had forgotten to close it.

"Tina, for Christ's sake!"

She heard voices and had no choice but to follow. She could hear Tina rummaging around in the kitchen.

"There might be some food we can nick."

The kitchen was small but beautifully kitted out. A small plaque said it had been funded by the Rotary Club. Mel felt a sudden rush of anger.

"My dad was in that. Least he said he was. Probably out with some woman."

Tina wasn't listening. She was too busy foraging, but the fridge was bare. She rammed a small canister of table salt and sachets of tomato ketchup into her pocket.

Suddenly a door slammed, and they could hear voices. Mel and Tina froze and ducked down. The hatch of the kitchen led into the main hall, and they could just make out denim-clad bikers milling around, swigging from bottles of cider and boisterously pushing one another, but they could not see their faces. They smelt of sweat and beer. A lone voice commanded for quiet, and there was almost instant silence. Tina tried to crane her neck but could see very little.

"This is an official meeting of the Sealtdock chapter." There was the sound of a thud as one of the bikers, who was still talking, was kicked. "I said shut up," the leader continued, his voice raised. "That's not something you take lightly. Brothers have rules. Anyone who breaks them gets the consequence." He lingered over the word emphasising its importance.

Mel was sure she could see the gleam of a large knife. The group fell silent. Pausing for dramatic effect, he pointed to one of the group.

"Richard here; he wants in." The group parted, and a younger boy not much older than Tina made his way into the group. "That's right, hint it?"

"Yit, that's right," the boy managed to mouth almost inaudibly.

Tina strained but couldn't quite see what was in his hand. It was some sort of leather holdall that he swung around his head and threw at the nervous boy.

"Open it...lay them out on the ground." He appeared to pull out a pair of Levi's. "Git your jeans off. Now!" Tina watched in amazement as the boy stripped to his white underpants. He stood nervously, covering himself up with his hand. "Hope you lot have all had enough beer tonight."

"Yit ready to burst."

"You go first, Danny and then the rest of you."

One by one, they all urinated on the jeans then the leader kicked the corner of the material up with his foot.

"Right, you put them on." The boy hesitated, and the

group crowded around. "You got a problem with that, boy?"

"No, course not."

"You don't take them off for a year. You don't wash 'em for a year. That's what you have to do." The boy picked them up and pushed his foot into the sodden legs. When he had done them up, the others circled him. "That is an honour. Don't let us down."

The boy stood beaming in the middle and was patted on the back by the other bikers. One offered him a swig of the cider.

"One of us now," said the leader solemnly.

"There's a party at Davey's tonight," chimed one of the boys excitedly.

The bikers, thirsty for more booze, filed out. The leader followed them and, on his way out, threw the chair covers into the puddle of urine. He spat and walked away. Mel and Tina looked at one another, horrified.

"Cawd der hell, if that had been me, I'd be right down that seafront and in the water," said Tina.

"Wouldn't want to meet him on a dark night."

They had been unnerved by the initiation ceremony. Tina had heard of these sorts of rites of passage but just assumed they were exaggerated. She thought back to her gang in Trotham. They might just shout at people or scratch the odd car, but it never felt like they would physically harm anyone. No, there was something malevolent about that man. She hadn't seen his face, but deep down, she knew it was Vince.

CHAPTER 11

Pauline strode down the high street past the numerous posters. They were everywhere: on the post box, bus stop, village hall and even The Bell had one on its front door. It made her feel relieved but also more anxious, bringing home how serious the situation was.

The women had divided the street up into sections, and every household was to be interrogated with a series of set questions. It was, as Clive had named it, a 'military manoeuvre'. Pauline looked at her list. The old Almshouses by the bridge were in her patch, and it seemed like as good as any place to start.

The houses, once built for the poor, were very beautiful. They were made of knapped flint, on one floor, and were ideal for the elderly residents who mostly lived there. Unlike a lot of the villages, they had not been sold off to 'furriners' from London. She knocked on the first two doors, and while the occupants were sympathetic, they had not seen a thing. Pauline reminded herself that they were very old and rarely left the house, except perhaps to go to the shops.

Tina's mother's house was the third one along. The other houses were well kept, but this house was a mess. An old carpet lay rotting outside, the rubber back flaking and blowing away in the breeze. A broken wooden chair lay in pieces on what had once been a lawn but was now knee-high in weeds. All the curtains were drawn, and a broken pane had been amateurishly boarded up with chipboard. Pauline knocked on the door and waited. There was no sign of life, but she saw a shadow move behind the window and knocked again.

"Tracey, it's Pauline. Can you open the door?"

More time passed, and then a thin hand reached around the door.

"What you want?"

The figure dressed in a faded, stained dressing gown appeared. Her face was lined, and her eyes squinted at the light. She stank of cigarettes and looked emaciated. Out of the corner of her eye, Pauline saw a large, surly man in the background.

"What you want?" Tracey repeated. Some of her teeth were missing, and she spoke between rasping coughs. Pauline explained about Mel going missing and asked her if she had seen anything.

Tracey laughed. "My Tina hint bin around for a few days. You don't see me making no posters about it."

Pauline looked appalled. "How old is she?"

"Seventeen. I had a baby by that age. She'll be off with them biker boys."

The man in a vest came to the door, and he aggressively chipped in. "Come back when she's ready."

He pulled Tracey in and shut the door. Pauline stood there, slightly dazed. She had always had a soft spot for Tina. As a child, she was out in all weather, without a coat. Her hair was unkempt, and her clothes were dirty. Her mother was a well-known drunk and was often in fights at The Bell. In more recent years, she had ventured out less, and Pauline assumed she just drank at home or worse. As Tina got older, she rarely spoke to Pauline but would nod when her gang of friends were not looking. The situation with Tina made her uneasy. She carried on to the other houses and looked forward to meeting up in the afternoon with the other women. Anxious for any snippet of information, she trudged on.

At 7.15 pm, everyone already had their seats. The village hall was crammed with people eager to help. Pauline knew a lot of them, and some by sight only. While grateful, Clive wondered how many had come to watch the spectacle. Nothing ever happened in Trotham. Most, while well-meaning, were curious, if not nosey.

Pauline paced up and down. She was desperate that someone would know something. Denise, a friend of many years, had offered to take minutes, "In case we forget something." Everyone agreed this was a good idea.

The police had said they would make an appearance, and Clive hoped it would add more urgency. He patted the pile of posters on his lap and took a deep breath. Pauline stood at the front, nervously rubbing her hands together. The clock hit 7.30 pm, and Pauline made an announcement.

"I know we said we would start at half-past seven, but Constable Butler hint here yet. I reckon we should give him another ten minutes."

There was a murmur of agreement in the room. Emma, bored, looked at Clive out of the corner of her eye. She recognised his jacket, although old, was a traditional tweed. His shoes, battered as they were, were Italian leather. Wear had enhanced the pattern and showed how expensive the leather had once been. Clive was what her mother would call a 'proper gentleman'. She had done well with Alan. He drove a fast car, a Porsche and, like her, enjoyed wearing expensive clothes. When they had moved to Trotham, it had been a culture shock. There was only one shop, and the people grunted more than spoke. They had gone to the local pub on their first night, which didn't even stock bitter lemon. She doubted if the surly landlord had even heard of it. Alan had tried to get into the spirit of things and had drunk four pints of Abbot. She was furious when she virtually had to carry him upstairs. Their first night in their new house had been spent listening to Alan throw up. Unable to sleep, she lay awake wondering if the move had been a massive mistake.

The first few months had been lonely. After the holidays, when the children started at the new school, she met some of the other mums. They were like her, affluent families, and she soon had a wide circle of similar people to have coffee with. She enjoyed inviting them around to her house, and it was certainly one of the largest in the village. They had knocked two houses together, and the building work had taken four months longer than expected. They had already spent a fortune on renovations and had had to stay in the Angel Hotel in Bury St Edmunds while the work was being completed. Once inside, she had enjoyed decorating and had chosen everything herself. Alan indulged her and allowed her a very generous budget.

"Where's Alan tonight?" Carole asked innocently.

"Oh, working again. Got to keep the wolves from the door."

They had both laughed, but Emma felt a pang of annoyance. He was rarely around these days, and when he was, he seemed tired. Her eyes fell back to Clive. With a bit of grooming, he would be a very nice catch.

One of her friends leant over to her and whispered, "Have you seen Pauline's shoes?" They chuckled at the Scholl sandals, which were frayed on one side. "Very stylish."

At last, the constable arrived, and the hall was suddenly silent. Pauline felt overwhelmed and held on tight to Clive's hand.

"Thank you all for coming tonight. This is now a missing person investigation. I want you to think hard about what you have seen in the last few days. Let us know anything, however small, that could be of help to us."

The officer passed over to Pauline. The policewoman methodically went through what they knew about the day. She invited everyone who had knocked on doors to report back.

"Hint no news from the buses, Paul. Ted asked around and went up to the other depot at Ipswich. He put posters up and everything," Betty said.

"I went around the Saniclifte Estate, and no one had seen nothing," added Doreen. Emma nudged Carol at the bad grammar.

The officer who had been listening intently read from her notebook. "Mr Saputo reports he heard some girls fighting by his shop but did not really think much of it."

Pauline looked at the shopkeeper, her neighbour of over twenty years.

"I wish I could tell you more, Pauline. I was serving Betty Cooper about 10.30 am."

"That's right. I'd come in for my crochet magazine. He has to order it," Betty piped up, feeling very important.

"I heard some shouting. I looked out the window and saw Tina Green. She was chasing someone up the road, but I couldn't hear much," Mr Saputo said weakly.

"That girl," someone whispered audibly.

"I am so sorry, Pauline. Those girls hang around my shop a lot. They are not bad, really. I didn't think much of it."

Pauline smiled at the old man. He had a gentle face, and she could understand how he would dismiss a teenager scuffle. It was probably not even Mel. Tina was always in trouble.

"That girl could create trouble in hell," someone whispered, but everyone heard.

Pauline looked at the policewoman and revealed that Tina had not been seen for days.

"I spoke to her mum today. She doesn't seem too worried," said Pauline.

"That's a surprise," said Denise as she held Pauline's hand. "Could they have gone off together?"

The policewoman took some notes and promised to follow it up immediately. Pauline thought it was probably just a coincidence, but it made her feel better to know that there might be two of them missing. She instantly berated herself as she would never wish harm on a child, but it meant Mel would not be alone.

At last, the meeting ended. There was no other new information, and Clive and Pauline felt deflated. They walked back home and tried again to call Julian. Pauline picked up Mel's orange gonk and stroked its synthetic hair flat.

"Tomorrow's another day, and we can go out and talk to the houses that were missed yesterday."

Pauline nodded, and they wandered up the stairs to bed.

***

The next day, Clive found Pauline sitting on her own in the garden. It was cold, and she only wore a flimsy top. She was sitting underneath the rowan tree and was touching its bark with her hand. Clive hesitated before calling out to her. He knew she drew strength from the old traditional beliefs, and he was sure, in her way, she was asking for help. When they had renovated the house, they had found a child's shoe and a dead cat in the walls—ancient superstitions of protection. Clive had wanted to throw them away, but Pauline had insisted they remain.

Clive loved her knowledge of the countryside. Not just recognising the birds but delighting in them. Before they met, he only knew a handful, but he now could spot all sorts of varieties. Her love of birds was infectious, and he found himself hiding behind the hedges to get a better look. He was aware that she had been brought up in poverty. Having experienced the power cuts of the seventies, she would often wrap butter in plantain leaves. Her parents, now long dead, had taught her to supplement foods from the land. Books had taught him that the Romans had introduced ground elder to Britain to eat, but Pauline taught him how to pick the tender younger leaves and cook them.

"We hint having none of that in the garden. That'll spread like wildfire."

Unusually for Suffolk, she was an only child. Her parents had tried for years to conceive. Clive knew she blamed herself for their lack of children. He often wondered what a child would have brought to their lives, but he loved her so completely. To him, she was enough.

He rubbed his wife's shoulder and tried to reassure her that it would all be fine. Pauline looked up and smiled.

"Well, that no good sitting around here feeling sorry of myself. Going to go out and see what else I can find out."

Clive nodded. "We'll do it together."

"Still got a few houses to talk to."

Pauline had been surprised and slightly hurt that Maureen had not come to the meeting or the subsequent one at the village hall. While she was still working through her list of designated houses, she felt the need to see her. She banged on the door.

Maureen was awoken by the knocking and did not dare move. She had been in bed all day, only venturing out to the toilet. That had hardly been an issue as she had not eaten or drunk anything. The knocking persisted, and she placed a pillow over her ears.

"Just go away," she whispered to herself.

Pauline looked at the drawn curtains and the milk that had been out all day. It had congealed, and the top had been pushed off by the expanding liquid. Pauline looked through the letterbox and wondered if she was ill. They had been friends for many years, and she was sure she would not have forgotten to take in the milk, especially in this weather.

She walked around the side of the house and tried to peep into the kitchen. The lace curtains were hard to see through, but she did notice some bread on the floor. Again, this was very uncharacteristic. Maureen's house was always immaculate. She used to laugh at Pauline about how she liked to never throw anything away. It was something she had inherited from her mother after the war. It was hard to throw off the austerity, and she found herself saving everything, even old bits of rope.

The little blue Mini, normally parked outside, was missing, so she assumed she must be away. Maureen had no family, and it was very unlike her to go away on her own. Pauline felt uneasy, but the milk and lack of car certainly suggested she was out.

Maureen was relieved when her visitor left. She sat up in bed. Her scarlet face was bloated from crying. With all her energy, she hurled her legs over the side of the bed and tried to stand up. It had been two days now, and she had eaten nothing. Pain pounded behind her eyes, and she realised she was dehydrated. Feeling numb, she desperately tried to quell the thoughts of Alan and dragged herself up.

CHAPTER 12

Tina had announced she was going into town, and Mel had been happy to lie in bed. She had eventually walked down to the sea and was delighted to see the pink ice cream van. Eddie leant across and opened the door for her to jump in.

Mel was pleased to have him all to herself, but Eddie seemed quiet. His usual casual humour was replaced with silence, and Mel wondered if she had done something wrong.

"You all right?"

"Yeah." His voice was flat.

Mel looked down. He had never been like this. She instantly felt it was something she had done or said, and he sensed her unease.

"Sorry, Mel, my mum's birthday today." Mel glanced at Eddie, and he looked like he might cry.

"Oh, sorry." Feeling inadequate, she squeezed his arm. "Does your family do anything?"

Eddie scoffed. "Haven't even remembered." They drove on in silence.

After a while, Mel asked, "Where is she buried?"

"She's not. Got her cremated. Probably cheaper." Eddie's face was dark. "I scattered her ashes on the heath. Mrs W came with me."

Mel was surprised as Mrs Wilbraham never left the house. She was obviously very attached to Eddie and loved his mother.

"It was a spring day. Really cold, and we stood on the fen road opposite Sealtdock. It was funny. We opened the urn, and a wind came up. The dust almost danced on the breeze. It flew right across…the sun also came out." Mel looked at Eddie, and she knew he was remembering it in his mind. "It was beautiful." Eddie blushed. "Sorry, I sound like a twat."

"No, it sounds lovely."

"I think she would have liked it, to be amongst the birds and wildlife."

By now, they had reached Sealtdock church. Mel recognised it as a perpendicular design, but the nave was much older. Curved Norman arches framed the windows, and she wondered how many times it had been rebuilt.

The flint work was ornate and suggested a time when Sealtdock had been an affluent fishing town.

Eddie walked through the old wooden gate. The graves near the front of the church were much older. Most were so worn you could hardly read their inscriptions. Others were for families and were substantial concrete blocks, but many had crumbled at the corners and were overgrown and decaying. They were careful not to walk on the graves. Eddie wandered around to the side and made a beeline for one of the more modern headstones. It was overgrown, and a jam jar of wildflowers had been there for some time. Eddie was on his hands and knees, clearing the weeds, while Mel peered to read the inscription.

Douglas Wilbraham 1910 – 1976 husband and artist.

She helped Eddie clear some of the weeds.

"Does Mrs W ever come here?"

"No, don't think she can." Mel guessed it was more than her health. "I come sometimes and give it a bit of a clean-up. Never really do it right."

Eddie walked over to the church wall and picked up some rusty discarded shears. He began to hack at the grass, trying to make it flat. Mel scanned the graveyard and picked some mallow and clover. The pink and white combined beautifully. The tap on the side of the church was stiff, but she managed to fill up the jam jar and arrange the flowers.

"Won't last long," she said.

They stood back and admired their handy work. Eddie looked wistful.

"Mrs W was never really the same after Doug went. He used to be quite a famous painter, exhibited in London. His work was worth a bomb. She can't bear to part with it, any of it. My mum told me she's got a room full of his paintings. She only saw it once when the roof leaked. Mrs W was doing her nut that Doug's work would be ruined."

"Was it?"

"No, the leak didn't reach that far." Mel touched the top of the grave and tried to imagine what he looked like. "She's never picked up a paintbrush since."

"Is that when she started drinking?"

"I think they were both pissheads. They'd drink and paint together. It was fun. Now? Well, I don't think she enjoys it." Eddie took one last look at the grave and announced he would have to go back. He climbed into his van and donned his hat. "Can't let the children down."

Mel turned down the offer of a lift and ambled down to the town. The sun was not too hot, and she felt happy. She had enjoyed Eddie's company and felt privileged that he had let her know his private thoughts. His mother's death had hit him hard. She thought about her own mother. At least she was still alive. Well, sort of.

Pauline entered her mind, and she was struck again by guilt. She knew her aunt would be out of her mind with worry. Twice she had nearly called her but had panicked.

She blocked her thoughts. She was not ready to face the consequences. They had stolen a car, and Tina would be furious. Breathing in the salt air, she made her decision. No, she would leave it.

***

The next morning, Tina had disappeared. She guessed she had wandered down to see Norman. Wary of him herself, she was glad of Tina's friendship with the old man. It meant they were less likely to be found out. Stretching, Mel felt the sun warming her face through the window. She waited briefly for Tina but then decided to explore her surroundings. Instead of following the road into town, she turned in the opposite direction.

Walking for what seemed like hours along the sandbanks, she enjoyed watching the various marsh birds picking their way and stopping to look for food across the hardened mud. The environment felt completely foreign. It was nothing like the oppressive endless hedgerows and narrow lanes of Trotham and so far removed from the busy streets of London. It also felt clean. The sky seemed gigantic, and there were few clouds in the sky. She had not met a soul.

Mel reckoned she had walked about two miles away from the campsite. While the beach had initially started as sandy, it was now stony, and she crossed the various marshy spots on ancient wooden bridges. She came across an old, dilapidated barn full of old nets and on the other side was a road with a row of 1950s houses, which seemed out of place in the wilderness of the shore. She stopped to eat an Opal Fruit, which she had found in her pocket. It took a while to unwrap the paper that had stuck infuriatingly to the sweet.

She looked at the line of houses. Most were well kept and had neat washing hanging outside, but one house stood out from the rest. It resembled a junkyard with an assortment of cars with rusty hulks, and various lumps of metal were strewn across the garden. They had been there some time, and weeds grew out between the metal, which had weathered to an orange-brown.

It was then she saw him—a man smoking. His grey, greasy hair was Brylcreemed back, attempting a Teddy Boy style. Lines criss-crossed his face, so his features were almost gone. He sucked relentlessly on his roll-up, never taking it out of his mouth. His skin had been hardened into permanent creases by the sun. White hair spiked in tufts out of his filthy vest, and his arms were adorned with faded but garish tattoos. He kept pulling up his trousers, which were far too big.

Mel instantly disliked him and found herself hiding behind the barn door. As she did so, she saw Eddie's ice cream van tearing up the road. It pulled into the house, narrowly missing the gate. To Mel's surprise, Vincent came out of the house and waited with who she presumed was their father. The older man shouted at Eddie.

"Get in, bah." There was some sort of exchange that Mel could not hear until Eddie almost screamed.

"I hint doing it."

The older man grabbed Eddie by the neck and forced

his face close to his ear. "You do as you are bluudy told, boy."

He did not let go of his grip and marched him to the door, pushing him inside. Vincent stood a distance apart and laughed. Then the door shut. Mel stayed hidden in the barn, unsure what to do. Terrified they would see her, she remained in her hiding place for a good ten minutes. Walking as fast as she could, she made her way back to the caravan.

Once on the coastal road, Mel heard a beep and saw Eddie grinning from behind the wheel of his van.

"Get in."

"You ok? I saw you earlier. I went for a walk, and I saw your dad shout at you. I wasn't spying, honest."

Eddie stared straight ahead, and they drove on in silence. Mel wished she hadn't said anything. Anxiety built inside her, and she felt she had made a terrible mistake.

"You know my dad's a bastard too?" She just blurted it out. "I've just found out he's got another wife," her voice broke, "and another family as well." When Eddie spoke, his voice was low.

"My dad's a shagger too. That bastard did it to my mum."

"My dad's more than a shagger. He's got another wife and family, and he's not even in Singapore. He's with his whore and her spawn." Eddie stopped the van and looked at Mel. Her cheeks were bright red. "Bastard."

"Where's your mum?"

"Oh, she's in the nuthouse." Mel laughed and then started to cry.

Eddie put his arm around her, and they sat in silence for a while. He then jumped up and fetched a couple of ice lollies. Mel felt exhausted, and the ice sugar water gave her much needed energy while the frozen juice coated her throat. After a while, he drove her back to the campsite, where he grabbed her hand and smiled.

"Thanks for the ice cream."

Walking slowly back to the caravan, she stopped at the toilet block to splash her face. She wondered whether to tell Tina about what she had witnessed.

CHAPTER 13

Tina meandered back to the caravan. The sun was hot, and her legs felt heavy. Vince was at the corner of the road smoking a cigarette. He was kicking the pavement and throwing tiny stones against the wall.

"All right?" he asked.

"Yit."

"Want a lift?" He gestured with his head towards the bike.

"Hint got no helmet."

He offered her his, but Tina pushed it away and clambered onto the back of the bike. She was grateful that she had been on bikes before and knew to hold on underneath rather than around Vince's waist. She hoped he would notice. His hair cascaded down and stuck to his neck with sweat, and he smelt of oil and grit. As he turned to speak to her, she could see the individual stubbly hairs on his chin. He revved the engine, and she felt a jolt of excitement.

"Ready?"

The bike roared away and caught Tina a little by surprise. She momentarily wobbled until she found her balance. Vince shouted over the engine's noise to ask if she wanted to go faster, and she shouted that she did but doubted if he could hear her.

They careered around the road, weaving in and out of cars. He stuck his fingers up at a couple who chastised him and revved his engine more. Once out of the town, they sped along the coastal road back to the campsite, and the sea flew past in a continuous stream of blue. Her knuckles were sore from the pressure of holding on so tightly, but she felt exhilarated and did not want the ride to end. Eventually, Vince came to a standstill, and Tina clambered off.

"Thanks, Vince."

"Aim to please." He pretended to tug at his forelock. Tina struggled for something to say and asked him about his T-shirt, which had three black claw marks and the word Shuck.

"Hint never seen that afore," she said.

Vince smiled. "That's my band, that is." Tina was impressed.

"Cawd der hell. You any good?"

"Fuckin brilliant. Come and see us. We're at the community hall. Ask Eddie. He'll show ya."

He turned the bike around and disappeared. Tina watched him until he was a tiny dot. She had enjoyed the ride, and there was something about Vincent that she liked. He felt slightly dangerous.

She suddenly felt a hand on her shoulder.

"Hold yew hard." Norman was standing next to her. He was slightly out of breath. "Are you deaf or summin? Bin hollering for ages. I got summin you might like."

Tina followed him into what she assumed was his house, which doubled as the campsite office. Norman looked at her, and his face darkened.

"That boy, he hint no good. I'd keep away from him if I were you."

The kitchen, which had very little furniture, had a large pot bubbling on the stove. The cupboards looked handmade, and a pile of junk sat on the wooden table.

"Reckon you might like this." He pulled out a camping stove, which had two rings and a small canister of gas. "Don't think that has bin used. Them London lot left it. Then I thought you hint got no cooker or nothing, have ya?"

"Thank you, that's grut." Tina felt a little bit

overwhelmed by his kindness. Norman smiled, and she noticed he had a few teeth missing, and some were black. He put a kettle on the stove and offered Tina a cup of tea.

"Hint got no sugar, but I 'ave got some biscuits in that ole tin." Tina rummaged around and found a scratched tin full of custard creams. It struck her as slightly bizarre. Norman clearly had a sweet tooth as he demolished about six biscuits dunking each one in his tea.

"How long you been here then?" she asked. Norman told her how he used to work in the field as a labourer, occasionally helping out on the fishing boats.

"That is till I went to war."

"How old were you?"

"Bout the same as you, I reckon."

He told her how the town had changed from a rural backwater to a holiday resort and how all the old industries had died.

"Lots of furriners moved in—artists, tourists and Londoners who got all the grut old houses. But they only live in them two week a year. Local people, they can't afford no house round here now." Tina enjoyed talking to Norman, but he suddenly made a move. "Got a go, gal. Got a new lot coming in."

He grabbed a set of keys and stuffed them in his frayed pocket when Tina noticed his trousers were tied with string. She picked up the stove, and he handed her four potatoes, salad cream and a tin of tuna.

"You might as well have these. They always leave stuff behind, and I don't like tuna." Tina thanked him. "Oh, and I was going to chuck this but reckon you and the young 'un might like these." A large pink vanity case was handed over. Tina had never possessed such a decadent item, and she ran her fingers over the seams. For years, she had washed her hair in washing-up liquid, and her bathroom had one bar of soap. She clutched the case to her chest, balanced the camping stove in her hands, and almost skipped back.

Once back at the caravan, she showed Mel her hoard. They were grateful for the food and excitedly opened the vanity case. It contained all manner of makeup and potions, and they took them out, one by one, lining them up on the table. There was an inner bag stuffed with more makeup, including Maybelline eyeshadows in various purple shades. Tina was particularly pleased with the black eye pencil and cooed with delight. Mel pulled out a large pink bottle of Salon Selective shampoo, toner, moisturiser and a bottle of Tramp perfume. In one of the pockets at the front, Mel triumphantly pulled out a blue Tampax holder with two tampons.

"Thank Christ for that."

Tina grabbed it. "Bloody brilliant these are for holding spliffs." She emptied it and rammed one inside that she had previously rolled. "That don't get all battered, and it keeps the tobacco fresh. Bloody brilliant."

She put it in her pocket while Mel rubbed some of the moisturiser on her hands. It soaked in and smelt of cocoa butter, which reminded her of being on holiday. Bright sunlight was still streaming through the window, and Mel felt warm and content. They lay back and surveyed their new belongings. It had been a good day.

Mel told Tina about visiting the grave and spending time with Eddie. Tina grinned.

"Reckon he fancies you." Mel found herself blushing.

"Oh, I don't think so."

"Can't be a virgin forever."

Mel looked at Tina. She hadn't even kissed him. Tina laughed and told Mel of her ride on Vince's bike and about his band. She was still smiling to herself when they eventually went to bed.

CHAPTER 14

It had become a regular pastime to hang out with Eddie in his van. Mel had darted into the front, determined that she would not always be in the back. They drove aimlessly along the coastal road to the other side of town, where the houses were much larger. It was the most affluent area, and many of the enormous buildings were second homes. Eddie drove along, pointing out the houses he would like to live in.

"Pub?" he suggested.

"Got no money," said Mel.

Eddie grinned. "Got a mate. Works at The Ark."

He swung the van around, and they parked on the verge. The Ark was an 18th-century tavern with old, heavy, timber beams. It had been done up for the tourists and had lost much of its charm. Over-furnished, with red and green carpet, it was trying too hard. Pictures of black and white fishing boats adorned the walls, and there were photographs of people in old-fashioned swimsuits paddling in the sea. Other pictures depicted the town as it had been in 1900. Mel squinted to see if she recognised anything. The caravan park was non-existent, but many of the guesthouses remained.

Mel nudged Tina and nodded towards a sign advertising 'Sealtdock's very own, Judith Stamford-Dailey, artist-in-residence'. Her prints, lining the wall, were tastefully displayed with their exorbitant price tags.

"Jesus! £800 quid," said Tina.

Various groups of families, with bored teenagers, sat eating lunch. They chose a secluded booth away from the holidaymakers, where Tina expertly rolled three fags while Eddie walked up to the bar.

"Dave…All right?" said Eddie.

Dave, a bit older than Eddie, was dressed like all the local youths in a AC/DC T-shirt. His hair was lank, and he looked exhausted. They exchanged knowing looks.

"Sort me out later?" said Dave, and Eddie nodded. The girls couldn't understand what was being said, but no money appeared to change hands.

Eddie was soon back with pints of Abbots. Mel had experimented with smoking, and while she still was not sure if she enjoyed it, she managed to inhale without coughing. The cigarette made her thirsty, and she greedily drank the beer, which tasted delicious.

"Slow down," said Eddie. Mel had become quite accustomed to drinking pints and soon polished hers off before Tina was halfway through hers.

"The apprentice becomes the master." Tina quickly gulped down the rest of her pint and grinned. Eddie hurried back to the bar and returned with three shots of tequila. Mel looked at the clear liquid and smelt it.

"Jesus, Eddie, smells like petrol." She was unsure what to do. Following Eddie's instructions, she hesitantly lifted it to her lips.

"Don't spill it," said Eddie. She drained it and then followed it by sucking the tart lime slice and salt. Each one of them pulled a face.

"That's disgusting."

"Don't want another one then?" laughed Eddie.

"Didn't say that."

The liquor surged down her throat and rested in her stomach, heating her from the inside, and she felt in fine form. The alcohol had lifted her, and she laughed and joked along with the others. She momentarily wondered what Jennifer and her friends would be doing in Italy. While missing out on a glamorous holiday still hurt, she doubted if she would feel so relaxed. Time passed quickly, and soon there were numerous empty glasses on the table.

A well-dressed man in a purple Pringle jumper asked them to keep the noise down. They just looked at one another and laughed. Mel saw him go up to the bar and complain, and she nudged Tina.

"He can fuck off," said Tina.

Before, Mel would have been embarrassed, but with Eddie and Tina beside her, she felt untouchable. Eventually, Dave came up to the table.

"Sorry, Twat wants you to leave. Noise and language." Dave raised his eyebrows. Eddie looked over to the bar, and the man was shaking his head at him. He whispered in Dave's ear.

"Drop it round tomorrow, mate."

Tina glared at the man and deliberately smashed a glass on her way out. The whole bar stopped to look at them.

"What you looking at?"

No one dared catch her eye. They all continued to look at their dinners as if they were the most fascinating things in the world. Once outside, they laughed.

"Fuckers!" said Tina.

"Probably the most exciting thing that's happened all their holiday."

Eddie announced he was too drunk to drive and was starving. They sat on the kerb and, between them, scraped together eighty-three pence. They managed to buy one bag of chips and sat by the sea, sharing them out. Eddie had put on too much salt, and Mel nearly tipped them on the floor, trying to get the bottom layer.

While they were fighting over the chips, they saw the man who had complained about them getting out of a large blue car. As he walked into the local shop, Eddie jumped to his feet and reached in the bin. He pulled out a portion of fish that was half-eaten and had obviously been in the sun all day and smelt rancid. Casually walking past the car, he hurled the offending fish onto the front seat.

All three of them hid behind the bins laughing. The man came out and lit a cigarette, and he leaned against the car for ages.

"Bluudy poser," said Eddie.

Eventually, he sat in the seat. They crouched down, shaking with laughter as the man hurriedly got out. His light-coloured slacks were stained with the residue of the rotting fish. He looked around furiously, and they ducked down, nobody daring to move. Eventually, he drove off.

"That'll teach that bastard." Eddie looked at his hands and ran down to the sea. "Going to have to wash these."

When he came back, he lifted Mel over his shoulder.

"Don't, Eddie! For Christ's sake."

He hurled her into the water. The sudden coldness shocked her, and for a second, she went completely under. Eddie and Tina looked at each other, then burst out laughing when Mel came out spluttering.

"Bastards!"

While Tina was laughing, he picked her up and hurled her in as well. Eddie ran off, followed by the drenched girls.

They waddled back to the campsite, complaining that their shoes were squelching. A few people smirked and pointed them out. Still dripping, Mel was relieved for the pile of stolen clothes and gratefully put them on. Her eagerness was not lost on Tina.

"Happy I nicked them now, aren't ya?"

She picked up the wet ones and unceremoniously dumped them on the grass outside. Tina pulled out the tobacco from her jeans. It was sodden.

"Rizlas have had it."

She laid what was left of the Golden Virginia on a plate and put it by the window to dry out. Mel leaned back and read a copy of the Radio Times. It had been a good day and she hadn't thought about her dad once. She felt a pang of guilt but chased it away, determined not to spoil what had been a fantastic day. Her lips tasted of salt, and her skin glistened from the seawater. She was too tired to contemplate anything and just needed to sleep.

CHAPTER 15

It was early and Tina had a slight headache. She had woken up with pain behind her ear, and it had gotten progressively worse. Mel had been talking nonstop, moaning about how she should be in Italy and washing in the sea, not outside a filthy toilet block. Tina had ignored her, but she was beginning to grate.

Back at the caravan, people were busy moving into the caravan opposite.

"That's all we bluudy need. Neighbours!" Tina glared at the boy sitting outside, who had a pudding-basin haircut and was shouting.

"Mum, Mum, got any crisps?"

A packet of Monster Munch was hurled out of the window. The boy was occupied with an Evel Knievel stunt motorbike figurine toy. He continued to wind up the red plastic handle and release it onto the path. It ran past Mel's legs and fell over, and she picked it up and gave it back.

"Watch it," Tina hissed.

The boy was oblivious, but Mel was annoyed with Tina. She had been in a mood since she woke up, and she wondered why she had to be so aggressive.

Once inside the caravan, Tina lit a cigarette. Mel sat at the table and pretended to read another *Radio Times*. She could hear the boy winding up his toy and retrieving it until he was called in.

"Going out," Tina announced.

"Where?" asked Mel.

"Just bluudy out."

Tina marched along the path and felt overwhelmed with irritation. The neglected child sitting outside had reminded her of home. Mel, although they had fun together, was not like her. She had never gone hungry or had to fight off the pawing of one of her mother's latest men.

The whining about Aunty Pauline also annoyed her. Pauline had a good heart, and she had given her food when she was hungry when there was nothing at home. She thought back to when she was about eight, wandering the high street, cold and bored. Pauline had stopped her and, careful not to embarrass her, had rubbed her tummy and pretended to be full.

"Oh, I'll never eat all these."

It never seemed strange that Pauline would have sandwiches with her. Ravenous and grateful, Tina would hang around outside her house, hoping she would invite her in for tea. On one occasion, she had been standing outside all day. It was freezing, and she had walked up and down the road, trying to keep warm. Pauline had given her a pair of woollen gloves, telling her she had knitted them so badly they would only go into the bin. Tina still remembered how Pauline had rubbed her hands together to warm them up and slipped a chocolate bar into her pocket. Mel didn't know she was born.

She spied Norman watering the plant tubs outside his office while cramming biscuits into his mouth. Bizarrely, he seemed only to grow vegetables, which was strange, as he had such a sweet tooth. Tina nodded, smiled, and he summoned her to come over.

"You all right, gal?" Tina nodded. "You and that young one been causing trouble in town. Ole Norman hears everything." Tina found herself blushing as he looked at her sternly. "Don't care what you do in town, but don't bring it to the campsite. You hear?" Tina realised she had been told off. Norman grinned and offered her a custard cream.

"Sorry," she managed to mutter.

Norman looked at the dishevelled girl in front of him. He beckoned her to follow him into the campsite office and pulled out a chair. Pouring her a large cup of tea, he thrust another biscuit in her hand. He noticed how she chipped away at it slowly, trying to make it last. Each bite she savoured, and she licked her fingers to get the last of the sugar.

"Hint you eaten for a while?"

Tina said nothing but blushed. She blew on the tea to cool it. The hot liquid warmed her through, and she looked at Norman and felt the same warmth she had from Pauline all those years ago.

Norman went to the back of the office and began throwing various things on the floor.

"Where is that bugger?"

Eventually, he pulled out a heavy-looking box jammed under a pile of tools. With both hands and a lot of swearing, he hauled it onto the table. Wiping away the dust, Tina lifted the lid. Inside were hammers, bits of broken metal, odd shoes and boots. Nestling amongst them were various tin cans, and Norman pulled them out and lined them up on the table.

"Beans, soup, spaghetti hoops and..." he pulled a face, "tuna."

"I love tuna."

"You're a strange one. That's good for cats." He handed her some loose potatoes. "I'll never eat all these afore they go green."

Tina thanked him and ran back to the caravan. It was

still early, but she felt fortified by the tea and biscuits. The tins she clutched meant they would not go hungry and should last them a few days. She would have to hurry as they only had half an hour before they started work with Mrs Wilbraham.

***

As the girls waited in the corridor for their orders, Mel felt the presence of the older woman studying her. Her eyes rested on her ponytail.

"You dress like someone who is not a native to this godforsaken town. Not really a tourist either, are you? In fact, you seem a very strange pair." Mel mumbled something about looking after her aunt's caravan, and this job was for extra cash.

"Need to raise the money to visit San Fruttuoso…with my friends. We're booking a villa."

Mrs Wilbraham looked at Mel again and nodded. This seemed to appease her, and Mel sighed with relief.

"I've read this is a centre for art and about someone exhibiting. I think they have the artist-in-residence, Jennifer…."

"Stamford-Dailey." She spat the words out and pulled a face. "Fucking artist-in-residence. *'Poppies at Dawn'*, *'Getting in the Fish'*…whoring herself for the tourist pound. Such bloody insipid shit." Mel stared at the floor, and to her relief, Tina returned to the room from the hallway. "Sells that shit for £800. To bloody idiots! Painting by numbers for those with no imagination. You can buy better stuff in Woolworths." There was an awkward moment before she continued. "Now I need the lounge attacked today and the hall. The lounge hasn't been used for a while, so it may be somewhat dusty. There are cleaning utensils in the scullery and dusters under the kitchen sink. Chop, chop." They looked at one another. "I'm having a lie down."

They watched as Mrs Wilbraham wandered to the bedroom. The stink of strong smoke wafted into the hallway, and they could still hear her muttering.

"That bloody woman! Bloody artist-in-residence."

Tina wiped her hands on her T-shirt. "Let's get on with it," she said.

"Reckon she's lying down for a bit," said Mel.

"Smokes that shit, and she will be falling down. Reckon she'll be at the bottle as well."

"She did seem terribly upset by that artist-in-residence. Perhaps she thinks it should be her."

"Piss-artist-in-residence, more like." Tina mimed guzzling wine and they both laughed. Despite laughing at her behind her back, they needed the money.

Tina was excited by the prospect of dusting as it seemed like something only aristocrats would do. Her own house was caked in grime, and their furniture was battered Formica. The corners were chipped so badly that the chipboard underneath fell out in clumps. She had already thoroughly wiped away the dust in the lounge as best she could and had not even been aware that there was such a thing as furniture polish. She hid how she felt, acutely aware of how ridiculous she was being. The heavy wooden table seemed to drink in the polish as if she was feeding it. Changing colour, the wood shone under her gentle strokes. Mel wandered into the room.

"Bloody hell, it stinks in here." Tina was jolted out of her daydream. "Open a window." Tina had been overzealous with the spray, and the fumes were overwhelming. Tina realised her eyes stung and were beginning to stream.

She had enjoyed the dusting and made a beeline for the cabinet in the corridor. Every inch of the yellow cloth groaned with thick dirt. She would need another duster. The kitchen cupboard had a variety of old bottles, but all the cloths had been used when they had cleaned on the first day.

Tina looked to see if she could find another cupboard. At the end of the corridor was an old, bleached-pine, Victorian door. The handle, once brass, was tarnished with age. Tina tried to turn it, but it did not budge. Assuming the door was just stiff, she pushed her shoulder against it, and it creaked but remained tightly closed.

A hand rested on her shoulder and pulled her away with some force.

"No, you don't." Tina spun around. "That is out of bounds. Nothing to see in there." Mrs Wilbraham stood behind her. Her face was bright red, and her voice alarmingly aggressive. "What are you doing in there?"

Tina, thrown at her overreaction, managed to splutter some words out about looking for a duster.

"I think you had both better go." Mel pulled a face behind and, twisting her finger next to her head, gesticulated that Mrs Wilbraham was mad. The girls scuttled away.

"Bloody nutter," said Mel.

They thought better of trying to argue, but Mrs Wilbraham was drunk, and they were anxious not to antagonise her further. They turned and walked out of the front door, which slammed behind them.

Mrs Wilbraham took some deep breaths. She knew she had not behaved well, but she couldn't open that door. She could not face it. It had been ten years. Walking into the lounge, she lit a cigarette. The room stank of polish, but she did not care. Reaching into the drinks' cabinet, she pulled out the brandy and poured herself a generous helping. The burning liquid felt familiar and calmed her almost immediately. It had been a while since she had been on the hard stuff but today felt right. Draining her glass, she helped herself to more. Settling into the chair, she sloshed the brown liquid around in her glass and began to breathe more evenly. Suddenly exhausted, she put her head back and tried to sleep.

Tina and Mel had almost run away from the house and made their way back to the caravan.

"She's a right nut job," said Tina.

"No wonder nobody stays."

Tina felt slightly alarmed by the incident. While she was not fazed by being shouted at, she needed the job. Mel was more disturbed by Mrs Wilbraham's erratic behaviour.

"Do you think we should go back?" she asked.

"Reckon? Let's have a drink."

They opened a bottle of Liebfraumilch. Grabbing the mugs, Mel gave one to Tina but then guzzled it straight from the bottle herself. It was warm and acidic. Mel's stomach was empty, and she was pleased and slightly surprised when Tina started to cook.

The old gas stove proved very efficient, and soon a pan of white potatoes was bubbling away. Tina used an old plate to drain the potatoes and mashed them. She then added a tin of tuna and dolloped a serving of salad cream on top. It had been out in the sun and was slightly congealed, but Mel was so ravenous she did not care.

"That looks a terrible mess, but it tastes all right."

"Eton mess," Mel quipped.

"Not sure what that is, but it's a fucking mess," Tina replied, and they both laughed.

It was surprisingly delicious, and the girls scraped their plates until nothing remained. They continued to drink the wine.

By now, it was dusk, and the people in the next caravan drew their curtains. Their clothes flapped outside on a makeshift washing line, and Tina jumped up. She gestured to Mel to hold the door while she quickly grabbed the T-shirts and jeans and threw them at Mel.

"One each."

Mel looked shocked. "They'll know it's us."

"It's Saturday, and they'll be gone tomorrow."

Mel looked at the clothes. She needed the T-shirt. It was not quite dry, so she laid it on the table. Despite feeling uneasy about taking other people's things, she reminded herself that 'needs must'. She looked at the T-shirt, which was black with a heavy metal band motif.

"Iron Maiden." Tina smiled triumphantly. Mel resigned herself to stealing the clothes. A day of cleaning and walking back in the heat had taken their toll.

They finished off the bottle of wine, shared a joint, and trudged to the toilets. On their way back, they saw the group of adolescent schoolboys. They were parading past the caravan and wolf-whistled. They had been drinking, shouting, pushing and tussling with each other. One of them looked straight at Mel.

"Want some of our cider?"

"Does your mum know you're out?" Tina hung on to the door and scoffed. The tallest boy in the group pulled a packet of cigarettes out of his top pocket. He lit it and took a drag. "Give us a fag, and you can drink your cider in here."

"Tina!" exclaimed Mel.

The boys filed into the caravan and sat down on any floor space they could find. They instantly stopped their raucous behaviour and, not able to think of anything to say, became mute. The confident one with the cigarette was the leader. He was handsome and knew it. 'The Jennifer' of their group, Mel thought to herself and instantly disliked him. Tina snatched a cigarette for herself and threw one at Mel.

"Only got two mugs." They looked at her nonplussed as she grabbed the bottle. "So, me and Mel will have those. You lot can drink out of the bottle." She poured out two generous helpings.

After a few minutes of awkward silence, the boys relaxed, and the confident one asked, "Where you from?"

"London. Ever been?" said Mel.

"Been to Norwich."

"Well, London's got bigger shops…even Harrods." Tina looked at Mel and nearly spat her cider out.

Each boy took a cigarette, and the caravan soon filled with smoke. Suddenly, their teacher bounded into the caravan. He was overweight with a mop of curly hair and dressed in green corduroys. He was the sort of teacher who was young and tried to be one of the boys.

"Right, you lot, out." He gestured with his thumb. Tina ran across the caravan and shouted into his face.

"This is my property. Get the fuck out." The teacher looked shocked. "Get the fuck out." She physically grabbed him and started pushing him aggressively out of the door. Following him out, she continued to shout. "Now fuck off!" Mel looked with astonished admiration. The boys sat open-mouthed.

"Err, we better go," one of them suggested. They quietly got up and filed out.

Mel looked at Tina. She was magnificent. She came back into the caravan. In their haste to leave, the boys had left the packet of Bensons and Hedges. She lit one of the cigarettes and inhaled deeply.

"Can't beat real fags."

The sun was going down, and the girls felt content. They had eaten a meal and were full. Tina laughed about the first time she had seen Mel with her dad.

"Should have nicked your dad's car," said Tina.

"You should have. Cares about that a lot more than me."

Mel found herself telling Tina all about the fact he had

another family and even about her mother. Tina sat and listened. She was uncharacteristically quiet and did not comment or even nod. Mel was surprised and slightly alarmed, and she broke the silence with a random question.

"So, doesn't that man who owns the shop mind you lot hanging about?"

"Mr Saputo? I stop anyone nicking stuff from that shop."

Mel looked puzzled. The man had seemed old and not the sort of person that Tina would have any loyalty to.

"Mr Saputo is an Italian prisoner of war and used to work on the orchards. After the war, he stayed and married his wife, Doreen. She's been dead years. He once saw one of my mum's boyfriends hit me in the shop. He give me a right ole slap."

"Christ, Tina. What did you do?"

"Nothing. But Mr Saputo kicked him out and took me around the back of the shop and gave me tea and cake." Mel looked at Tina, astonished that she was so matter-of-fact. "He gave me all of the cake, not just a slice. I stuffed it in my parka pocket and ate it in my bedroom. I didn't get any tea that night, but I was all right," she said triumphantly.

"Where was your mum?"

"Pissed with Terry."

"How old were you?"

"'Bout seven."

"What happened to Terry?"

"He fucked off, probably dead now. Bastard."

"Did your mum have any more boyfriends?"

Tina laughed. "A few, all wasters, except Dave. He was ok. He gave me a copy of the *Guinness Book of Records.* He didn't last. Adrian–Ady - he's the last one. He's a…." she paused, "he won't leave me alone." She trailed off. Tina was silent for a moment and threw a wine cork at Mel.

"Ouch."

Tina smiled a little. "Now pass me the Golden Virginia."

Mel took a moment to comprehend what she had said. She had seen this man and seen how he had pushed her, but Tina was hinting at something much worse.

They sat up laughing for another hour and eventually went to bed. Mel relived the teacher being so unceremoniously thrown out and found herself laughing out loud. Tina was impressive. But later, Mel couldn't sleep. The conversation about her mum's boyfriends unsettled her, and she replayed what she had said and wondered what she had meant.

CHAPTER 16

They followed the thudding music to the venue. It was an old village hall with posters outside advertising playgroups, things for sale, and a faded picture of a lost cat. Mel wondered if it had ever been found. Motorbikes screamed up and down the road, and throngs of leather-clad teenagers huddled together, drank White Lightning, and smoked cigarettes.

Tina strode confidently towards the entrance. She had drawn thick kohl pencil under Mel's eyes and commanded her to wear a leather jacket she had stolen. Mel felt only half-dressed. Her hair, shaved at the back, was so out of place with the flicks that the other biker girls sported.

They joined the queue to pay, and Mel could feel the anxiety in her stomach building, but Tina was enjoying herself. Mel had never been to a gig before and was not sure what to expect. The girls from school had gone to see The Teardrop Explodes, but she had not been invited as there was 'not enough space' in Jennifer's dad's car.

At last, it was their turn to pay. A tough-looking biker smoked furiously on a roll-up and took their money. Vince poked his head around the door and grinned.

"These two don't need to pay." Mel mouthed the word thank you, and Tina strutted ahead like royalty.

Once inside, the music was deafening, and Mel was struck by how dark it was. The band on stage stood with their legs apart, hammering out their songs. According to the flyer, they were the support group called The Loose Stools. They donned incredibly tight trousers and swung their manes of hair around in a circle. To Mel, the audience appeared to be in layers. Those nearest the stage were manically rocking their heads back and forth like they were in some sort of satanic ritual. As the mass of people thinned out, those at the back were just watching and drinking beer. Mel was unsure what to do, so she took her lead from Tina. She was standing at the side, lighting a cigarette, watching the band, and nodding her head in time to the music.

"Let's find the bar," Tina suggested.

"What?" shouted Mel.

"Bar."

Mel was relieved as they moved away from the jostling mass. The bar was a hatch in the wall and was packed. Throngs of leather arms waving money reached across her. As far as she could tell, they were only serving beer in plastic cups. Not perturbed by the volume of pushing bodies, Tina ploughed her way to the front.

Mel felt a tap on her shoulder and was relieved to see Eddie. The music was still incredibly loud, and he beckoned her into a corner. Reaching under his jacket, he produced a plastic bottle of White Lightning cider, and Tina returned with the beer.

"Neck that," instructed Tina. She thrust the cup towards Mel, who did as she was told. The fizzy beer momentarily made her gag, and Tina and Eddie laughed.

Eddie passed Tina the cider. "Hint got no glasses."

Tina took an enormous swig and drained her glass. You have now."

Mel did the same, it was warm, but she did not care. They edged their way back into the main hall, where Vince and his band were on stage. All of them were dressed the same, in denim and leather, with the band's distinctive claw logo on the drum set. There was a momentary lull as they tuned their instruments.

"Weren't sure you was going to come," said Eddie.

"So, what is Vince's band called?" asked Mel.

"Shuck. It's a devil dog. They say it ran into a church and killed people about five hundred years ago."

"Bollocks," said Tina.

"No, that claw is an actual copy of what's on the church wall when it left. I've seen it. I drew the logo." The girls looked at Eddie, impressed.

"Do you do art?" asked Mel.

"I painted the back of Vince's jacket and a couple of others." Mel remembered the grotesque painted design of a skeleton. "I just copied an Iron Maiden album cover. Art was the only lesson I was good at."

"I'd like to see what else you've done."

Before Eddie could answer, the band started to play. Guitars mingled with drums in a pounding frenzy. Vince strutted around the stage, and while he had a powerful voice, Mel could only decipher the odd word. More and more people crowded into the room, raising the temperature and knocking into her. It was hot and uncomfortable, and as Tina and Eddie pushed towards the front, Mel felt claustrophobic and mouthed to them.

"Going for a wazz."

She pushed her way past scowling, leather-clad girls stood under a sign that read 'ladies'. It was empty with two cubicles, but neither had seats or toilet roll. Cigarette butts littered the filthy floor. The sinks were full of lager cans, and one was full of vomit. She immediately walked out. Anxious to get away, she opened a side door that led outside. The fresh air was welcoming. She could still feel the vibration of the music and hear the cheering and yelping. Mel had not dared take off her jacket, eager as she was to fit in while sweat poured into the small of her back. Sitting on the wall outside, she was grateful for the reprieve.

Out of the corner of her eye, she saw two men holding

someone up against the wall. They had their hands around his throat and were shouting into his face. One of them punched him in the stomach and let him fall to the ground. They then ran past Mel laughing. Cowering into her jacket, she prayed they wouldn't see her.

The person on the ground had been winded but got up relatively easily. He wiped his mouth and checked his hand to see if he was bleeding. Mel's view was obscured by a bush, but she was certain the person attacked had been Eddie. She rushed over to him, but he was gone.

Mel wandered back into the hall and saw Tina. She was standing against the wall smoking. She anxiously scanned the room for Eddie, but he was nowhere to be seen. Vince commanded the stage and continued to strut up and down. A mass of identical leather-clad bikers head-banged rhythmically to the music. They pushed and jostled one another aggressively. The room was roasting, and the noise seemed unbearable. Mel tried to make her way over to Tina but was continually pushed back by the thronging crowd. One of the girls from the shop barged into her shoulder.

"Out the fucking way."

Mel gave up and retraced her steps to the outside of the building. Eddie was nowhere to be seen, and she felt alone. While relieved to be out of the hall, she chastised herself for not enjoying the band. Tina seemed so at home, but Mel hated it and wanted to be back at the caravan.

Mel found the loud music too much and was overwhelmed with a feeling of claustrophobia. She needed to leave. She had tried to tell Tina she was going but had not been able to find her. While she felt guilty for not telling her, she knew she was with Eddie and would be fine.

She questioned why she was not able to relax and enjoy herself. It was much more than not liking the music. Recently, she had begged her father to let her go and see The Teardrop Explodes but had been secretly pleased when he refused. All the girls at school were in love with Julian Cope and were desperate to see him. The thought of going to the Hammersmith Odeon, even with her friends, had just seemed too much. Jennifer and her band of followers had done nothing but talk about their adventures, and she had beaten herself up for her cowardice.

She started the long walk back to the caravan park. Suddenly she saw lights coming behind her—it was Eddie, and he smiled at her through the window.

"Hop aboard." Mel looked relieved.

"What about Tina?"

"Don't worry about her. Vince will give her a lift home. Find me a light, will ya? Desperate for a smoke."

Mel rummaged around in the glove compartment, and as Eddie tried to help, an envelope fell out, cascading drawings onto the floor. Mel picked them up slowly and began to look at them.

"Bloody hell, Eddie. These are brilliant. Did you do them?" Eddie blushed.

"Hint shown them to no one before."

The envelope contained crayon pictures of birds and landscapes. Many were on bits of old torn card or brown paper. Mel was always above average in art at school but never in the same league as the truly gifted. Eddie had talent. He looked at Mel and pulled out one of the sketches.

"This one is a bittern. I drew this in February when the reeds died down. He was a noisy bugger. Make this sort of booming noise." He did a quick impression. "I nicknamed him Basil and followed him around. Following that sound, boom, boom. Does that make me sound like a nutter?"

"Yes." Mel looked closely at the drawing. He had captured the bird's movement as well as its colours and plumage.

"I had a few colours then. Vince made me draw an Iron Maiden album cover on the back of his jacket, so I used the rest of the paints for these." Mel had seen the jacket, a grotesque skeleton-like creature emblazoned on the back. She assumed it had been bought like that. She quickly shuffled the papers in her hand.

"You're really good."

"I showed Vince this lot once. He said, *'Art is for poofs.'*"

"He still got you to paint his jacket." Eddie's face darkened.

"He showed some of my drawings to my dad, who got all weird. Says he doesn't like birds in the house; someone will die. He threw everything I'd done, loads, on the fire. That's why I hide it."

Mel looked at Eddie. Although her dad was a liar, he had never tried to hurt her. Everything she ever did was *'fantastic'* and *'great'*. Empty praise, but it was what parents did.

"I can take them to the caravan if you want. The lock's a load of rubbish, but at least your brother and dad won't find them."

She continued to leaf through the bundle while Eddie described what each bird was called. He had a surprisingly comprehensive knowledge of the local birds and described in detail their plumage and habits.

"Never had you down as a bird watcher."

"I think you'll find the term is twitcher. My mum got me into birds. She knew a lot more than me."

Mel was a little bit surprised. It seemed so strange that someone like Eddie would spend his days drawing birds. She liked it and the fact that he could talk to her about it.

She then took a deep breath and asked him about what she had witnessed outside the gig. Eddie took a long drag on his spliff.

"Those are the Ellis twins." Mel looked incredulous. "My dad…." He stopped. Mel looked at him to continue, "he got drunk and gambled two thousand quid. Fucking idiot! That was a reminder that we owed it. They're a local family. You just don't mess with them."

"What are you going to do?"

Eddie shook his head and laughed drily. "Avoid at all costs."

After Eddie had dropped Mel at the caravan park, he reluctantly drove home. He hesitated before he entered, keen to avoid his dad and brother. The house seemed deserted. Ravenous, he rushed to the kitchen and quickly threw together some bread and a bit of stale cheese.

Eddie hurriedly took his sandwich up to his room and closed the door. Picking off stray dog hair from the bread, he took a bite. The whole house heaved with their shedding fur, and he hated the filthy beasts. The hoover, covered in dust, lay in bits in the cupboard.

Since his mother had died, he had fended for himself. Snatching food while avoiding his father, he escaped to his bedroom at every opportunity. His room was like every other room in the house—it had seen better days. Ripped childish wallpaper hung down, and his curtains were precariously nailed into the wall. Despite its dilapidated state, he kept it as tidy as he could. Sometimes the dogs would lie on his bed, covering his blankets in their grimy fluff, leaving their wet smell in the air.

Eddie rummaged in his bedside drawers and found an old, chewed biro. He could see that it was still half full of ink and hoped it worked. He started to sketch on an old envelope he had found discarded in the bin earlier. The act of drawing always made him feel calmer. He thought about Mel and started to draw her face. Her features soon took form, and he sat back and admired his work. While her nose was a bit thinner, he had captured her essence. He was a little bit surprised that he had drawn her so effortlessly. There was something about her that drew him to her. She seemed interested in everything he did, and he always felt at ease in her presence. Tina was fun, but his connection was deeper with Mel.

He heard his father climbing the stairs, so he hastily put the picture under his pillow. The steps, thankfully, bypassed his room, and he could hear someone relieving themselves in the bathroom. The door banged, and they walked back downstairs. It was about ten o'clock, and Eddie felt tired. He knew Vince would be out until all hours, and he was keen to sleep before his father started swearing and shouting, as he did most nights. Laying down, he patted the pillow. Perhaps tomorrow, he would give the picture to her.

CHAPTER 17

The next day Mel and Tina returned to Mrs Wilbraham's house. Met with the same standoffish response, they wondered if she had even remembered her drunken behaviour. It was not mentioned, and Mel was dispatched to the garden.

"I need my roses cut back and the path cleared. The front really has got out of hand." Tina waited for her instructions and was told she would be, "Responsible for the lounge."

Mrs Wilbraham's Georgian house had once been grand. The antiques oozed class, and despite being layered with dust, they imposed themselves on Tina. She marvelled at the marquetry, the cut of the wood, and most of all, how solid it felt.

Her own house wasn't so much furnished, as an assortment of chairs that had been given so long ago that she wondered if they had ever been new. The green draylon chair in the sitting room was the worst. The arms were worn to white, peppered with burn marks and stank of beer and urine. Her mother regularly fell asleep there, including one time with a cigarette that burnt a hole to the size of a fist in the foam. Her mother would pick at it when she was drunk.

Mrs Wilbraham's house was like another world. Paintings were on every space and the curtains, while dirty and faded, were voluptuous. She started to wipe away the dust, and the furniture almost came to life from a grey colour to warm mahogany. The polish nourished the wood, making it shine. Tina stood on the arm of the settee and stretched to take down the heavy curtains. She dragged them outside, laying them over a chair and began to beat them with the handle of the broom. Like a sleeping dragon, they came to life with swirling colours of green and gold. Tina ran her hand along the material and admired the weight and lustre. She worked fastidiously on every inch of the curtains until she was coughing with dust and her arms ached. She needed water. Even the tumblers in the kitchen were heavy, and as she gulped down her second glass, she noticed her hands were black. She could feel the sweat running down her back.

Mrs Wilbraham had stood at the doorway watching Tina work. She had not been in the lounge for so long that it felt foreign. She had seen it slowly slipping into grey as if reclaimed by the sea. Then she saw Tina working conscientiously lovingly restoring the colour and life into the room. Something was endearing about her. She looked like a Victorian foundling. She seemed grateful for the job, but there was something more.

"Come here, Tina. You can stop now. It will still be here tomorrow."

"Looks a load better, doesn't it?" She looked like a child beaming at her accomplishment.

"Yes, a good start. Job well done. You can finish it another day." The older woman almost smiled.

Tina regaining her composure asked, "Gonna pay us for today?" Mrs Wilbraham was slightly taken aback.

"Five pounds sufficient?"

Tina snatched the money and mumbled, "Thanks."

Grabbing Mel on the way, she skipped out of the house with the money flapping in her hand. They were sweaty and filthy, but they didn't care. They stopped at the local grocer's and made their way triumphantly back to the caravan.

"Fags, potatoes and wine," cheered Tina.

Mrs Wilbraham had watched the girls leave. She enjoyed them coming to the house and felt a pang of guilt that she had behaved badly the previous day. It had been Tina trying to open that door. Forcing herself to look at it, she chastised herself for being so weak. She slowly walked over to it. It had been nearly ten years. The Victorian pine door was identical to every other in the house, but she dared not touch it. The key had been placed in the cabinet and remained wrapped in an old velvet cloth. She took a deep breath and retrieved it. The material had faded on the edges, but the fabric was bright red where the key lay. She lifted it and turned it around in her hand.

"Old fool."

Cobwebs hung from the door frame, and the key proved stiff to budge. The door eventually swung open, and she peered into the gloom. Once, it had been a vibrant place where she had bounded with ideas and enthusiasm. Dust sheets covered every surface. They surprised her as she had forgotten she had placed them there, masking everything underneath like a shroud. Once white, they were now battleship grey, caked with years of dirt.

The room had lost its smell of paint and plaster, replaced with dust. It coated her mouth and inside her nostrils and momentarily made her sneeze. She felt a discarded paintbrush under her slipper and scooped to pick it up. Its handle had been snapped in the middle exposing sharp splinters of wood and it still had a smidgen of flaky blue paint on the tip. Holding a corner, she tentatively lifted the edge of a sheet. The colours underneath startled her. Reds and oranges leapt out of the picture below. She was instantly transported back to the time she had painted it. A woman's face stared back at her. She lifted the rest of the sheet to reveal numerous sketches of the model. Palettes of paint, dried into hardened rock, lay next to half-finished canvases. She ran her fingers across them.

Slowly she crossed the room to the old butler sink. Doug's chipped mug nestled next to paintbrushes in old jam jars where the methylated spirit had now evaporated. She tentatively lifted the mug and rested her lips against the rim. God, she missed him. The mug suddenly fell from her hand. She desperately tried to catch it but could only watch it shatter on the stone floor.

She bolted out of the door and slammed it shut. Blood dripped from her hand onto the tiles, and she realised she was clutching jagged wood of the old paintbrush. Running her palm under the tap, she winced in pain as she checked for splinters. The blood in the sink reminded her of the picture she had uncovered. Stopping to hurl the paintbrush in the bin, she stopped. Instead, she placed it gently on the side and poured herself a large glass of wine.

***

On their way back through the caravan park, Norman gestured for the girls to stop. Mel instantly thought that he had discovered their identity or had witnessed them stealing, and she was relieved when he said he only needed to talk to Tina.

"All right?" said Tina.

"Got a proposition for you, gal."

Tina nodded. "Listening."

"Got a lot of them old caravans to clean. 'Ave to get them ready for the next families. That can be a rush."

"Yes."

"Hint getting no younger and need some help. Can't pay you much or promise regular work, but I could do with a hand now."

Tina looked at Mel. "Do you need both of us?"

"No. You'll do."

"What about all the stuff they leave behind?"

"Well, that's meant to go to lost property, but no bugger ever come back for it. S'pose if that's jewellery, give that to me. Otherwise, you can keep it. Got some ole salad cream here…hate the stuff."

"When you want me to start?"

"Number six, that need a good ole clean. Want to do that now?"

Norman walked back into his office and returned with keys, a bucket full of cleaning fluids and cloths. Tina felt ten feet high as he had chosen her, not Mel, and she skipped over to the vacated caravan.

The rented caravans were much better equipped than the 1960s one they had. They all had little cookers, fridges and sinks. She was amazed at the mess the previous tenants had left this one in. Beer cans littered the floor, and mounds of rubbish were piled everywhere. A foul-smelling liquid was seeping under the fridge door, and she assumed it was leaking milk. When she opened the door, she discovered that the fridge was stuffed with half-eaten food. Tina marvelled at the opened butter, ham and sausages. She snaffled up as much as she could, including a packet of custard creams that lay unopened on the bench. She would enjoy telling Mel about her new job and surprising her with her hoard of food.

While Tina was cleaning the caravans, Mel wandered back along the dusty campsite path. She saw a young girl fall and cut her knee, and her mother gently picked her up and rubbed her better. The sight brought a sudden memory into her mind. When she was five, she had fallen off her bike in Muddy Lane and cut her face. Pauline and her concerned mother carried her home and laid her on the settee. Pauline had made some of her 'magic' ointment, and they had lovingly stroked her hair until she stopped crying. All that day, she was treated like a princess. Holding her head, she fingered the small scar that had formed that day. Mel thought about her aunt and felt sick with guilt. She willed the thoughts to stop, but they tumbled unabridged into her brain. It was not her aunt's fault she had run away, and she was probably going out of her mind with worry.

When she was very young, her mother was always there. While never gregarious, like her dad, she was always singing and happy. Slowly she had withdrawn from life. Even as a child, she could sense her slipping away. The last few years, she had virtually disappeared. Mel walked faster and tried to stop the images in her mind. She tried to block them, but her mind raced to one of the worst times she had ever seen her mother.

Pauline had squeezed her hand. Neither spoke. The waiting room had worn green plastic chairs incongruously screwed to the floor. She had sensed the older woman wanted to put her arms around her, but the proximity of the chairs did not allow it. A white clock had clicked away on the wall. Eventually, they were called.

"Pauline Melrose."

"That's us." She had managed a weak smile.

They followed the nurse through the heavy, white, locked door. More doors followed, and long corridors all painted in the same insipid green. The hospital had once been enormous and housed over a thousand patients. Only a fraction of it was used now, but it was still imposing. The sheer scale of the place felt like the further you went in, the harder it was to get out. Mel looked at Pauline, and she knew she felt the misery of the place as well despite her heroic attempts at joviality.

They trudged on until they came toward ward 730. Again, it was locked. Off the main corridor, women sat in beds, hardly moving, while some shuffled around in their dressing gowns. Mel did not dare catch their eyes.

"Come on, gal. Let's go and find yer mum."

They were led to a side room where Mel's mother was propped up on the bed, hugging her knees. Mel remembered not knowing what to say and taking her cue from Pauline.

"Alice." Pauline had tried to sound as upbeat as she could. Alice stared straight ahead. Mel approached and took her hand. She leant forward and half-whispered.

"Mum."

Her mum had turned her head and looked at her. She mouthed as if to say something, but no words came. Mel remembered the smell of disinfectant. It felt cold, but it wasn't the temperature, it was the atmosphere. Mel had stared at her mother's translucent skin. Her veins were visible and gave her complexion a ghostly hue. For a moment, she was fascinated by how pale she was. She hardly looked alive.

"It's the drugs. She knows you're here. Alice, would you like some water?" There was no reply, but Pauline still poured her a glass and continued the stilted one-sided conversation.

"Mel's been busy at school, haven't you?" Mel managed to nod. "Clive's writing another book. Haven't really seen him for days. You know how he likes to lock himself away."

Mel had tuned out Pauline's prattle and could not stop gazing at her mother's skin. The prominent veins did not look like they belonged to her mother, and it looked like some strange demon that had entered her body. Mel could hear Pauline continuing the endless efforts at conversation, and at last, it was time to go. She felt relieved but at the same time guilty at wanting to leave.

"You get better, Mum. See you soon." The figure on the bed just looked vacantly at her. Pauline leaned over, kissed Alice and wrapped the blanket over her bony frame.

The nurse greeted them both, and Pauline took her to one side. Mel was glad she could not hear the hushed conversation, although the odd muttering about 'sedated' and 'progress' did reach her ears. Pauline had tried to reassure her.

"It's just the drugs, darling. She knows you're here."

"I doubt that!" Mel snapped.

They walked in silence through the corridors and endless locked doors until they reached the car. Pauline turned around to look at the building. Cold East, what a name for an institution. Mel had been studying the poor laws at school and knew full well that the building had once been a workhouse before it housed the mentally ill. It reeked of misery, and she felt that some of that energy had seeped into the very fabric of the building.

They drove off in silence. Pauline did not know what to say and just gave Mel an inadequate rub on her shoulder. Neither turned around to look at the building. Mel had not spoken for several hours. The trip had frightened her in so many ways.

The memory was still so clear. A dull pain was beginning to grow in her chest, and she was not sure if it was anger or guilt. Mel walked as fast as she could to try and push the thoughts out of her mind until she found herself at the shore, breathing in the salty air. Piling up pebbles, she counted them before stacking them again. The rhythm of the sea helped to soothe her mind, and she lay on the beach staring at the clouds.

It took Tina a long time to finish cleaning the caravan, but she was keen to do a good job. She stood at the door and felt a surge of pride. Collecting her cleaning bucket, she made her way back down to Norman. He was sitting outside whittling a piece of wood.

"All right?"

"All right?" Norman beckoned for her to come in and gave her a mug of tea.

"Want to go and see what I done?"

"Trust ya. Got a few more for you to do ammorra, if you hint too tired."

She suddenly felt tired but also exhilarated. No one had ever picked her out, let alone given her a job.

"Dint find no jewellery. Just some food."

"You need feeding up. See ya, ammorra." He turned and then said more seriously, "You keep safe."

Tina was slightly taken aback. She knew he disapproved of Vincent.

"Nothing ever happens around here." Norman raised an eyebrow and turned away. Tina continued with a headline delivery, "Holidaymaker drops their ice cream." Norman looked her straight in the face. His face was suddenly solemn.

"Plenty fishermen tell you different."

"Yeah, but they're out to sea. Nothing ever going to happen here."

The older man sighed and took down an old black and white photograph in an ornate silver frame. He handed it to Tina. The picture showed a man posing stiffly in rolled-up trousers with a handkerchief on his head and a woman who was laughing, holding his hand. Tina studied the photograph and laughed.

"Who are they then?"

"That's me."

"When you had hair."

He only half-smiled. "My wife, Joan."

"Wife?"

"Been married ten years."

Tina looked down. She was not sure what to ask next. Whatever she asked, she imagined the answer would not be good.

"The sea took her," he said simply.

"How?" Seeing his expression, she regretted asking as soon as the words were out of her mouth.

"1953, the most terrible storm blew down this coast. It were a beast. It rained like the sky was falling, and the wind would blow a man over. She never stood a chance. Over fifty people died that night."

"Jesus."

"He didn't help us. That swept away houses and everything."

Tina felt the pain of the older man. She gently passed back the photograph, and Norman took it and lovingly placed it on the shelf. Feeling inadequate, she put the packet of custard creams on the table and left.

Tina did not go back immediately to the caravan but followed the old worn path down to the sea. It was deserted, and the sun was beginning to set. She looked at the great expanse of water. The light shone on the top, and it looked like a silken gown. The tide had come in and small waves broke at the edge. She tried to imagine the storm. It seemed almost impossible.

A small spit of water hit her face as the tiny pebbles were clawed underneath the waves. She felt suddenly uneasy. It was the enormity of the water which unsettled her. She thought about Norman and the chaos of that night—fifty people, it was unbelievable. He had not given her any details, and she dared not ask.

As she walked back to Mel, she could still hear the waves relentlessly lapping behind her, but she did not turn around.

CHAPTER 18

Tina walked down to the toilet block. As she passed Norman, she went to wave and noticed he was limping.

"What's up with you then?"

He turned around. The pain was evident in his face. "Can you give me a hand?" Tina noticed he was hugging his leg. "That's ole arthritis. That ole doctor say I've had what's called a flare-up." Tina saw that his hands were swollen, and the joints had a bump like a knuckle. He was wincing. "Got to clean up four caravans this morning."

They had all meant to be going for a drive to the famous 'devil dog' church that Eddie had been telling them about, and she had been looking forward to it. She looked at Norman, and he suddenly looked very old.

"I'll do it."

"Can't afford to pay..."

Tina held up her hand. "You can give me a custard cream."

When she got back, Mel was flat out on the bench, which filled Tina with irritation. She always rose early and never struggled with getting up while Mel dragged herself out of bed like she had run a marathon. She briefly told her about Norman.

"But we were meant...."

"Yeah, well, you can go, but I'm helping Norman." Tina stormed out.

Mel sighed. She was annoyed by Tina's moods. Throwing her jeans on, she decided that she would have to help. She wrote a hurried note for Eddie and stumbled out. Not sure what caravan she was in, Mel knocked on several that looked empty.

"Fuck off!" said a grumpy man in a vest. She apologised but had laughed to herself. A month ago, she would have died of embarrassment. Casually, she kicked over his shoes that were outside, and it felt good.

Eventually, she found Tina. The enormity of the task surprised her as the caravan was filthy. Rubbish had been left on the floor, and the small hob cooker was caked in oil and fat. Tina was on her hands and knees, scraping chewing gum off the floor.

"Came then?"

"Two hands and all that."

"Wouldn't you rather be with Eddie?" Tina couldn't keep the sarcasm out of her voice.

"Wouldn't you rather be with Vincent?"

Tina threw her a cloth, and Mel got to work. Neither of them spoke. She had never been as efficient as Tina, but she put her back into it. Despite it being early, it was hot, and Mel could feel sweat running down her back. While they did not speak, Mel could tell Tina was beginning to thaw.

Tina dramatically opened the fridge. "What's for tea?"

There was only a half-eaten jar of mustard with the lid off, and they felt deflated. Tina looked at Mel, who was dripping with sweat. She was grateful she had come to help and felt slightly guilty that she had felt so much irritation. They moved on to the next caravan expecting a repeat of the carnage, but it was spotless. The bedding was neatly folded, as were the towels.

"Shame, really, as I have to put new in each one."

"Can't you just leave it?"

Tina sighed. "No, I want to do it properly for Norman."

Mel stood by the fridge and made a drum roll sound as she revealed a half-eaten loaf of Slimcea bread and some butter. A green bottle of Perrier water was in the door.

"Who the fuck buys water?" exclaimed Tina.

They made quick work of the inside and moved on to the next caravan, where Mel found a copy of *Forum* magazine under the bed.

"Wear gloves with that."

They sat down and laughed at it, particularly the section entitled *Readers' Wives.* Tina was glad Mel had come. She had jealously guarded the work Norman had given her, and Mel had often offered to help her, but she wanted to keep it for herself. She had been thrilled to be chosen.

"If we get the next one done, we can still go out with Eddie," said Mel.

Tina looked at Mel and realised that she was a little bit jealous of their friendship. Much as Mel irritated her with her whining about her aunt, she was a best friend. At school, she had always been the dirty kid, the one other families wouldn't let their children play with. It was only when she was excluded that she had found her tribe of teenagers. She was the undisputed leader. Mel was someone she would never have been friends with, but they had a connection. She was the only person who had punched her and got away with it. She smiled to herself at the memory.

"Come on, let's finish this off, then we can go." Tina looked at Mel. She was excited. "You go with Eddie. I'll check on Norman." Mel looked down.

"Tina, I don't want you to miss out."

"If I come, you might miss out." She raised her eyebrows. "Although wash your pits, you stink."

Mel skipped to the toilet blocks and quickly stripped off. There was a young family inside, but Mel felt no embarrassment. She laughed at how coy she had been before. Back at the caravan, she tried to make herself look less dishevelled and waited for Eddie to arrive. She could see his van as he pulled into the caravan site, and she rushed to meet him.

The drive from Sealtdock was much longer than Mel had anticipated. The van had laboured around the bends, occasionally throwing out plumes of black fumes. It was a bumpy, uncomfortable ride, but Mel had enjoyed Eddie's company. They drove down a labyrinth of narrow lanes and eventually saw the steeple of Blythburgh church. It was located at the head of the River Blyth mudflat that stretched for great distances in front of the water. Eddie told her it had once been a harbour but had long silted up.

"How come you know all this?"

"My mum. It's a great place to see wading birds." They looked at each other and laughed as it seemed an incongruous thing to say.

Mel was amazed at how impressive the church was. Enormous and extremely beautiful, she recognised it immediately as perpendicular style. The trips she had spent with Clive and Pauline had paid off as she could name several of the features. The exterior was decorated with flush work. Large gargoyles stared down at them from the entrance, and Mel stopped to put her hand in the ancient stoup. Worn down by fingers of the congregation, long dead, the act of feeling the stone made her feel a strange connection to the past.

They pulled open the old wooden door and wandered inside. There was a medieval scratch dial used for centuries before clocks were invented, and the roof was adorned with beautifully carved angels. Mel knew from Clive that very few angels survived the ravages of the Puritans. She had always enjoyed the story of Holy Innocents in Great Barton, where the angel's heads were all cut off, but the last one remained as the person hacking them off fell and died as if in some holy revenge.

The atmosphere in the church was still. The stone kept out the searing heat, and although the light was slightly muted by the windows, it was light and airy. They walked around the church and admired the beautiful medieval carvings and stonework.

"Want to see the devil's fingerprints?" Eddie led her to the north door, where black scratch marks were clearly visible. Eddie put on a scary voice. "Legend has it there was a terrible storm. Everyone had gathered in the church, and a demonic dog ran in and killed some of the people praying."

"Shut up."

"Not just here but in Bungay too." Mel looked closely at the scorched marks. They were identical to the band logo that Eddie had drawn. He whispered in her ear. "They say this is the claw of the devil. Want to touch it?" Mel felt suddenly alarmed. While she believed it was all superstition, something was holding her back. Her hand faltered, and she felt apprehensive. Eddie, as if reading her mind, said quietly, "Me neither...don't want nothing to do with the devil."

"Nor me."

They sat in the pews and looked at the carved angels above. There was a room at the top of steep steps labelled 'the priest's room'. They walked up the steep steps and looked out over the church from the small window. It afforded a good view of the surrounding countryside.

They wandered out to the graveyard and walked amongst the gravestones. A group of tourists descended on the church, and they decided to leave. Walking down to the marshes, Eddie pointed out several wading birds.

A group of Americans who had heard of the Suffolk devil dog asked for ice creams. Eddie opened up the freezer and obliged. They walked down to the marsh and looked out over the mudflats. Eddie excitedly pointed out a snape and explained about their long beaks. They sat watching as it rummaged in the mud for insects. Mel enjoyed listening to Eddie, who enthusiastically regaled her with facts about their habits and habitat.

"So today we have enjoyed church architecture and done some bird watching." Eddie smiled.

"Oh, the youth of today," said Mel. They joked that they would have to make up a story for Tina that they had stolen a candlestick. "Or the collection."

Eddie put a piece of grass between his thumbs and blew. The high pitch startled Mel, and she tried several times to do it herself but failed.

"No...holding it all wrong." She dropped the piece of grass again. He clutched his hands over hers and guided the blade of grass between her thumbs. "Now try." A pathetic blowing noise was all she could manage.

They sat for an hour, enjoying the scenery and each other's company. Mel felt relaxed, and she began to blurt out information about her mother. Eddie did not interrupt but sat facing forward and grasped her hand.

"Just scared I'll end up like her."

Eddie smiled and pushed the hair out of her eyes. "You won't."

"How do you know?"

"Just do." There was a silence. "I'm nothing like my dad. Nothing." Mel was taken aback at how vehement the words sounded. "Bastard." She sensed he wanted to tell her more, but he suddenly got up and pointed. "Look, a tern." It had come quite close to them, and Mel could see the joints of its legs as it circumvented the mud.

The moment had gone.

It was now half-past six, and they were surprised at the time. Eddie rolled around the money he had earned from the American tourists.

"Enough for a pint."

They went to the local pub, The White Hart, and ordered two pints of beer. Fittingly, it was an ancient inn, and Mel sat down and admired the large inglenook fireplace. Eddie returned and offered her a cigarette. Her mind wandered to Jennifer in Italy, and she smiled to herself. If only they could see her now.

On the way back, the van started to jolt.

"Shit! No petrol," Eddie said.

Mel looked alarmed. "We're in the middle of nowhere." Mel strained to see if there were any houses, but it was getting dark. "Thought we'd be all right."

Eventually, the van came to a standstill. Eddie got out.

"You'll need to steer." Mel panicked but grabbed the steering wheel. "We need to get off the road," Eddie shouted from the back of the van and Mel felt it lurch as he started pushing. There was a gap in the hedge that tractors used to access the field. "Pull in there."

"Got a petrol can?"

"Yeah, but it's too late now. Everywhere will be shut. I'll keep an eye out for cars but doubt anyone will pick us up this late." Mel felt a surge of anxiety. "It's ok. Got a sleeping bag." Between the freezers, there was barely enough room for one. Eddie looked at Mel. "It's ok. I'll sleep in the front. Nothing to eat or drink as usual."

Mel produced a glass bottle of Corona that she had emptied and filled up with water. It was warm, but it was better than nothing.

"Bathwater?"

They sat on the lip of the van and looked at the stars. Without streetlights, they seemed infinite.

"Every star is like our sun," said Eddie.

"Could be billions of planets out there," added Mel.

"Do you believe in aliens? Did you hear that some were supposed to have landed in Rendlesham Forest a couple of years back?"

"Aunty Pauline's always going on about that. Reckons it's a government cover-up." They sat in silence, contemplating the enormity of the universe.

"And I'm stuck in Sealtdock."

"You could leave."

"How?"

"You could go to art college."

"In London?"

"Have to get a haircut. Like mine. Wouldn't fit in as a heavy metal greaser."

"With or without the ponytail?" He playfully pulled it.

"I like it."

"I like it, too."

Without warning, he leant over and kissed her. Eddie immediately felt scared, but Mel gently kissed him back. They looked at each other, held hands and then continued to stare at the stars.

"Got to pee," Eddie announced.

As Eddie relieved himself behind the van, Mel lay down on the floor in the back. The old sleeping bag was thin, and she lay on top of it while Eddie lay his jacket over her.

"But you'll be cold."

"Don't matter."

"Come here." She lay on her side and indicated that Eddie lay next to her. "No funny business." They both laughed, and it broke the tension.

It was a tight squeeze, but with his back to her, they managed to fit into the space. She put her arms around him and could feel how warm he was. Eddie lay very still, and he could feel her breath on his neck. It was a strange mix of excitement but mainly comfort. They were soon fast asleep.

They woke up with aches and pains. They listened and could hear a car approaching. Eddie grabbed the petrol can and attempted to flag it down, but the driver did not stop. They started to walk hand in hand. They had no idea of the time, but it was early morning. Eddie pointed out a water vole in the ditch.

"It's a rat."

"It's not."

Eventually, they saw a car and an elderly man pulled alongside them.

"Broken down? Where you heading?" asked the man.

"Sealtdock," replied Eddie. There was something about the young couple that the old man liked, and he soon pulled away with his two extra passengers.

"You're lucky I'm visiting my sister. I've come from Aldeburgh."

The driver prattled on about the weather. While they answered him, they were remembering the night before.

Once they had been dropped off, Eddie awkwardly kissed Mel on the cheek.

"What about petrol?"

"I'll nick some, siphon it...won't cost." Mel surprised herself that it seemed the most natural thing in the world. "I'll hitch back to the van. See you."

Mel skipped back to the caravan. She couldn't wait to tell Tina.

***

Early morning, few people were around. Eddie positioned himself between two cars and quickly siphoned off some petrol. In his haste, some of it went into his mouth. Spitting it out and wiping his tongue, he slipped back onto the road and stuck out his thumb. He felt good. A van going to the docks stopped, and a French driver asked him for directions. Sharing a Gitanes cigarette, they spoke in broken English. Eddie directed the driver and hopped out where he could pick up the ancient road. He thought about Mel and smiled, the sun was warming, and he was happy to walk the extra mile to the van.

Soon he was steering the van back to his house. Running the petrol dry had forced impurities into the tank, and black choking smoke flew out of the exhaust, eventually settling down. He patted the steering wheel.

"Come on. You can do it."

It was only midday, but he needed to go back and get ice cream supplies. Despite the early hour, he hoped his dad would be at the pub or passed out. Perhaps there would be some bread, and he could grab a handful and take it to his bedroom.

He was in high spirits, and as he turned the corner by the barn, he noticed an unfamiliar van in the drive. It was battered, and two men were getting out. He pulled into the old wooden building opposite and crouched down to watch. Straining, he could just make out the features of the two men. They were both about forty and wore black singlet vests. They were pushing his father around, and twice he fell to the floor. The dogs trapped in the kitchen were frenziedly barking. Part of him felt he should go and help, but he knew there was little he could do. The taller one pushed his dad against one of the rusted cars, and lifting him by his collar, spat in his face. His father cowered on the ground, covering his face with his arm.

Eddie waited until they left, and his father was inside before he got back into the van and drove in the gate. Once he reached the door, he stopped, anxious his father would take it out on him. Taking a deep breath, he entered the kitchen. The older man was sitting in the chair stroking one of the dogs. He was whispering in the dog's ear, and he looked at Eddie.

"They kicked Betsie."

"Who?"

"Them Ellis boys. That's got to be sorted, boy." His father had opened a bottle of cider and was drinking straight from it. He continued comforting and petting the dog. "There, there, gal. You're all right."

Anger shot through Eddie, and he turned away. He scanned the kitchen for food, but apart from a half-eaten Weetabix, there was nothing. In the distance, he could hear Vince's motorbike. Expecting an argument, he slipped upstairs. The euphoria he had felt with Mel had all but gone. Opening the door, he saw that the dogs had been in his room as there was dried slobber on his sheet. Flinging the sheet in the corner, he lay on the filthy mattress. Taking out the drawing of Mel, he clutched it to his chest and waited for Vincent to start shouting.

CHAPTER 19

Maureen heard the letterbox swing, and a small white envelope dropped onto the mat. She picked it up. There was no name on the front. Ripping it open, she read out loud.

HOLY INNOCENTS CHURCH AT THE BACK
6.30 PM.

It was written in non-descript capital letters and was not signed. She knew it was from Alan.

Trotham Church was on the outskirts of the village. It had been a plague village, and the centre had moved as the villagers escaped infection. The church, however, had remained constant. It would be quite a walk and very muddy, due to the local river, even during the summer months. Maureen did not care. It was clearly from Alan; that was enough.

Looking at herself in the mirror, she was still wearing

the same clothes she had worn that day. She quickly turned on the immersion heater. She needed hot water and quick. It would take a good hour, but she still could not face the kitchen and lay back down in her bed.

Later, she tentatively eased herself into the hot bath, trying not to aggravate her sunburn. It was still raw, and she cried out loud. Once immersed, she let her head flop back and allowed the water to calm her mind. She lay under the water and counted. It was something she had done as a child. Managing thirty seconds, she came up spluttering. The water in her ears strangely made her feel more alive. She still had nearly two hours to get ready, not factoring in the walk. She stayed in the bath until the water was nearly cold. The tank, emptied of hot water, forced her to get out.

Maureen smiled at herself in the mirror. She had bought two outfits before they had met in the field as she had been unable to decide. Her favourite one was torn and filthy from charging through the hedge. She had bought a modern polka dot shirt and spent ages arranging the shoulder pads. She applied her makeup and put extra foundation under her eyes, which were still bloated from crying. At last, it was time to leave.

Alan waited around the back of the church. He had taken his poodle with him, and he congratulated himself that if anyone was to see them together, it could be explained by the dog. His wife Emma had also been impressed, and he had earned some much-needed brownie points.

He surveyed the churchyard looking for Maureen. He

knew her mother was buried somewhere here, and she often tended the grave. He looked along the line of more recent headstones and tried to work out which one it was.

He saw her walking towards him, waving. God, why was she so clingy? It had only been a bit of fun. He could have anyone he wanted. Why had he lumbered himself with this middle-aged monstrosity? He reminded himself that it would have been unprofessional to mess around with the girls at work—too close to home. He had met Maureen at one of the ghastly village events that Emma had dragged him to. He had flirted with Maureen, who was on the Tombola and then bumped into her in town. It had been too easy, but he had needed a distraction. It was supposed to be just a laugh.

Maureen saw Alan's head poking above one of the graves. Despite the care she had taken choosing her outfit, she questioned if she looked good enough. Crickets were abundant and she heard their loud scraping legs all around her. Many of the gravestones were very old and had inscriptions that were only just legible. Others were clearly family tombs and had all members buried underneath. She did not like to tread on the graves and meandered her way through the grass. Alan muttered under his breath. He was keen to get this over and done with.

"What the bloody hell is she doing?"

Maureen was tired from the walk and realised she had not eaten. Adrenaline kept her going, and she hurried the best she could. When she eventually got level with Alan, he was looking down. He kicked at the grass and took a deep breath.

"It's been fun, but this...whatever this is…."

"Alan?"

"Never happened."

"But you said...."

"Come on, grow up!" He pushed his face close to hers and shouted. "Never happened!"

"How can you say that?"

"I am high up in the Council. Soon to be Head of Council. You are a cleaner." Maureen felt sick. She turned around to look at him, and he almost seemed to be enjoying himself. "Look at you. What was I thinking? Jesus!" Crushed, Maureen fell to the ground.

"But you said...."

"I'm married, you stupid woman. You were only ever a bit of fun. If you can call it that."

"Bastard!" She spat the words out in frustration. "I'll tell." He spun around, and for a split second, she thought he might strike her. His face was mocking.

"And who are they going to believe?"

"I'll do it."

His voice became very low and controlled. Grabbing her arm, he whispered in her ear, "You live in a two-bedroom council house. I am a councillor. One word from me and you will be rehoused in a one-bedroom flat, shall we say, in Thetford. Or shall we say miles from here?" He let go of her arm and pulled the dog away. "Come on, Polly. Let's go home to Emma."

Maureen stayed on the ground. She could hardly believe what had just happened. Trying to move, she fell back down again. The shock of his words was too painful. He had been threatening, but worse, so cruel. She managed to pull herself to her feet and started the walk home, praying she would not meet anyone, just fixed on getting inside and shutting the door.

***

Pauline pulled into the car park. She had forgotten how imposing the building was. Clive read the council sign over the door. 'Welcome to Cold East Mental Health Services'. It seemed so out of place against the stark, Victorian, gothic brickwork. He wondered if it had once been a workhouse, like many institutions. It had a strange atmosphere that he could not put his finger on, and he thought about the number of souls that had been incarcerated here. He held Pauline's hand, and they ventured inside.

"That looks like it should be in a bloody horror film," she said. Clive nodded, and together they walked into the reception.

The woman who greeted them was young. She hardly looked up, mumbled something about it being the drugs round, and they were told to wait. Directed to old plastic chairs, they tried to sit down. Battered and uncomfortable, several of the legs had their stoppers missing, and it took them a moment to find one that did not wobble. Everything about the reception felt grubby.

Pauline shifted uncomfortably in her chair. Neither of them spoke and the wait seemed interminable. Despite it being hot outside, the reception felt cold. Clive could see the goose pimples on his wife's arms. After twenty minutes, Pauline marched up to the desk.

"Still the drug round? We've come a long way."

"Visiting times aren't till one."

Clive felt his wife tense. The disinterest from the receptionist was too much for Pauline, and raising her voice, she blurted out.

"She hint on no section. She here voluntary, so you can't stop us from seeing her."

The young girl raised her head and sighed. She almost looked amused by Pauline's frustration. Clive placed his arm on Pauline and leaned over the desk.

"Perhaps you could point us in the right direction."

"Like I said, visiting isn't until one," she replied aggressively. Pauline's face was now almost purple. She slammed her hand down on the desk and stared into the eyes of the young woman.

"She isn't on no section. So, she can walk out now. Now

tell me where she is, or I'll find her myself." A more kindly-looking woman came to the desk.

"Is there a problem?" Her tone was neutral and professional. Clive explained that they had driven for three hours and needed to see his sister. The older woman was an experienced nurse. She glanced at the receptionist, and Clive could sense from her expression that she was not impressed. "These people need help, not your attitude." Clive and Pauline were taken aback and meekly followed the nurse through the labyrinth of corridors.

"Not the easiest place to find your way around," she smiled jovially. "What is your relative called?"

"Alice Styles," answered Clive.

"Oh, Alice." She almost cooed. "She'll be glad to see you."

They walked for what seemed like an age, along corridors and passing rooms where the residents sat slumped. Occasionally they would hear cries, but they never saw who caused the noise or why. Eventually, they saw Alice. She was sitting in a chair facing the window. A doctor, in civilian clothes, was standing by the drug trolley. He was issuing instructions to a junior nurse. He looked up but did not acknowledge them.

"Oh, you're in your own clothes." Clive shot a look at his wife, but he also recognised why she had said the first thing that came into her head. Alice lifted her eyes but didn't speak.

Her lips were cracked, and her skin translucent. Pauline could see the resemblance to her brother, but unlike Clive's face, her colour was almost alabaster. He took her hand and squatted down so they were at eye level.

"Hello," Clive said gently. Alice turned her head slightly, and her lips pursed together. She laid a white hand on his. Clive was shocked at how thin she was, and her hand hardly weighed anything. As gently as he could, he whispered, "We know about Julian. So does Mel." His voice trailed away, and he questioned why he had been so direct. Pauline never could couch anything in niceties. Perhaps she was rubbing off on him after all these years.

"Mel...." Her voice was croaky and faint. "My Mel...."

Pauline squeezed her hand and looked around the room. There was a photograph of Mel in her school uniform smiling for the camera but very little else. Like the rest of the hospital, it smelt of disinfectant, an astringent smell that got into your nostrils. She looked at Clive, so lovingly stroking her hand and, taking a deep breath, she announced loud enough for everyone to hear.

"Right, Alice, you are coming home with us." The doctor who had ignored them previously strutted straight over to Pauline.

"That's not wise." Pauline looked at the consultant. He had a similar accent to Clive and appeared very senior in the hospital.

"And you are?"

"Mr Henchard. We need a clear plan with Alice. She requires medication."

Pauline looked at Alice. "That's what your medication does, makes her into a zombie." Alice remained slumped in her chair. "She's not staying here."

"I am the senior doctor here, and I am saying this patient is not fit for release." Pauline rose to full height and put her face close to the consultant's.

"Mr Henchard, she is coming with us, and legally there is nothing you can do to stop us." Clive looked at his wife. He wasn't sure if this was true. "I work at the library, and I have read up on what you can and can't do legally. Her section has now expired, and Alice no longer has to stay here." She turned to look at Clive and then tenderly said to Alice, "Want to come home with us?"

"She's not capable of making a decision," sniffed the doctor.

Alice looked at Pauline and mouthed the word. It was hardly audible.

"Yes."

The nurse that had shown them to the room smiled. Avoiding the doctor's gaze, she gently touched Alice's shoulder. "Looks like someone is going home." The consultant, not used to being challenged, tutted and glared at the nurse.

"There are procedures for release. Nurse, nurse, where are the notes?"

"In the filing cupboard where they normally are." She shot him a look. He blustered around but was ignored by everyone in the room. The nurse leant over to Pauline and whispered the words. "Well done."

Pauline gestured to Clive to gather the meagre collection of clothes and toiletries. The nurse gave them a wheelchair, and together they pushed Alice out of the room. Pauline lay a cardigan over Alice's bony frame and held her hand as the nurse led the way. Clive was unsure if security would swoop in at any moment, but he knew he must get Alice out of that dreadful place. After what seemed like an hour, they reached the front door, and Clive turned around and spoke to the nurse.

"Thank you."

"You are welcome. She will fare much better with you. People get lost here."

"Will you get into trouble?"

"Well, it is a bit unorthodox, she should have a release plan, but you can go to your GP. Just get her away from here."

"What about you? Will you get into trouble?"

"Probably, but they should be closing this place anyway. Should have closed it years ago. Care in the community…taking a bit longer than everyone thought."

Uncharacteristically, Clive grabbed her hand and hugged her.

"Thank you so much."

"Get her to the GP as she will be coming off some heavy medication." Pauline thanked her again, and as gently as they could, they put Alice in the car. She was so light they could virtually carry her.

Before long, they were driving down the Suffolk roads away from the hospital. The window was open, and Alice enjoyed the breeze on her face. She looked at the beautiful Suffolk countryside whizzing by. For so long, she had only seen the four walls of her room. Her drugs kept her mentally locked inside, and while she felt a sense of anxiety, she knew this was the right thing to do.

Clive looked at his wife in the mirror and felt a surge of admiration. He wondered if he would have had the strength to take Alice out if it hadn't been for her. He felt weak, and even though he had had so much more education and opportunity than Pauline, she was the one driving the search to find Mel. He resolved to try and be braver. He looked at his sister and sensed that she was happy. Although he was sure he had imagined it, he thought she had regained some colour, and he squeezed her hand.

CHAPTER 20

Mrs Wilbraham rolled onto her side, and the pain in her knees was worse than normal. All night she had tossed and turned, but nothing would relieve the aching. She had lain awake since four listening to the birds. Normally, her arthritis was a dull, heavy pain which she managed with marijuana and red wine, and it took the edge off the intensity. Occasionally the thunderous burn would flare up, and there seemed to be no pattern to it.

It had been raining lightly, and the morning was fresh. The pain was unexpected as she had not been drinking as heavily as she sometimes did. This had coincided with the girls cleaning. Having them in the house had strangely brought her some enjoyment, and they were company. Perhaps not the edifying, mentally stimulating company of old friends, but they brought youth. She laughed when they discussed the nude she had hanging in the hallway. Tina seemed very perturbed that she could not be sure if it were male or female. She had studied it closely and pointed triumphantly.

"That could be a dick."

Mel seemed much more educated. They were a strange mix. While she was not sure she believed their story about working through the summer, she was happy to go along with it.

Deciding to rest a bit longer, she tried to shift her weight around. Nothing would work, and eventually, she hauled herself out of bed. Each step was excruciating, and while she felt cold, she could not make the extra effort to reach her dressing gown. Slowly and deliberately, she wandered into the bathroom. Her bladder control was not once it had been, and there was some urgency. Reaching into the medicine cupboard, she found the bottle of codeine, and after an initial struggle, managed to loosen the lid and gobble down the small white tablets. They had worked before; they could work again. Her warfarin was in the kitchen. She had been warned by a very young arrogant doctor that she must take it for her heart. To spite him, she had always washed it down with a good red.

She stumbled along the corridor. Despite it being summer, the flagstone floor was cold on her toes. It was barely six o'clock. She grabbed her pills and snatched a bottle of red wine and a crystal glass. She would have a quick nightcap and go back to bed.

Walking back to her room, she stopped to pick up and look at a picture of her late husband. Tina had wiped the layers of dust away, and Doug looked as fresh-faced as he had all those years ago. The picture had been taken in Holbein in the rain. She ran her hand over his face, and still clutching the picture, stumbled into the lounge. She had taken to placing it in there now since it had been so lovingly cleaned. Gratefully sinking into her favourite chair, she pulled the rug over herself, and as the sun began to rise, it warmed her through. The codeine had also started to take the sharpness of the pain away. She poured herself a glass of wine and stared at the photograph.

After most of the bottle had gone, she needed the toilet. The wine and pills had wrapped her in a film of velvet, and she felt fine. Once she stood up, she began to feel the full effects, stumbled and held on to the table. Steadying herself on the various bits of furniture, she slowly made her way to the bathroom.

Suddenly, her legs give way, and as if time slowed down, she felt herself falling and her head colliding with the basin. It took a second for the pain to register with her as her body slammed against the floor. She tried to get up but was too exhausted.

"You silly bloody fool."

She tried to move her limbs. Had she broken anything? How was she going to get up? She tried again to lift herself, but the pain was too much. She felt herself slipping out of consciousness and suddenly became very calm. Then, there was blackness.

***

Tina and Mel washed in silence. Their meagre supplies were virtually gone, and they were not looking forward to working on an empty stomach. Mel tried to make conversation but was met with grunts. They walked back to the caravan in silence.

"Going for a walk," Tina announced.

Mel watched as she stomped off across the campsite. She could not quite put her finger on when her relationship with Tina had begun to change. Now she felt the same rush of anxiety that she had around the girls at school. She found herself trying to please her and reading second meanings into everything she said.

Her heart pounded, and the familiar worries about her sanity began to surface. She never had a name for it, but she had become aware of her panicky feelings when she was eleven. Wandering down to the fenland behind Pauline's house, she had stumbled across a dead wasp's nest. It had been sprayed white with poison, but the beauty of the intricate chambers encasing the wasps had fascinated her. She had stabbed at it with a stick and broken bits off to look at it more closely. The wasps were lined up as if in tiny shrouds inside the incredible encasement.

On returning from the field, she had told her aunt all about it. Pauline, uncharacteristically, had been quite strict. She told her the poison was strong and to make sure she washed her hands properly before tea. That was when it had started—the fear that she had already ingested the poison. Even though she was sure she had not touched it with her bare hand, the irrational fear remained. Mel scrubbed her hands until they were sore. She ate the sandwiches made for her tea but was careful to leave the corner where her hand touched the bread. All night she lay awake thinking she would die.

Remembering that day, she realised it was a watershed. Even now, whenever she stayed with Pauline and Clive, she would scrub her hands several times a day. The tap in the bathroom would also have to be cleaned, and then she would check that it had been switched off, often getting out of bed three or four times. She would often rush to bed so that Pauline would go in the bathroom after her, and then she could be sure the tap was off.

Over time, those thoughts had waned, but when she was stressed, she would notice the old behaviours creeping back. Her main anxiety was that she would become like her mother. She had inherited her translucent skin and delicate features, and it was a fear she had carried around and resented her mother for.

Mel looked out of the window for Tina and guessed she had already made her way to Mrs Wilbraham's house. She would give her another five minutes. Eventually, she decided to leave. Shutting the door and locking it, she counted to ten five times, saying the last number out loud, so she knew she had done it. The lock would have been easily broken, but still, she carried out the bizarre ritual. She trudged down the path beating herself up for her stupidity.

Nearing Mrs Wilbraham's house, she saw Tina. She was quite a way ahead but was not hurrying. Mel felt a stab of anger that she had left without her. She hadn't even had the decency to tell her she was leaving. She quickened her step and was soon within shouting distance. With every step, her anger swelled. She eventually reached her.

"Wait up," she shouted. Tina ignored her, which enraged her more, and she grabbed her by the shoulder.

"What's up with you?" Tina spun around and glared.

"Just fuck off."

"Why are you so bloody moody?"

"Why are you so...?"

"So what?"

"Annoying and lazy." Mel looked at the other girl. Her face was bright red. "Never clean up."

"I…."

"Messy bitch."

"You make all the mess, and how come you've got the bedroom? Didn't ask me! Just took it."

"Yeah, well, I work harder for Norman and Mrs Wilbraham. Twice as much."

"I would if I could...."

Tina mimicked a posh voice. "Tina, what shall I do? Tina, how do I clean this? Tina, how do I wipe my arse? Fucking hell," she shouted. "Work it out yourself."

"That's not true."

By now, Tina was in full flow. "Moaning on about your aunty. She's all right. Lucky to have her." This completely incensed Mel, and she screamed.

"What do you know?"

"A lot more than you." By now, some people were watching, and Tina glared at them. "What you bluudy looking at?" They turned away and stared at the ground. One little boy in a red shirt, under the protective arm of his father, stared, fascinated at the two young girls shouting in the street.

Tina stormed off towards Mrs Wilbraham's house. Mel had not finished. Tina's words had hurt her; she was still angry and had more to say.

"What is wrong with you?"

Tina ignored her and walked up the path to the house. She banged heavily on the door. There was no answer, but sometimes when the older woman's arthritis was bad, it would take her a while to reach the door. Still, they waited.

Tina looked at Mel. Her face, contorted with anger earlier, was now full of concern. She stuck her finger in the old brass letterbox and struggled to peer through the gap. There was a brush trim inside, and despite pushing it down, she could see very little.

"I'm going around the side and check the door there," said Tina. They both walked around to the lounge doors. The curtains were drawn, but they could just see through the cracks.

"She never goes out," said Mel.

"She might be in the loo." Tina climbed on the

drainpipe but could see nothing through the swirling patterned glass. Jumping down, Tina picked up a heavy piece of flint from the flower bed, lifted it above her head and went to smash the window.

"Tina, for Christ's sake."

"What else?"

Tina threw the rock, and it smashed through the glass next to the door handle. The key was still in the lock. She wrapped her hand in her jacket and stretched to unlock the door. Shards of glass had shattered everywhere. Looking at the mess, Mel wondered if they had done the right thing.

Tina had already gone. She ran into the hallway and checked every room. Eventually, she found Mrs Wilbraham on the floor, unconscious. For a moment, Tina thought she might be dead. She shook Mrs Wilbraham violently and the older woman began to moan. As they heaved her up, Mel was taken aback by the dead weight. Her arms screamed in pain as she hoisted her up, and a wide gash on Mrs Wilbraham's forehead spewed blood onto her hand. She recoiled and nearly lost her grip.

"For Christ's sake, hold her. Come on." Tina's voice was commanding, and Mel noticed the large wet patch on the floor. "Yeah, she's wet herself." Mel turned her face to Tina for her next instruction. "Now get her on the settee."

The older woman, despite being a bag of bones, was surprisingly heavy. Mrs Wilbraham began to moan. She was vaguely aware of the figures pulling at her, and her bird-like arms thrashed about as she tried to push the girls away.

"Get off…get off me."

Tina spoke clearly and calmly. "You've had a fall. We need to get this seen to."

"No doctor."

"You have to…."

"No, no!" She almost screamed.

"You might have a concussion, and you've pissed yourself."

"Tina!" said Mel.

"Well, she has."

Mrs Wilbraham looked so frail. Her hair, normally tied back, hung over her face in grey strands. Mel secretly thought it made her look like a witch. Beads of sweat rolled down her face, which had turned translucent pale grey. Mel could smell alcohol mixed with ammonia from the stale urine, and she thought she might faint.

Once Mrs Wilbraham was safely on the sofa, Tina took Mel into the kitchen. She held her by the shoulders and barked instructions.

"Get some water, tear up a towel or something. I'll sit with her." Mel rushed around doing as she was told, glad to be away from the struggling woman.

"Shouldn't we call a doctor?"

"You can't force her. My mum's always falling over."

"Drunk?"

"Yeah, my mum's a pisshead, just like her. But she's not a bitch. Hurry up."

Mel did as she was asked and ran back into the lounge. Tina screwed up one of the cloths and pressed it against the wound, stemming the flow of blood.

"That always looks much worse than what it is." Tina dipped the cloth in the water and dabbed away the blood. The sheer flow of it was alarming, but the cut was not as deep as the volume of blood suggested. Mrs Wilbraham winced with pain. Mel was amazed at how tender Tina was.

Mel rushed into the bedroom, found an old sheet, and they attempted a dressing with it. Mel had once trained with St John's Ambulance and had been taught how to dress a wound but could remember very little. It was a mess but seemed to do the trick. The older woman seemed calmer.

"I'll stay with her in case she's concussed."

"What about the doctor?"

"If she pukes, I'll call a doctor," Tina almost shouted.

Mel was grateful that Tina was in charge. She caught a glimpse of her ashen face in the mirror. Her back was dripping with sweat while Tina, in contrast, seemed in control. Mel felt her glaring at her.

"Stay with her while I make her some tea. I'll try and get some water down her."

Mel looked at Mrs Wilbraham. She felt a surge of admiration for Tina. She was not sure what to say. She pathetically patted Mrs Wilbraham's hand and stared at her in silence until Tina returned.

"What else can I do?"

"Roll me a fag."

Mel clumsily tried to roll a cigarette, but what she produced was loose, fat and falling apart. Tina knocked it out of her hand.

"For Christ's sake." Mel felt useless. "Go if you want. I'll stay here. Make sure she's ok."

"Are you sure?"

"Yes."

Mel meekly offered to clear up, but Tina told her to go. She repeated herself more forcibly this time, and Mel could sense the irritation in her voice. Relieved, she almost ran out of the house and back to the caravan. She chastised herself that she should have stayed and supported Tina but had felt totally out of her depth. Her mind raced that she was weak, and by the time she returned to the caravan, anxiety was tearing at her stomach.

***

Mrs Wilbraham opened her eyes. The pain in her leg was sharp and momentarily made her breathless. Her head was throbbing, and she realised she was on the settee. She felt Tina's hand squeeze hers and was surprised to see her concerned face.

"What time is it?"

"'Bout seven. You've been asleep all day."

"What happened?"

Tina explained that they had found her lying down in the bathroom after breaking in. Mrs Wilbraham told Tina off for breaking the window but knew that she was being unreasonable, and Tina pouted like a petulant child.

"Next time, I'll bluudy well leave ya."

In truth, the fall had frightened her and reminded her how infirm she was becoming. Her head ached, and she had bruising down her legs. They were a motley shade of purple and blue, and they quite fascinated her. Tina had changed her clothes, and the embarrassment of wetting herself was more painful than the injuries. She sat back in the chair and looked at Tina. She had stayed up with her for hours.

"All right?" Mrs Wilbraham managed to smile. "Tea?"

Tina scuttled off to make a pot while Mrs Wilbraham surveyed the room. A pang of anxiety crept into her head about what might have happened if Tina had not broken in. She looked at the bottle of wine and pills where she had still left them. Despite knowing that they had caused her fall, she wanted a glass of wine more than anything. Tina returned with the tea, and they sat in silence.

"Going to need a glazier to fix that door." Tina nodded. "Look in that chest." She pointed to the Edwardian bureau. "Got a list of workmen in there. Red book."

"Ok."

"Think there's a Yellow Pages in there." Tina dutifully did as she was commanded and pulled open the heavy drawer. It was stuffed with papers, photographs and letters. "Bring it all here." Tina grabbed the contents and laid everything out on the table in front of Mrs Wilbraham.

"Who's this?" Tina held up a picture of a distinguished-looking man. It was black and white, and he was smoking.

"Doug just before he died." Her voice choked up, and she chastised herself.

Tina looked at the frail woman. She looked old, and she could tell she was reliving some distant memory. Tina rummaged in a pile and found a small red book, and she handed it to Mrs Wilbraham.

"Will cost an arm and a leg. Broke the whole door panel.

Perhaps Eddie could have a look," Tina suggested.

"Yes, ask him." Mrs Wilbraham uncharacteristically squeezed Tina's hand and mouthed the word. "Thank you."

"You got a load of letters in here. Not been opened."

Her voice trailed off. They were bills, and Tina was well aware of what final demands were. In her household, their electricity had been cut off numerous times and they rarely had a working phone. Mrs Wilbraham snatched them off her but knew that Tina had grasped what they were.

"Just problems, Tina."

Tina looked at the older woman. Despite the antiques and size of the house, she was obviously in debt. This was serious. God only knew how long before she had her electric cut off or worse.

CHAPTER 21

Tina almost skipped along the path to meet Vincent. She had met him on the way to Mrs Wilbraham's earlier that day. He had skidded his bike next to her and pretended to run her down. She had carried on walking, and he had driven his bike beside her before casually inviting her to come and hang out at the barn, where his band practised. They were going to have a session that afternoon.

There was something animalistic about him. So much larger than Eddie in stature, with a roughness about him that was undeniably attractive. She wasn't sure if he liked her or not. He would flirt but was never overtly attentive. It made her only the more anxious to impress him. She had washed her hair and stolen a Judas Priest T-shirt off an unsuspecting family's washing line. It had been a good find. She still had some eye kohl from the makeup bag that Norman had given her, and she had enjoyed drawing the dark lines under each eye.

Glad to be away from Mel, she was happy to have

somewhere else to go. The barn was not far, and she was enjoying the anticipation and the walk. Birds wandered across the mudflats in search of their lunch. There was a slight breeze, and the salty air lifted her spirits. The day was hot, and she took her time, keen not to arrive with sweat-stained armpits.

Before she could see the barn, she heard the thumping bass of heavy metal music. Surprisingly, there were three Norton motorbikes parked outside. Tina was a little bit perturbed as she had expected it to be just the two of them. Then she laughed and reminded herself it was a band practice. Vince was standing with his legs astride an old log. She could not make out the faces of the others, but they were dressed identically in black leather jackets and jeans. Laughter carried in the air, but there was another sound she could not quite make out. As she got nearer, she ducked behind the old oak tree to check her appearance. She looked again toward the group and saw a small white dog cowering between them.

Without warning, Vincent kicked the dog, which flew through the air. It was booted back like a football by one of the lads. The dog screeched in pain, and the assault continued—each ferocious kick sapped the helpless animal's life. Tina was overwhelmed with revulsion. The dog lay on its side, gasping for breath. Vincent kicked it one more time, and there was silence. They all cackled in unison. Vincent lifted the dog by its collar and unceremoniously tossed it away.

Shocked and unsure what to do, Tina jumped into the drainage ditch. Crouching down, she tried to make sense of the enormous cruelty she had witnessed. She remained there for about fifteen minutes until she heard the motorbikes revving up. They screamed past her, and she stayed in her hiding place until her heart stopped pounding.

Running back to the caravan, she could hear frantic voices searching for their dog. A woman shouted to her.

"Have you seen our puppy? He's wandered off."

Tina managed to mutter, "No." Covering her ears with her hands, she eventually reached the sanctuary of the caravan.

***

The force of the first blow took Eddie by surprise. He stumbled and grabbed onto the kitchen sink for stability. His father punched him in the stomach and kicked him in the shins. He could smell stale tobacco on his breath as he pushed his yellow teeth close to his ear.

"You will do this job, bah."

Eddie tried to move out of the way as another fist came crashing into his chin.

"I don't want...."

"You will!" His father's voice was shrill. "I tell you what you will and won't do." Eddie lifted himself to his full height and pushed the older man away. Momentarily startled, he fell back, but the shock on his face was soon replaced by amusement. "Trying to hit me back, are you?"

"Fuck off!" Eddie tried again to hit him, but the older man was too quick. He picked up a saucepan and slammed it into Eddie's head. He could feel the blood pouring from his mouth and running down his shirt.

Vincent came into the kitchen and took the saucepan out of his father's hand.

"He hint no use if you kill him."

The older man laughed and lit a cigarette, and he pointed at the frightened boy.

"He'll do as he is bluudy well told."

Eddie tried to get up, but the pain in his head was too much. A boot came crashing into his rib cage and winded him. His vision was blurred, and he felt desperately thirsty. Vincent glared at his brother.

"Git up, bah. We have to plan this."

"Can't."

The two older men turned away, and Eddie saw his chance. He ran blindly out of the house and along the sea path. He knew Vincent's bike couldn't manage the footbridge and stile, and it would give him a head start. Twice he stumbled and nearly fell. Sweat poured down his back, and his body burned with pain. Eventually, he reached the sea wall and sank into the gritty, wet sand behind it. He clutched his side and gingerly lifted his shirt. A visible boot print glowed angrily on his skin.

"Just rest," he repeated to himself.

He was breathing heavily, and each breath sent a searing pain down his side. If he could just stay out long enough, his dad would get drunk and eventually pass out. Vincent would be looking for him, but for the moment, he felt safe.

"Eddie?"

Panicked, he turned around and was relieved he recognised the voice. Tina stood over him. He was jumpy, and she could instantly tell something was wrong. When she got closer, she saw the state he was in. Blood had run down his shirt, and his face was a purple and black mess. He raised his T-shirt, and she gently touched the bruise.

"Ouch."

"Sorry." Tina pulled out the bandana stuffed in her pocket and ran to the sea. "Saltwater, that'll help." She dabbed it on his face and his side. "Was this Vince?"

Eddie remained silent then he spoke quietly. "No, my dad." His voice shook, and for a moment, he was worried he was going to cry.

Tina sat next to him on the sandy pebbles and offered him a roll-up. They sat in silence. The sound of Vincent's motorbike suddenly became audible. It got closer, and they instinctively ducked down behind the concrete wall. Vince was above them. They could smell the petrol as he revved his engine and felt the vibrations of the Norton. He shouted again, and they could sense his prowling eyes.

"Eddie, for fuck's sake."

They remained still. Eventually, the bike roared away. Eddie looked at Tina, his face serious.

"You need to keep away from him. He's da...."

"I know." She told him of what she had witnessed that afternoon. "It was sick."

"Jesus!"

"That poor bluudy dog. He chucked it in the ditch like it was rubbish." Eddie saw the disgust on Tina's face. Seeing the dog beaten so senselessly had affected her. While she always seemed harder than Mel, there was a vulnerability about her.

"Fucking psycho," said Eddie.

"Your dad's not?"

"Both bastards."

Tina lit another cigarette. "So, what was this all about?"

"I can't tell you." Tina pulled a face. "He wants me to do a job, and it's a big one. If I get caught...."

"What sort?"

"Drugs, not dealing the odd bit of dope. This is slabs of it from the docks."

“Fuck, Eddie.”

“Yep, bluudy twenty years if I get caught.”

“Just don’t.”

Like a spectre, Vincent appeared behind them. “There you are, boy. Now git the fuck home.” He had ditched the bike and snuck up on them. Eddie's face drained of colour. He was not sure how much Vincent had heard. “Got to take this boy home,” Vince said to Tina “His dinner’s getting cold.”

Eddie compliantly sat on the back of the bike, and they drove off. Tina watched the bike weaving away. The sound hung in the air long after they had gone. Suddenly, feeling exhausted, she rubbed her eyes, trying to soothe the headache that was forming. She needed to lie down.

***

Back at the caravan, Tina found herself irritated by Mel. She thought about Eddie and how lost he seemed. Mel was sitting up proudly clutching a bottle.

“Come on, got some wine.”

“Don’t want it.” Mel looked defeated. Tina did not have time for this. “Just leave me alone.”

“Have I done someth...?”

"Just fuck off, will you?" Tina went into her bedroom and slammed the door. She lay on the bed and thought about Eddie.

Mel picked up her bottle of wine and walked out of the caravan. She could feel the heat of tears beginning to gather behind her eyes. What had she done? She had thought the wine would please Tina. The same pattern was being repeated that had been at school. Always on the edge of the group, never sure if they were genuine. For a while she had thought Tina was different.

Mel walked away from the town and sat down by the blackberry bushes where they had devoured the fruit with such glee. Many of the berries had been eaten by birds, but a few were left. Scratching her arm, she pulled a couple away. They tasted bitter, and she spat them out. Pulling them apart, they seemed to be covered in a sort of white 'mange'. The season was over, and rot had begun to seep in. She wiped her red-stained hands on the grass and took a swig from the bottle.

***

Back at the house, Vincent told Eddie to go to bed. His father was pacing the house, and he wanted to talk to him properly about the task. Shouting was not going to help, and he needed to get everything organised. Vincent moved the tins of beer off the table and pushed the bowl of dog food away with his foot. His father was still relatively sober, and he laid a battered map on the table.

"The drugs are going to land here." He pointed to an inlet further up the coast. Vincent knew the land well, and he had checked it out on his bike numerous times. The land was perfect for landing a shallow boat, and the layout of the rock and heath meant it was not overlooked. Suffolk had a long history of smugglers, and it made Vince laugh that he was just following a tradition. "I've got the exact times of the tide."

"Right."

"We take the stuff and load it into a boat here. The tributary goes inland. The boat is a tourist boat, so it won't raise suspicions. I've got people waiting to get it on board. They're good boys."

"You have to be careful, bah."

Vince looked slightly irritated. "There is no fucking about. There'll be three heavy pallets. I need Eddie to help me load 'em."

"What vehicle?"

"A van is too obvious. We need to look like tourists. We'll nick a car. We can change the plates. We'll just dump it when it's done. The Dutch boys have given me the drop-off points for their contacts. We get to keep ten kilos."

"What's that in English?"

"Shit loads, and we get cash for the drop-off."

"Can we trust them Dutch boys?"

"If anyone gets caught, we are all fucked. I've done

dummy runs and timed how long each journey takes. I've even checked out the moon. It's going to be waning, so it'll be dark. This has to run like clockwork."

"Shame about this bloody arm. I could have done this."

"Eddie will." His father scowled. "Don't worry. I'll make sure he's onside."

"How you going to do that?"

Vincent looked at his father. His eyes were black. "I'll pay one of those girls a visit. He won't dare say no when I've bluudy finished."

His father slumped back into the chair and lit another cigarette while Vince continued to pore over the maps.

When they had got home, Eddie had hoped his father would be crashed out in the kitchen. Often, he would fall asleep with his cigarette still burning, and the ash would balance to over an inch still clutched in the old man's hand. Eddie had hoped, one day, that he would set himself alight.

Vincent had commanded him to go to bed, and he had slunk up the stairs to his room. The relief of being alone overwhelmed him. He lay on his side as the pain from his rib cage was too much. Shifting from side to side, he tried to get comfortable. His mind raced. Staring at the Artex ceiling, he traced the swirls with his eyes. It was mindless but kept him distracted. He thought of his mother and desperately tried to remember her face. He missed her so much.

***

The next day, Eddie left as soon as he was awake. Careful not to wake anyone in the house, he crept out, putting his boots on in the van. The sun was not yet up, and he drove down the tiny lanes to the sea. He enjoyed the birds and beauty of the landscape. He watched as a tern tentatively walked on the sand, its long legs stopping it from sinking. Driving for a good twenty minutes, he eventually pulled in behind the sand dunes. The area was much more barren here, and there were only a few holiday stores, selling garish buckets and spades. As it was barely six o'clock, they were locked behind bright blue shutters.

The sun was not yet up, and Eddie was slightly chilly. Mel had left an old blanket in the back, and he wrapped it around his bare arms. He was hungry and realised he hadn't eaten since breakfast the day before, so he helped himself to an ice lolly. He pulled down the vanity mirror and surveyed his face. He had a black eye which, surprisingly, was not painful unless touched. The real discomfort was his ribs.

His mind raced. He would have to do as he was told. Who could he tell? No one was on his side. He suddenly thought of his mother. Wrapping the blanket around himself, he tried to sleep. If he went to see Mel, she would question him about his injuries. He could say that he fell off the bike. Tina would go along with it. Craving a friendly face, he decided to go and see them. They might even give him breakfast. Exhausted, he rested his head on the back of the seat and tried to forget the last twenty-four hours.

CHAPTER 22

Vince watched Mel as she wandered down to the town and started on the path to the caravan park. He aggressively pushed past Norman, who was watering the herbs growing in buckets outside his office. His frame was a lot heavier than the old man's, and he easily unsteadied him. Norman spun around and shouted.

"You git out of my park, bah."

Vince looked at him and grinned. "You going to make me?"

Norman lowered his tone. "I'll git the police on you. You see if I don't."

Throwing his cigarette down, Vince spat, narrowly missing Norman's boots. Furiously, Norman followed in pursuit but was stopped by two holidaymakers. Standing with his hands on his hips, Vince laughed. His face darkened as he remembered Eddie's defiance the night before. He would make him pay for that. Patting his breast pocket, he purposefully strode towards the girls' caravan.

Tina uncharacteristically woke up late. Mel had gone, and she was grateful for the peace. The distance between them had been her making, and she felt guilty. She could not keep her irritation at bay. Lifting her hands above her head, she surveyed her bright red hands. They were raw from being constantly in water. The nail varnish in the vanity case had helped, but her nails were torn and ragged. Yes, she deserved to take it easy today. It had been hard scrubbing out the caravans, and her arms ached.

An old, discarded Radio Times lay open beside her with a picture of David Bellamy on the front. She picked it up. Another half an hour wouldn't make any difference. Leafing through the pages passed the time but very little registered. Unable to relax, she kept replaying the events of yesterday. God, Eddie had been in such a state. She needed to see him to make sure he was all right. It seemed like a week ago that she had witnessed Vince so cruelly kill the puppy. She felt a stab of revulsion and could still see its lifeless body. Vince was a bastard.

She heard Vince before she saw him. He was whistling The Ace of Spades. Pulling the curtain back slightly, she glimpsed the heels of his boots as he walked around the caravan.

"Christ, no." She froze and dropped down on the bed. If she was quiet, he might not see her.

Vince tapped on the window above her head. She sensed his eyes peering through the gap in the curtain.

"Wake up, Tina." He banged again, and Tina panicked. He had seen her. Her mind raced. She would have to do something. Trying to sound as casual as she could, she shouted.

"Not dressed...."

She quickly rushed around as she had only pants on and an old shirt. Grabbing a towel, she wrapped it around herself and walked out of the bedroom. Her heart was beating fast. Vincent was dangerous, and she felt vulnerable.

As calmly as she could, she said, "Hold on."

Pulling back the curtain, she frantically looked for Mel, hoping she might come back. Norman was in sight but was walking in the opposite direction. She felt trapped.

Vince grinned through the window. "Smoke?"

Tina gestured for him to come in. He smiled and pulled a rolled joint comically between his thumb and finger from his pocket and presented it to her. Tina leaned across and lit it, and she could feel him stare at her. He pulled out two cans of beer.

"Fucking Father Christmas, I am."

Tina opened the beer. For once, it was cold. The joint began to make her feel woozy. God, it was strong. She took another swig of beer and spilt it on her thigh. Vince rubbed it away and commanded her to take another swig. Tina did and spilt it again.

"Anyone would have thought you did that on purpose." His heavy hand rubbed the stain. He laughed, but Vince did not remove his hand. It lay heavily on her knee, and she offered him the smoke. "That's all right. I got wankered before I got here. You catch up." She did as she was told. He began to move his hand further up her thigh. Tina felt unable to move. "Want a blowback?"

Before she could answer, he took a deep draw and blew the smoke into her mouth. It took her by surprise, and it burnt the back of her throat. The room felt strange, and her vision began to blur. Christ, she was wasted. Coughing uncontrollably, he offered her the can. The cool liquid helped, and she greedily guzzled it.

"Got some tobacco on your mouth." Tina tried to move, but before she could flick it away, he gently brushed her lips with his large dirty fingers and leaned in. "Got to take a closer look." He pushed his lips against hers, the sensation of his rough beard startled her, and suddenly his tongue was in her mouth. She did not dare move. She could not move. He left his heavy hand on her leg and began to squeeze. She felt it creep up to her thigh and further, all the time kissing her harder. His hand roughly pushed its way into her pants. His other hand lifted up her bra and squeezed. He was hurting her. She was not sure if it was her bra digging into her or his nails. His rough beard scratched her face as he lowered his mouth to her ear. His breath smelt of alcohol and cigarettes, and he squeezed her breast tightly and pulled her even closer. Tina felt out of control. It was all moving too fast. She felt hot and sick. He then lowered his voice to a gasp. "I know you've been warning Eddie about our business."

It took Tina a second to register what he said. He thrust his fingers inside her, hurting her and squeezed her breast even harder.

"Stop...."

She managed to say the word, but it came out as a whisper. His mouth was on top of hers, and she couldn't speak. She tried to move her mouth away, but he was all over her, his hands large and forceful. She felt sick and was in pain, but he wouldn't stop. The drugs made her feel sick, and she felt totally out of control.

He suddenly pulled away. "Keep your snout out, slag!" He stood up and readjusted his crotch. "Slag...put something a bit stronger than dope in there." He spat on the floor and left, leaving the caravan door wide open.

Tina felt numb. What had just happened? She could still feel where his fingers had been clasping and grabbing at her. The smell of his tobacco and sweat was all around her. She felt disgusting. Her head pounded, and she felt nauseous and weak. Trying to lay back down, the room kept moving, and her heart was exploding in her chest. She couldn't process what had just happened. Sweating, she clung to the table. Soon it would pass. The word 'slag' kept ringing in her ears.

Tina held desperately to the tabletop. Her vision blurred, the floor moved up and down, and nausea clutched at her throat and stomach. She could feel the sweat searing through her clothes, and she was drenched.

She was not sure how long she had sat there clinging

on. Her hand hurt, the muscles strained, holding on to the only tangible thing she knew was there. Eventually, she felt the efficacy of the drug lessen. The room began to return to normal, and the floor remained still. She could feel her body ebbing towards normality, but she still felt weak.

Her palms were raw and itched. She realised she had been ferociously scratching at them. Lines of blood oozed down the back of her hand. Sitting very still, she tried to piece together what had just happened. The back of her eye pounded, and she wanted to be sick. The bile merely burnt her throat and then subsided. She tried to get up but felt too shaky. She stayed still and waited. Clutching her legs, she became aware that she was rocking back and forth. The door to the caravan swung on its hinges, but she did not have the energy to shut it.

At last, she felt well enough to stand. She could still smell his breath and the musty tobacco. Pulling on a pair of jeans, she stumbled out into the bright sunshine. She could not stay in the caravan. Without looking back, she ran towards the town. Her feet hurt, but she carried on running. She realised in her haste to leave she had bare feet. Some tourists had shouted, "It's Zola Budd," and she heard their self-congratulatory laughter as she dashed past them. She did not stop until she reached Mrs Wilbraham's house.

***

Mrs Wilbraham found herself looking forward to the girls coming. The house had almost had breath blown into it, and it was noticeably lighter. While the years of dust had been removed, it was more than that. Tina initially had been surly and aggressive, but she had softened and had made a wonderful nurse after her recent accident. She loved to throw herself into tasks and thrived on approval. Mrs Wilbraham enjoyed seeing the broad grin on her face when she praised her. It was funny that while she had seemed the older and certainly more vocal of the two, she was eager to please. The other one was more of an enigma. They made a strange team.

Eleven o'clock came, and they had still not arrived. She found herself checking her watch, and she could not shake a sense of unease. Finally, the doorbell rang, and Mrs Wilbraham almost ran to the door.

"Where have you been? You're an hour…." She attempted to chastise Tina, but one look at the dishevelled figure before her made her stop. Tina's eyes were black with kohl, and it ran in tramlines down her face. Shocked, she realised something was desperately wrong. "Come in, child," she said tenderly and beckoned her into the house.

Tina obliged. Her eyes were red, her skin white, and she burst into tears. Mrs Wilbraham instinctively put an arm around her shoulder and felt the young girl shake. She put her head on her shoulder and continued to hug her. She had no idea how long they stood there. Eventually, Mrs Wilbraham took her by the hand and laid her on the settee.

"I'll make some tea, and when you feel better, you can tell me what the problem is." She heard how inadequate her words were before they even left her mouth.

Once in the kitchen, she began to recognise the strangeness of the situation. For years she had lived alone, and very few people had got close to her, just Eddie and his mum. Tina had come, and she had embraced her. She found herself enjoying that sensation. Once back in the lounge, she took one look at the child and those feelings instantly turned to guilt.

"I've made you a cup of tea." Tina just stared blankly at her. "I want you to drink it. Then I might let you have one of my cigarettes."

Tina, shaking, sipped at the cup. Mrs Wilbraham put a rug around her and told her to drink up. She would not force her to tell her what had upset her, but she was concerned it was serious. This wasn't some teenage break-up. No, something terrible had happened.

"You don't have to tell me what. I won't insult you by asking you." Tina meekly nodded. "You're safe with me. Stay here as long as you like."

Tina managed a couple of sips of tea. Her lips were parched, and although thirsty from running, she was too tired to drink it. She meekly lay down on the settee and closed her eyes. Mrs Wilbraham sat by her side. She plumped up the cushion she used as a pillow and tucked the blanket around her. Tina was grateful for the tightness of the covers, and they helped her feel safe. She felt the adrenaline leave her body and her bones felt like lead. Exhausted, she curled up and slept.

CHAPTER 23

Mel walked back from the town. The sun was hot, and her clothes stuck to her uncomfortably. She kicked at the gravel on the road and tried to make sense of the last couple of days. Tina had been frosty. It reminded her of school. Jennifer, and her inner circle, sometimes included her and other times made her the butt of their jokes. She had been thrown by their behaviour. Sometimes Jennifer seemed genuinely happy to see her and praised her clothes or hairstyle. Mel bathed in her attention. More often than not, she was on the periphery, clinging on to the group. When she'd had the haircut, she had been ecstatic that they liked it. For a few days, she was accepted and felt like a queen. It was the haircut that had led to the invite to Italy. Only three girls were chosen, and she remembered the face of Katie Shaw when she was told she was not one of them.

"This year, there simply wasn't space for her."

Mel had savoured that moment, relieved that for once, she was in the inner sanctum. Tina, however, was different.

She did not communicate with half meanings or snide comments. For a while, they had become inseparable, and she had even told her about her mother. There was no judgement with Tina. Why had she suddenly become so distant?

Mel kicked a stone along the path. Twice it fell in the gutter, and she scooped it up. Out of the corner of her eye, she saw Eddie. He was leaning against the entrance to the pet shop, looking at snakes in glass cases. She called over.

"Eddie, wait up."

He looked up and stared at her. He did not acknowledge her greeting or even nod. Vincent put a hand on his neck and pulled him away. Mel looked after them, stunned. She felt a physical pain in her chest and mind, which had been momentarily distracted by the pebble. Thoughts tumbled out, drowning her.

Why was he being like that? What have I done? Perhaps I said something? But what? Who do you think you are, thinking that Eddie was interested? Why would he be? Never had a boyfriend. Never would. What have I said? Why do I always get it so wrong? First Tina, but I don't know what. She grasped her head and screwed up her eyes. *What is wrong with me? Just like my mum....*

The thought was almost too unbearable to contemplate. It had always been in the back of her mind that she would inherit her mother's mental health issues. She had never been brave enough to voice them to anyone and ignored them. She certainly could never tell the girls at school. She survived on the edge of anxiety. Sometimes she could tame the beast and remind herself that things would get better. Most of the time, she was treading water, permanently struggling, and second-guessing what she said and did. It had been different with Tina. In the last few weeks, she had felt more in control. Strange, as she was so far out of her comfort zone. Perhaps she looked down on Tina and so was not constantly trying to impress her. She thought about her dad and how the anger had carried her through. Now she was alarmed that the same old pattern of being on the outside had wormed its way in. This was what she was.

Once back in the caravan, Mel shut the door. They liked to keep it open as it could get oppressively hot, but Mel wanted to shut out the outside. She found a mug and tipped out the dregs of wine from the night before. A thick red residue lay at the bottom, but she did not care. A half bottle of red wine sat on the bench, and she poured herself a generous helping. The first warm mouthful burnt her throat. It was warm and just added to her thirst.

Tipping Tina's jacket on the floor, she found a packet of Rizlas and her tobacco tin. It contained everything she needed. She had watched Tina and Eddie roll joints so effortlessly. With all her concentration, she stuck three Rizlas together and slowly crumbled in the black resin. She was not sure how much to put in but had seen them do it enough times to hazard a guess. When she rolled it, she had used too much saliva, and it was baggy and unsmokable. She unravelled it and transferred the content to another set of cigarette papers. While not perfect, this attempt was pretty good, and she admired her work. It reminded her of the first time she had smoked with Tina and Eddie and how they were always boasting about what experts they were.

The concentration of rolling had focused and calmed her mind, but the memory again flooded her with doubts and questions. She took another swig of the wine and lit her work. As before, it made her choke, but she persevered. Each puff she matched with a swig of wine and had soon drained her glass. She slumped onto the seat and lay down. She was suddenly exhausted.

Mel woke to find several hours had passed. The sun was no longer blazing, but the air felt close, and it was still unbearably hot. Behind her eye, there was a pulsating banging and her throat was dry. A discarded bottle of Fanta lay on the bench with only a dribble inside. She greedily swallowed it. The sudden sugar made her gag. Tina had boiled some water for tea the day before and Mel swigged out of the spout. While warm, the liquid made her feel much better. She was unsure how long she had been asleep, but the sun was going down. The events of the day replayed over and over in her mind. She found her thoughts pouring out, criticising, questioning and deriding her. The wine and dope had numbed her, but she now felt the overwhelming need to leave the stuffy caravan.

She ran down the path to the beach in a daze, grateful that few holidaymakers were about. It was deserted apart from a few dog walkers in the distance. The odd yelp carried on the wind but seemed far away. There was a stillness to the air that seemed almost ungodly. Black clouds billowed in the distance and the sun was swallowed on the horizon. She stared at the sea, normally so blue and clear, it was now a dark green and coming in.

Out of nowhere, a sharp wind whipped around her shoulders, and she began to feel cold. Swirling waves crashed onto the beach, each time moving closer and closer. Dirty foam edged towards her feet. Occasionally, the spray would spit against her cheek. Mel looked towards the dog walkers. They had gone and she was alone. The sea stretched out for miles until it met the sky. She had always enjoyed the vastness of the Suffolk sky, but tonight it only added to her feeling of isolation.

Trembling, she tried to steady her hands. Her heart pounded relentlessly, and she felt like it would come out of her chest. The sea continued to crash and encroach onto the sand. She felt like she couldn't breathe. Water filled her shoes, and the sudden cold jolted her out of her detachment.

It was dark and she was cold. Light droplets of rain had begun to fall, and she knew that a downpour was imminent. The clouds obscured the moon, and there was barely enough light to find the way back. Once on the familiar campsite path, she began to run past the tents and up to the caravans. The light through the orange curtains made them appear like demonic eyes lining her route.

Once inside, she sank down on the seat. She reached for the wine bottle and, without looking for a mug, gulped straight from the bottle. Her attempt at rolling a joint was half-smoked in the ashtray. Grabbing it, she hastily lit it. Throwing off her wet socks, she covered her feet with Tina's jacket, lay back and listened to the wind.

Sand at the bottom of her jeans rubbed her calves, and her feet were freezing cold. She took off her jeans, wrapped a towel around her bare legs, and sat in darkness. A torch that Tina had stolen was just in reach, but she was too tired to stretch for it. Hugging her knees, she tried to quell the noise in her head. Thoughts rushed and cascaded into her brain, criticising and berating. The wine was almost gone, and she drank the last remaining drops. She was too tired to roll another joint. The effort was too great.

Rain lashed against the side of the caravan, and deafening droplets hammered against the roof. Mel found herself alarmed. Up until now, the skies had been bright and there was nothing but the relentless heat. She heard a dog bark outside while the caravan walls shook with the ferocity of the rain and the curtain billowed despite the windows being shut. There was a drop in temperature and the atmosphere seemed almost unworldly. Mel pulled the towel around her tightly and hugged her knees. She looked out into the sky and could see lightning striking over the sea. The storm was getting closer. The dog continued to bark.

"Shut up! Shut up!" She covered her ears.

Mel picked up the bottle opener. The end where the finger went was smooth. She wondered if it was an antique. It was certainly solid and old and seemed strange to be nestled amongst the plastic 1970s knives and forks. She stuck the end in the table and spun it around. Pulling the towel down, she tentatively ran the sharp end across her exposed bare thigh. It left a thin white line without breaking the skin. Fascinated, she dragged it again, this time with more force. The sensation of pain slightly startled her. With total concentration, she pushed the end into her thigh and drew blood. The abrupt pain calmed her mind and focused her thoughts. The wound began to drip blood, and she watched in fascination as it ran like tributaries down her leg. Digging it in again, she almost felt an instant release. She lay back and felt the warm blood trickle down her thigh. The towel absorbed most of it, but some fell onto the cloth of the seat.

Mel was too exhausted to clean it up. She lay down and listened to the rain. It had begun to subside, and the dog's incessant barking seemed fainter. Pulling Tina's jacket over her, she lay down and tried to sleep. Periodically, she pressed the cut on her leg. The area was sore, but the resulting pain gave her an instant rush, and she breathed deeply. She sensed the storm had moved further away. Just the rain remained heavy but not ferocious. She felt her body relaxing, and she was soon asleep.

***

The next day when she woke up, she still had the old towel wrapped around her, and her legs felt stiff. She opened one eye. Tina was still not home, and the caravan was a tip. An empty wine bottle lay on its side and bits of tobacco were strewn across the table. While she did not feel great, her headache was not as ferocious as it had been. She slowly pulled herself to her feet and instantly noticed the sharp pain in her thigh. Lifting the towel, she saw the red welts from the night before. Feelings of shame rushed through her. It felt like a very bizarre thing to do. Tentatively touching the strips of broken skin, she winced, but the sudden sharp pain felt strangely pleasurable. She remembered as a child falling off her bike into a bed of nettles with Aunty Pauline. Dock leaves, while relieving the initial sting, were more of a ritual than a cure. The next day she had enjoyed the sensation of touching the red marks the nettles had left. She had been fascinated by those tiny stings. This was the same sort of pain.

Stopping to pick up some clothes, she made her way to the toilet block. The campsite looked different. Pools of water from the rain the night before had gathered along the normally arid path. The entrance to the toilet block was muddy, and various sized footprints littered the white tiled floor. Mel looked at her trainers. They were dirty and frayed. She remembered Jennifer telling her what was '*the best look*'. She had bought them to please her, but she had never really liked them. Relieved there was no one else in the block, she quickly splashed water under her arms and face. The cold made her feel instantly better. She looked at her face in the cracked mirror. Her eyes had black rings underneath them, and her hair, which had been shaved at the back, was growing out. She was a mess.

Once back in the caravan, she scrabbled around for food. There were some mashed potatoes hardened to the base of a saucepan and an empty packet of custard creams. She greedily wolfed down the stale crumbs at the bottom of the packet. She had drunk a mouthful of water from the tap at the campsite, but she was still thirsty. Hunger tore at her stomach as she realised she had not eaten for twenty-four hours, and she started to cry.

A month ago, she was due to go to Italy. Now her whole world was in turmoil. The same criticising voices raged in her head, and she sank down on the seats. The blood from the night before had hardened to a dark brown on the seat covering. She pressed on the wound over her jeans and felt the instant control that the pain gave her. Pulling down her trousers, she picked at the young scab that had started to form and instantly felt better. She had to do something. Mrs Wilbraham owed her money. Even if Tina were there, she would have to get it.

Mel walked with purpose down to the town. The sea was much calmer than it had been, and the sun felt good on her back. A tiny drop of salty spray landed in her mouth, and she licked it, enjoying the sensation. As she walked, her mind began to race. She had seen Tina and Eddie together, and their joint coldness had coincided. A rather desperate thought entered her mind that they were seeing each other behind her back. It all suddenly made sense. Tina had disappeared several times, and Eddie had suddenly blanked her. It had hurt so much. Anger welled in her stomach and chest. Thoughts continued to plague her mind, and she went over everything in minute detail. *'Yes, it all made sense.'*

Her initial optimism was replaced with despair. Thoughts continued to crash into her mind, and she wanted them to stop—each one feeding her anger. Remembering Tina's words on their first day, she repeated them under her breath. '*We've done the bluudy work. We need paying.*'

She knocked on the door and waited. There was no answer or movement inside. She knew Mrs Wilbraham never left the house, so she knocked again. She took deep breaths and readied herself. Eventually, Mrs Wilbraham came to the door. Mel quickly rehearsed her demand for payment in her head.

The older woman instantly disarmed Mel. Her face was

ghostly white, but it was her eyes that alarmed her. Normally so defiant, she looked like she had been crying. Her usual booming greeting was also missing, and she meekly gestured for Mel to come in. Grabbing her arm, she steadied herself.

"Come," she whispered.

Mel sensed something was wrong. She was led into the dark lounge and saw a figure lying on the settee with a loose blanket over them. In the dim light, she moved closer and realised it was Tina.

"What's wrong with her?" Tina was always so strong, so resilient. Nothing stopped her from getting up and bounding about. She was always the early riser and never slept in. A tumbler of water was by her side but had not been touched. Mel looked at Mrs Wilbraham. "What happened?"

The older woman looked down. She suddenly felt frail and old. Taking Mel's hand in her own she whispered.

"Vincent."

It took a moment for Mel to realise the implication of what had happened. The older woman's face was enough to convince her that something was desperately wrong. She looked back into the lounge.

"Should I?"

"Leave her. She needs sleep." Mel felt helpless, and she was grateful for Mrs Wilbraham's warm hand on her arm.

"She hasn't eaten, and I've got no food in. Could you buy something and cook it?"

As if reading her mind, she pushed a ten-pound note into Mel's hand. She grabbed it and ran to the local Mace store.

Mel had never cooked a meal at home in her life and, when faced with the ancient cooker, suddenly felt inadequate. Tina needed her, and she was not going to let her down. She remembered making spaghetti bolognese in home economics and could remember how to do that, and despite struggling to open the tin of tomatoes, the pot was soon boiling on the stove. Theatrically throwing in some pepper and a sprinkling of salt, she was happy with her efforts. Grabbing an old wooden tray, she plated the food up.

When she reached the lounge, Tina was sitting up. Her face was drawn and white. Mel was not sure what to do, but after placing the food on the table, she knelt beside her friend.

Hardly audibly, Mel mouthed the word, "Sorry."

Tina faced her and burst into tears, and they hugged each other. Tina looked Mel in the face and half-smiled.

"That was me that was a cow," Tina said. Mrs Wilbraham looked on and smiled.

"Right, the tables are turned now, lady," said Mrs Wilbraham eyeing the food.

"I couldn't...."

"Mel has spent an age cooking for you, so I demand that you eat."

Tina meekly did as she was told. The food was bland, and she only managed a couple of spoonfuls, but it gave her strength. It somehow warmed her from inside.

"Better than mashed potatoes and tuna," joked Tina.

"And salad cream," they chorused and weakly laughed.

Mel did not realise how hungry she was. Her father had taught her how to spiral the spaghetti around her fork, like Italians, but she merely sliced it with a knife and piled it into her mouth. The red sauce splashed onto her clothes, and again, she did not care. Mrs Wilbraham picked at her food but managed some of it and uncharacteristically turned on the television. They had never seen her do that and had forgotten that she had a set. They watched The Professionals and argued about who they both fancied. Mrs Wilbraham said it was *'utter tosh'*, but the girls knew she secretly enjoyed it.

The rest of the night, they merely sat and watched whatever was on and by two o'clock, Mel had fallen asleep. Mrs Wilbraham was drinking wine in a chair, half dozing, and Tina was staring out into the night.

"What time is it?"

"'Bout two-thirty."

Comfortable, snug, and warm, Mrs Wilbraham was happy for them both to stay. She asked Mel to fetch some blankets and told her she could sleep on the chaise lounge.

"Careful as it's an antique."

It was then that they heard the sirens.

CHAPTER 24

Maureen heard the letterbox clatter. She instantly thought of Alan. Despite his venomous attack on her, she held out some hope that he had had a change of heart. There was a crumpled piece of paper on the mat and she tentatively picked it up. The paper unfolded, revealing a picture of a young girl. Underneath the photograph was the word 'missing' with Pauline's telephone number scrawled across the bottom. Maureen was stung by the realisation that the girl they had seen fighting that day was Pauline's niece.

"Oh my God." She steadied herself against the door. How long had she been hauled up in bed waiting for Alan? All that time, this young girl had been missing. She looked about fourteen. "Jesus Christ."

Maureen stood very still, unsure what to do. Pauline must know. She would go there straight away, and she had to ring Alan. She took a deep breath. Chances were, he would have already told the police everything that he knew. It would all be ok, please God.

She slipped on her sandals, and almost running, she made her way to Pauline's house. Knocking earnestly on the door, she waited. Often Pauline would be in the garden, so she walked around the side.

"Paul? Clive?" Her voice sounded strange to her own ear.

She went into the shed and looked through the back door, but no one was home. She wondered what to do. Should she go to the police now? Every minute could be vital. Alan would know what to do, so she rushed home and frantically dialled his number.

The young girl who answered the phone was surprisingly officious.

"What was the nature of the call? Was he expecting her call?" Then a very curt, "Hold."

Linda returned to the call. "I'm afraid Mr Lucas is on official council duty and is unavailable."

"Listen, madam," Maureen could feel her voice rising, "this is very important...." But Linda had already hung up.

Maureen knew she had been fobbed off and felt a surge of anger. She was not sure it was directed at Alan or his little jumped-up, slip-of-a-girl. Pauline's niece was in danger, and if he would not take her call, then he would have to see her. She grabbed some money from the sideboard and rushed down to the bus stop. Buses were infrequent to town, only four times a day, but if she hurried, she could get the 1.30 pm.

***

Alan sat back in his chair, feeling irritated and slightly concerned. That woman was becoming a liability, and he would have to do something.

"Linda, can you come in? I need you."

"Of course." She guessed it was about the woman on the phone. While keen to appear professional, she was desperate to know what the commotion had been about.

"I need you to fast track a council eviction. That woman has taken umbrage with my decision to rehouse people who are in homes that are too big for their needs. Her mother is no longer with her, and there are needy families we need to house now."

Linda smiled. "Of course."

"The sooner we make this happen, the sooner she will leave me alone. I don't need the distraction."

Linda looked sympathetic and shot him an understanding smile. "Honest, hard-working taxpayers deserve better."

"Couldn't agree more."

***

Maureen's bus pulled into the garage, where she got off. The purpose-built council offices were virtually next door to the bus depot. Serving the whole district, they were laid out over several floors and were surrounded by endless rows of cars. The sheer size of the building made her feel uneasy. She took a deep breath and raced up the steps. Until now, she had planned just to see Alan. She had given very little thought to what she was going to say. To her relief, the receptionist was much friendlier than the ghastly secretary she had spoken to earlier, and she helpfully pointed her toward the lifts.

On the fourth floor, Maureen looked up and down the corridor. She saw Alan leaning over a desk laughing with a young blonde girl, and she guessed this was the woman she had spoken to. For a moment, she lost her nerve but seeing him so carefree infuriated her. The decision of what to do was taken away from her as Alan spied her and came rushing out.

"What the...."

"Alan, we need to talk...."

"I've said everything I need to say." He forcibly grabbed her arm and pulled her towards the lift.

"Alan, those girls we saw, one of them is missing. We need to tell the police. It's important."

Pushing her into the lift, he scrambled at the controls to shut the door. "Come on!"

When the door cranked shut, he turned his full fury onto Maureen. Grabbing her by the neck, he pushed her against the wall. Her head slammed painfully against the metal wall. She felt unable to breathe.

"Keep your mouth shut."

"But...."

"Shut!" He reinforced his command by tightening his grip and knocking her head again. Terrified, she tried to nod. "You want to keep staying in your house, you will keep it to yourself. Do you understand?" Again, she tried to answer, but all that came out was a guttural noise. "Yes, is the word you're looking for."

The lift came to a standstill on the ground floor, and Maureen rushed out into the lobby. She did not look back but heard Alan's familiar smooth patter. He smiled at the people entering the lift.

"What floor? Should walk, really." He patted his stomach and they all laughed.

An empty can of Coca-Cola rolled backwards and forwards underneath her seat as Maureen stared out the window at the flat landscape. The bus stopped under the railway bridge. The height was only just high enough for the bus. The driver had to approach it correctly to make sure he was right in the middle. Over the years, several had come 'a cropper'. As children, they had fought to sit on the top deck, and all screamed when they went under the bridge. Even as an adult, she still felt the same rush as the bus edged through the Victorian archway. This time, she felt nothing but a terrible numbness. The journey was a good half an hour and there was not another soul on the top deck.

The bus passed a field where the farmers were

harvesting. The dust of the corn filled the air and irritated the back of her throat. She was thirsty, and she coughed so hard she heaved. The sensation pulled at her stomach muscles. A large, red Massey Ferguson was cutting the corn into a tight square. The terrified animals that had not escaped would be forced into the enclosed space and trapped, then be picked off by the men with guns.

"Shooting fish in a barrel," she muttered to herself.

She could not see the men with guns until they cleared the hedge, but she knew they were there. The animals would have no chance. It was so unfair, and there was no sport in that. She felt surprisingly angry.

She was still feeling angry when she got off the bus. Lost in thought, a beep alerted her to someone waving. It was Pauline. She was in her Morris Minor and pulling into her drive. Maureen rushed past her bungalow and caught Pauline as she was getting out of the car.

Pauline looked up for a moment and hardly recognised her old friend. Her face was white and puffy, her hair wild, and her clothes looked like she had slept in them. This was so unlike Maureen. It was more than that; there was darkness in her eyes. Maureen leaned over and held her hand.

"Paul... I din't know."

Pauline looked confused. "Know what?"

"'Bout your niece."

Clive opened the door and they trudged into the lounge. He was also visibly shocked at Maureen's appearance.

"Oh, Paul...."

Pauline sat her down and commanded Clive to fetch her some water and a packet of crisps.

"Salt and vinegar in the cupboard, top right...you need the salt."

Pauline was grateful that Alice was still in bed as she had no idea what Maureen was about to say who began to sob hysterically.

"I'm so sorry." She told them the whole story of how she was with Alan in the cornfield and how they had witnessed two girls taking the car. "I din't know it was your niece."

Clive pulled a face when he told her that she had had to walk three miles and report it missing in the next village.

"I hint been out of bed. I din't see no posters." Pauline put her arm around her friend and hugged her. "If you'd known, you could have searched for the car. You might have found her...oh, Paul."

Clive, who had kept very quiet, piped up. His voice was strong and full of emotion.

"Alan Lucas, he knew. He didn't tell anyone in case they discovered his grubby little affair."

"Clive!" shouted Pauline.

"Sorry, Maureen."

"He told me he was leaving his wife, that she didn't love him, what a fool. I went to see him. He said if I tell, he'll make me move out of my council house and move me miles from here."

"He can't...."

"Says I don't need no two bed. He hurt my neck." She pulled down her top, revealing a livid red mark on her neck. Pauline and Clive look horrified.

"That bastard." Pauline grabbed Maureen's hand. "I know you've had a terrible time. But do you think you can come to the police station with me?"

Maureen nodded. "Yes. Of course." She was still sobbing, but she felt better for telling.

Pauline looked at her friend, who was brushing crisp crumbs off her lap. Vulnerable, especially after her mother had just died, Alan had taken advantage of her.

"Do you think you can come now?" she asked gently.

"Yes, Paul. Need to."

Clive grabbed the car keys.

CHAPTER 25

Bounding up the steps to his office Alan retied the causal sweater across his shoulders. His trousers were light brown and brand new, and he knew he looked good. Casually he plonked a box of Black Magic chocolates on Linda's desk.

"For all your excellent work, as usual."

Best to keep in with the secretaries. He had, in reality, chosen Linda because she was young and had nice breasts. Beverley would have been the obvious choice, as she was much more experienced, but he wanted a younger model. He sauntered past Beverley's desk and laughed as he knew she was glaring at him. Infinitely more qualified, but who wanted to work with someone the same age as their mother?

He opened his office door. If everything went to plan, soon he would have a bigger one. He sat down heavily on his leather chair, and leaning back, thought about the month ahead. In a few weeks, he would be Head of the

Council—he was sure of it. He congratulated himself on 'playing a blinder' when Linda poked her head around the door. She had brought in his morning coffee, anticipating his every need.

"Just as you like it."

"No one makes it like you, Linda."

She left the room. Always call them by their names; it was a trick he had learnt in his last job. The in-tray overflowed to his left, but it would have to wait. He pulled the balls on his Newton's cradle. It had been a present from his wife and was strangely hypnotic. The ball bearings clicked back and forth while he thought about the day. The coffee was a bit hot, and he decided his day would start when it cooled.

Raised voices outside made him sit up. Linda was forcibly telling someone to leave.

"Alan…," she corrected herself, "Mr Lucas can't be disturbed." Alan smiled to himself. He might as well get used to dealing with the public now.

"It's ok, Linda. I'll deal with this."

A woman bustled her way into the room. Alan immediately recognised her from the various fetes and bazaars he had been dragged to. She was a local, or 'an arable' as Emma had mockingly referred to anyone with a Suffolk accent. He could see why. Her crimplene skirt clashed with her shirt, and her Scholl sandals were worn and frayed on one side. Emma would never have been seen in public like this. This would not take long and would be fun. Probably some nonsense about a dustbin or an objection to a minor road extension. He went to shake her hand.

"Pamela, isn't it?"

"Pauline, and don't you shake my hand." He was taken aback. "Don't you dare!"

Pauline was surprised that her voice had risen to a shriek. Alan, through the glass panel door, could see Beverley straining her neck to see. She would be enjoying this. He calmly walked over to the door and pulled the blind.

"We need to...." Pauline started.

"Talk." He ended her sentence patronisingly.

Shutting the blind had given him time to catch his breath. He would make short shrift of this ridiculous woman, whatever the problem was.

"No, you need to bluudy listen." Her eyes narrowed. "I got one word for you...Maureen." Alan was knocked off-kilter. That bitch was meant to keep her mouth shut. It was still her word against his. "You are a piece of work, Alan Lucas. Treating her like that."

"There's no proof."

Pauline ignored him, and her voice lowered, calm and controlled.

"Threatening Maureen with losing her house. Abusing your position."

"She doesn't need a two bed...."

"Oh, and a man of your position takes an active interest in all his cases, do you?" Alan kept quiet. He was making it worse. "But worse still, and something I will never forgive you for, you knew about Mel and Tina. You saw them, and you kept quiet." Her hand on his executive toy, while she was speaking, had grabbed the strings, and twisted them into a tangled mess. Alan stood with his mouth open.

"What do you want?" he said simply.

Pauline had not quite finished ranting and her voice raised to almost a scream and then dropped to a threatening whisper.

"You are a...filthy bastard." He winced and knew that the secretaries outside would have heard every word. "There is nothing better I would like to do than tell the whole world what a bastard you are. But there is something I want."

"What?"

"Firstly, you let Maureen be. You don't talk to her. Ever! You stop this council swap today." He nodded. "You step down as council candidate. I don't want you representing me or my home."

"You can't...."

"Oh, I am sure everyone would love to know how you withheld information from the police."

He indicated for her to be quiet. "Ok...ok."

"So, you're not denying it?"

"What about my wife? The children?"

He looked pathetic, and Pauline was aware he was trying to manipulate her. In the drama of the moment, she had forgotten about his family. She did not like Emma, and she had shown herself to be a vindictive and desperate snob. She had all but ousted her from the Women's Institute and taken over the Summer Fete. Pauline took a moment to think.

"I won't tell her. But only because the poor cow is married to you. That's punishment enough."

"What about Maureen?"

"Can't speak for her, can I?" With this half-veiled threat, she took a biscuit from the plate. "But I *will* tell. So do as I say."

With that, Pauline left the office, walking past the secretaries, who both pretended to have their heads in typing. The older one could hardly contain a smirk.

Alan sat down heavily on his chair. He tried to untangle the ball bearings, but his hands were clammy, so he gave up and threw it down. His mind was racing with the threats that Pauline had made. Men were expected to have affairs;

that would be ok. But if it ever came out that he had withheld information from the police…he would have to withdraw his application for the Head of the Council. Pauline looked like a joke, but he did not doubt that she would follow through on her threats. He looked at his lap and saw that he had slightly wet himself.

"Jesus Christ."

***

Emma sat in the lounge. The cleaner had been and everywhere gleamed. Once the children were packed off to school, she had spent ages getting dressed. She had a new pastel top with batwing sleeves and was keen to match it with her trousers. Sitting down on the settee, she looked around the room. Although a new property, she felt it needed work and had been hinting to Alan that it needed an upgrade.

It was her favourite time of the day. Opening a magazine, she leafed through the pages highlighting the latest trends. Her eye was caught by a settee. It was American and had a befitting exotic name, Bruschur Fils Westbury in bouquet glaze chintz. She held up the blue pattern and imagined the lounge with the sofas as a feature. Her daydream was interrupted by the sound of the car pulling into the drive. Alan was in the driver's seat.

He sat there for what seemed an unnaturally long time. She was just about to get up when she heard the key in the lock and his familiar cheerful voice.

"Morning, darling."

"What are you…?

"Oh, had a bit of an accident." He pointed to the stain on his trousers. "Bit of a fight with a bottle of mayonnaise...don't ask."

"The Head of the Council can't be seen walking around with obscene trousers."

"Quite."

He returned from the bedroom with a new pair of slacks. They were her favourite ones and went so well with his pink shirt. He leant over to kiss her.

"Got a bit of a surprise...." She closed her eyes and held out her hand. "No, darling, it's not that type. I've made a decision."

"Yes! To the extension?"

"No," he hesitated, "not standing for Council Leader."

"But Alan, you said it's the natural progression to politics. I've already told a few of my friends it's in the bag…why?" Alan sat down and took her hand. He made sure he looked into her eyes and tried to sound as convincing as he could.

"Emma, I already work all the hours God sends. If I stand, you'll hardly see me. You're the most important thing in my life, darling."

He looked at her and could almost feel her

disappointment. She would need to be worked on. He would take her away for a holiday, a perfect mini-break; she would come around. Before they could talk more, the doorbell rang.

"Who the hell is that?" said Emma.

Alan took a deep breath. He was grateful for the distraction, and it gave him time to think. He heard Pauline's voice at the door. His mouth suddenly became dry, and he again felt the need to urinate. Pauline entered the room, followed by Maureen. He nodded to them both. His heart began to beat fast in his chest, and his hands ran with sweat. Time seemed to slow down as he waited for the inevitable accusations. He braced himself and waited.

Emma was all over them. They had not seen her house before, and she was busy showing them all her alterations and latest fashion applications.

"We were looking for a teardrop light, and, of course, it needs a dimmer. We decided on red and black for the kitchen as it just looks so modern and clean." Pauline and Maureen cooed and made all the right noises, all the time glaring at Alan.

At last, Pauline spoke. "As you know, I have had a few family issues, and we have our hands full. Emma, I wondered if you would like to take over the running of the Women's Institute officially and organise the Harvest Supper?" Emma beamed. "You have such an eye for detail."

"Guilty," she bragged.

"You always know what's going on." She threw a vicious look at Alan and continued. "We normally do a cold meat spread, but I know you have other ideas."

"Well, yes, that would be great."

"Maureen and I will continue the History Society, what with Clive's interest...."

"Oh, yes."

Maureen had so far been silent. She looked straight at Alan and said calmly. "Yes, it's important the village is run by someone trustworthy." Alan winced. "Trust is so important, isn't it, Alan?"

Emma puffed herself up. She was delighted with her new status. It almost made up for Alan not standing for Council Head.

"Tea? I have some Lapsang Souchong."

"Oh, these ladies are probably busy," Alan interjected.

"No, we have time. That would be lovely." Maureen smiled while Emma went off to the kitchen and began to busy herself preparing the tea. She used the best china and chocolate biscuits.

Pauline looked straight at Alan. "You'd better not be standing for Council Head."

He shook his head. "Please don't tell Emma."

"Poor cow, she deserves you." Emma appeared carrying a tray and placed it down in front of them. "Oh, Emma, this tea looks delicious," said Maureen.

"Biscuit?"

"I shouldn't give in to temptation, but sometimes you can't help yourself, can you, Alan?"

Maureen looked at Emma, saddled with such an obnoxious man. Pauline had made her come. She had thought she would be unable to face him, but now she saw him for the weak man he was. She enjoyed watching him squirm, and Emma was equally ridiculous. To think she had once been intimidated by her. She sipped her tea and helped herself to another biscuit.

Finally, they got up to leave. Alan was relieved to see the door shut behind them. He rushed to the bathroom and locked the door. His mind raced with anxiety. Looking in the mirror, he saw that his cheeks were bright red. Splashing his face with water, he took a deep breath and walked out as normally as he could.

***

That night, once back at home, Pauline felt exhausted and went straight to bed. Rolling over, she strained to see the clock. It was 5.30 am, and, unusually, Clive was already up. She quickly wrapped her dressing gown around her and padded down the stairs quietly so as not to wake Alice. She could smell the faint odour of burnt toast. Clive was sitting in his brown pyjamas, surrounded by Ordnance Survey maps. He didn't notice her standing by the door.

"Couldn't sleep?"

Startled, he looked up. Clive seemed distracted. His brow was furrowed in concentration. "Pauline, the police think the girls went to London."

"Yes, they reckon Mel will go where she knows."

"What if?"

"What?"

"What if they didn't go that way at all but went east?"

"Well, there hint much there."

Clive became animated. "Maureen said she put in £5 worth of petrol. If her car does about thirty miles to the gallon, they would only have been able to go so far."

"They could have filled up."

"What with? Mel didn't have any money, and Tina...well, where is she going to find the money?"

Pauline looked deflated. "Maureen said she'd just got paid...left her wages in the car."

Clive grimaced and swore. "They still could have gone east and…."

"The sea would have got in their way."

"Exactly." He slammed the pencil down triumphantly.

"So, they could be anywhere along this coast."

"Where?"

"Most of it is inhabitable, but it has a few towns."

"There's jobs they could have got. It is holiday season."

Pauline looked at her husband. She was not sure she believed his theory but, it could lead them to Mel and, she was willing to consider anything. Mel might know some people in London, but she would hardly be able to hide out at her friends' houses forever.

Clive picked up the flyers and posters they had made. "Let's drive to the coast and hand them out." Pauline grabbed his hand.

"I'll need to wake Alice and let her know. She might want to come. Then I'll get me get me clothes on, and I'll be right there."

CHAPTER 26

Vincent prowled around the kitchen, furiously smoking. His hands needed occupying, and he ripped up a Rizla packet into tiny shreds. He leaned into Eddie's ear.

"That's what I'll do to you if you let me down." He threw the tiny green pieces of card onto the floor.

Eddie said nothing and continued to stare at the sink. His lunch of a fried egg was still congealed on the plate in the sink and momentarily made him feel like he was going to be sick. Time was moving slowly, and they had been ready for hours. Eddie began to roll a spliff, but Vince hurled it away.

"Not tonight."

Everything had to be organised. His father came in and nodded at Vince.

"Going to take them dogs out for a walk." With the

word 'walk', the dogs became very animated and jumped up, barking. "Shut your noise."

Rushing past Eddie, they rubbed against his legs and left their hair. He tried to pick it off, but it added to his nausea. The dogs had never been pets and only reacted to his father. He kept them as guard dogs, but as a child, Eddie had often been frightened of them and he had been nipped on more than one occasion. He was glad when they eventually left, and their racket subsided.

At last, it was 10 pm, and Vince indicated it was time to go. Eddie was relieved to be doing something. The constant waiting was worse.

They crept along the path to the barn. There were car lights in the distance, and Vince told Eddie to jump in the ditch. They crouched down; it was important they weren't seen. Eddie, out of the corner of his eye, could see the rancid corpse of the dog that Vincent had killed. Its jaw was knocked off, and bits of its fur were still intact. The vision repulsed him. Vince laughed and booted it away, detaching its head.

They quietly entered the barn and pulled the tarpaulin off the car—a blue Ford Escort Estate. Vince ordered Eddie to get in. Children's crayons were on the floor, and there were various sweet wrappers.

"Nicked it fifty miles away." Vincent slammed the car into gear. He grinned at Eddie and drove out of the barn.

Eddie took a deep breath. His stomach burnt with acid. Vincent drove slowly as he did not want to attract any attention. The waning moon threw up very little light, and although he knew the roads, in the strange light, they seemed treacherous.

They drove out of the town into the darkness of the heath. Barren as it was, the intermittent trees created strange shadows on the road. The water of the tributaries, normally teeming with birds and fish, was black. They drove in silence.

Eddie's mind raced. He was scared. The strange light of the moon made him feel like this was happening to someone else. It was a strange detachment, for which he was grateful. His palms were running with sweat, and he wiped them on his jeans. Vince looked ahead; his eyes fixed on the road. If he was nervous, there was no outward sign. Slowly they edged near to the seashore. Vince cut the lights and they precariously followed the path until they could go no further. Vince grinned at Eddie. He was enjoying himself. He checked his watch.

"Bit early."

They sat in total silence. Eddie hated the waiting. His hands were clammy, and he could feel the bile rising in his throat. The sea stretched out for miles into the blackness, and the rhythmic crashing of the waves added to his sense of foreboding.

He tried to remember what Vince had been like when they were proper brothers. It felt like a lifetime away. Now he was kept like a trapped animal. Always on the periphery of Vince's plans, he never knew what was happening. As the youngest, he was forced to follow the demands of his brother. Unlike Vince, he had no appetite for thieving or scheming. This, however, was in a totally different league.

Eddie was not even sure what the cargo was. He suspected slabs of marijuana, but it could be worse. There was no point asking. He stared at the floor and resigned himself to the task ahead.

Vince continued to scan the sea and they sat there as time dragged. Eddie thought of Mel. He hated the fact he had ignored her. She had looked so wounded, but he had not dared try and talk to her. Vince had watched his every move and he could not risk any reprisal. He thought of how confused and upset she must be and wished he could be with her. God, how he hated Vince. His mind imagined what he had done to Tina, but it repulsed him too much. Vincent continued to stare ahead, his face set like stone.

"Git out, and don't slam the bluudy door."

Eddie followed him down to the shore. He dropped down onto the damp stones. The sea had deposited a mass of dark, slimy seaweed, and Eddie jumped as he put his hand in it. Although it was not a cold night, Eddie felt a chill in his bones. He wrapped the leather jacket around himself and hugged his knees. Still, they waited.

Eventually, they saw something in the distance and heard the faint noise of an engine. Vince stood up and signalled with his torch. There was a reciprocal flash, and Vince grinned.

"At bluudy last."

The small craft took a while to circumvent the waves. As it got closer, Eddie was surprised by how low down in the water it was—a small fibreglass boat completely non-descript. In his mind, he had been expecting a massive trawler. As if reading his mind, Vince whispered.

"Don't worry. You can get plenty on that."

He waded out into the waves. The person driving the boat also jumped out, and together they guided the craft to the shore. Eddie stood still.

"Git here...help."

Jolted out of his daydream Eddie, too, entered the freezing water and helped heave the boat ashore. He got a better look at the man. He, too, was dressed in black and wore a woollen knitted cap. He was unshaven and merely nodded.

Nobody spoke. Vince and the man jumped into the boat and began unloading. The drugs were on pallets—bricks of it wrapped in black plastic. They formed a chain and unloaded them one by one. Eddie was surprised at how heavy they were, and he piled them up a safe distance from the shore. They worked relentlessly until the boat was empty. Vince and the man pushed the boat back into the waves. Then Vince watched while the other man disappeared into the blackness of the night. They could still hear his motor as they surveyed the pile.

Vince barked at Eddie to help him get them into the car. He did as he was commanded and slowly heaved the parcels one by one to the car. A couple of times, he slipped on the gravel, grazing his shins, but did as he was told. The slight gradient of the beach and the poor visibility hindered them, but Vince did not want to use the light. Eddie painfully slipped and banged his hip, and Vince slapped him around the head.

"For fuck's sake."

Before long, the car boot was stuffed, and several had to be placed under the seats and in the footwell. Vincent went down to the beach to check they had got them all and then started the engine. He was smiling. Eddie tried to block out what they had in the car. His mind raced. What if he got caught? He had a caution for stealing a petrol cap from a lorry, which for some reason he had thought was a good idea, but that was two years ago. This was a whole new league, and it terrified him. He could feel the hard packet under him with his boots, but he dared not look at it.

Vince remained calm. As before, he did not put on the lights and weaved his way back to the road.

Vince smiled and patted the steering wheel. "Crap ole car but done the job."

Eddie could not even look at his brother. He knew he was revelling in what they had just done. He seemed manic. Vince leant over and frantically tried to find a radio station. The sound of Judas Priest 'Breaking the Law' blared out. Turning it up, he stretched over to his brother's ears and joined in with the words. He slapped Eddie behind the head.

They drove on into the darkness. The concentration and self-restraint that Vince had shown on the way there had disappeared. He began to drive faster and sped along the ancient roads. The moon gave out so little light that Eddie was worried they would end up in the ditch.

"Slow down." Vincent scowled at his brother and laughed, pressing the accelerator harder. He changed to a higher gear, and the car screamed. "For Christ's sake!"

Eddie wondered why he was acting like this. They still had the drugs in the car and were far from safety. Vince continued to stare forward, clenching the steering wheel, and singing. He looked like he was possessed.

They saw a faint light behind them, and Vincent checked it in the mirror. It was certainly unexpected, as there was so little traffic on the backroads, especially at this time of night.

"Probably someone just coming home pissed."

Vince, however, slowed down and checked his mirror again. The car seemed to be catching up. Cold sweat poured down Eddie's back. He hardly dared look in the mirror but stole a quick glance. Vince turned the radio off.

"Probably nothing." His voice did not have the self-assurance it had before.

The car behind was gaining on them and must have been driving faster. There was no way to see the driver, just two disembodied lights. Vincent looked at Eddie.

"They could just be catching up...probably nothing." He pushed down on the accelerator and sped down the barren road. The car behind matched them for speed. "Shit."

They continued to speed along the road and sudden bends. Eddie found himself flung against the window. The car made ungodly sounds as Vince changed gears, trying to gain more speed. The car was definitely in pursuit. They hammered past a T-junction, and another car joined the chase. It was evident it was a police car. The noise of the sudden siren made them jump and its piercing sound was deafening in the silence of the night. The blue flashing light looked almost surreal. Vince continued to drive faster and faster. Eddie shouted for him to stop, but there was no getting through to him.

"Fuck ... fuck!"

Vincent fell silent. He looked straight ahead and continued to accelerate. The blue light momentarily lit up the features of his face, contorted with concentration. Eddie clung to his seat. He was glad he had put on his safety belt. Vince had laughed at him and called him a poof, but its restrictive grasp had made him feel less anxious. It was the one bit of control he could have over the evening.

"Christ, slow down."

Vince stared into the distance. He knew the roads well, and there was a sharp corner coming up where he might gain some advantage from the cars behind. He accelerated, his face deathly white. The sirens wailed in his ears.

"Shut up…shut up."

The corner loomed quicker than he had anticipated. He misjudged the angle. Eddie looked at his brother, and they both knew they were going to crash. He saw the lights of Sealtdock; they were nearly home. The car jack-knifed around the bend. Time slowed down, and a sweet wrapper looked like it was floating through the air. Eddie caught a glimpse of his brother's eyes. He was expecting terror, but it was more a look of madness. He was almost laughing. The car swung around with considerable force and Eddie's head lurched violently sidewise before slamming into the seat. The car left the road and rolled over and over. Vince did not have a seat belt on, and Eddie could hear his bones crack as they smashed against the side of the car. When the car came to a standstill, there was a deadly silence.

Covered in blood, Vince looked grotesque. He was breathing in shallow rasps, and he reached for Eddie's collar.

"Package…take to the Ellis boys…it's the debt. Promise?" Eddie tried to speak, but no words came out. "Go...now." He slumped back down.

Eddie could hear men shouting in the distance. He momentarily hesitated and then grabbed the hard plastic package under his seat. He furiously hammered against the door, but it was jammed shut. Hurling himself through the shattered glass of the window, he landed heavily. Without looking back, he ran.

Lungs screaming with pain, Eddie charged across the heath. He threw himself down as he saw searchlights illuminating the ground directly behind him. He was grateful that he knew the terrain well. The numerous attempts to draw the bittern meant he had walked the heath on many occasions. Facedown on the ground, he could feel his heart loudly pounding. The recent storm had drenched the parched land, and he could smell the earthy dirt. Roots and twigs pulled at his clothes and impeded his progress. He still had the heavy brick, it was awkward to hold, and he needed both hands. Forcing himself to get up, he staggered on towards the town. He was vaguely aware of blood trickling down his face and into his eyes. His ribs hurt, and the overwhelming tightness in his chest floored him.

He tried to run, but it was impossible. He had to circumvent the tree roots and uneven ground carefully. While he was grateful it was so dark, the lights of the town were his only guide. He knew the barren landscape was intersected by numerous waterways. He wondered if he fell in, whether he would have the strength to pull himself out. Pushing himself, he continued crouching down every few moments in anticipation that he would be seen. Eventually, he reached the outskirts of the town.

The tarmacked road was much easier to run on, but he knew he might be spotted. Sticking to the shadows, he clutched the heavy brick close to his stomach. He had one thought in his mind. Vaulting over a walled garden, he could hear police sirens and dogs barking. Careful to stay out of the light, he stuck to the side roads. People excited by the noise opened their windows, and he shrank behind bins and cars to avoid their gaze.

Eventually, he reached Mrs Wilbraham's house. Until

now, reaching her had been his plan. Now he was suddenly anxious. What if she was too drunk to hear him? She might not want him to come in. She might send him away.

The police and their dogs were getting closer. He edged under the windows and banged furiously on the wooden door.

"Come on...come on." He had no plan other than to find Mrs Wilbraham. There was no answer. "Please...."

CHAPTER 27

"What the bloody hell is going on out there?" said Mrs Wilbraham.

Mel looked out the window but could see very little. Sirens blared in the distance, and dogs barked. By now, they were all wide awake and eager to find out what the noise was about. Mel strained to see but, despite the odd flashlight, she could see very little.

"Nothing ever happens around here."

Mrs Wilbraham wryly smiled. "It's not a hotbed of crime, but there was a murder here once. Jealous husband bumped off his wife."

"When was that?" asked Mel.

"1973...probably due a good slaying." Mel laughed at the older woman's remark.

They all remained very still, listening for clues, enjoying the drama. The police sirens were getting nearer, and they strained to hear more, when suddenly there was a thunderous banging at the door. All three of them jumped. The two girls looked to Mrs Wilbraham for guidance.

The knocking was incessant, and Mrs Wilbraham grabbed Mel's arm while they stood in front of the wooden door. The letterbox lifted, and she heard the anguished voice of Eddie pleading with her to let him in.

"Open it. Open it!" Mrs Wilbraham commanded.

In Mel's haste, she painfully sliced her hand on the latch as Eddie almost fell into the house. His eyes were wild.

"They're after me!"

His T-shirt and jacket were bedraggled and filthy, and his denim jeans were black with dirt and dust. His face, normally so jovial, was taut with anxiety. The gash on his face dripped blood onto the floor and he struggled to breathe. They could hear the voices of the police now shouting instructions to one another. Eddie looked like he was going to die. The police were knocking on people's doors.

Eddie tried to explain what had happened but only managed a few words.

"Vincent...drugs...crash."

He pushed the black plastic bag at Mrs Wilbraham, and his eyes met hers. She knew what the package contained, and they exchanged desperate glances. She ushered him into the living room. Tina looked at Eddie, visibly shocked at his state.

"Fuck, Eddie."

Mrs Wilbraham swung around and shouted instructions. Mel was told to go and make a pot of tea.

"Quickly, on a tray...don't worry about boiling the kettle. Get the Garibaldis." Mel nodded and rushed off. "Eddie, take all your clothes off. Stand on the blanket. Don't get mud on the carpet…all your clothes." She turned to Tina. "Pull this table forward, arrange the settees around it," she barked. Eddie did as he was told until he was completely naked. The older woman looked at the frightened boy. His thin white body was covered in bruises, and she muttered to herself. "That bastard."

She didn't have time for anger now. Eddie's face was filthy. She looked around and grabbed the old blue and white antique vase. The flowers Mel had placed there were drooping but not quite dead. Dipping a corner of the blanket in the stale vase water, she quickly rubbed his face until it was clean. The ingrained dirt, however, was still visible, so she reached into her art box and smeared green paint across his face.

Mel, by this time, had raced back with the cold tea. Tina was handed the paint and told to smear it over Eddie. She merely stared. Mrs Wilbraham snatched the paintbrush out of her hand and gave it to Mel.

"Artistically."

Eddie stood like a startled rabbit. Mrs Wilbraham arranged his limbs around the table and placed the expensive blue and white vase next to him. "Now stand like that," she said. Eddie did as he was told. He felt numb. Mrs Wilbraham rushed to her neglected art room and rummaged in a box.

"Come on, come on." She frantically hurled old artwork onto the floor, throwing up dust. Scrabbling around the piled canvases, she knocked over paints and brushes. "Where are they?"

It had been ten years since she had packed her pictures away. Eventually, she pulled out some sketches. They were rough pencil sketches she had done at art school. They were of a young man. For a moment, she stared at them, transported back. She ran her finger along the face; it was a youthful Doug. There was no time for sentimentality. She quickly tucked them under her arm and charged back to the lounge.

"Quick, take these." She hurled the pictures at Mel. "Arrange Eddie like this."

Mel glanced at the pictures and understood what she was trying to do. She clasped his arm gently and pulled him into position. His skin was clammy, and he was shivering. Mrs Wilbraham picked up a pencil and hurriedly sketched the blue and white vase. Her fingers, while arthritic, still retained the skill she had honed over so many years and neglected for longer. With a strong hand, she drew over the features of Doug thinning the nose and adding more hair. She worked fast and thrust the resulting sketches at

Mel. She grabbed the pictures and gave one to Tina, but she only looked blankly at her.

"Tina, sit here." Mrs Wilbraham sat on the settee and her eyes fixed on the clothes strewn across the blanket. "Quick! Give all that muddy stuff to me and the boots."

She lifted her dress and stuffed it all underneath her. It was bulky and uncomfortable, but she patted down her dress as best she could to disguise it. Suddenly out of the corner of her eye, she saw the plastic block that had been left on the table in all the commotion.

"Christ, give me that as well." For the first time, Mrs Wilbraham's voice sounded panicked. She quickly regained her composure and directed Mel calmly. "Grab it...plenty of room under here."

Mel dived for it and pushed it under the skirt. Despite their best efforts, the mass of clothes and boots stuck out awkwardly. Mel quickly picked up one of the blankets, folded it neatly and tucked it around the older woman.

Mel looked around the room. She poured out half a cup of tea and took a bite of a biscuit. Her mouth was so dry that she could hardly swallow it, but they needed to be convincing. Choking, she grabbed a mouthful of cold tea and forced the biscuit down. Mrs Wilbraham nodded to her. Eddie looked like he was going to faint. He was shaking and ghostly white. Tina uncharacteristically was silent. Mel was not even sure if she understood what was happening. She tightly clutched the sketch but had not even looked at it. They waited for the inevitable knock on the door.

In a desperate state of anxiety, they jumped at every sound. They could hear muted shouting in the street and then the unmistakable sound of heavy boots walking up the stone path. When the knock came, Mrs Wilbraham flattened down her dress, took a deep breath, and counted deliberately to fifteen.

"Mel, if you could let in our guests."

Eddie looked at Tina with frightened eyes. He was sure she could hear his thunderous heartbeat and he gasped for air. Mel pushed back the lock and let in the two officers directing them to follow her into the lounge.

One was much older than the other and had a slightly rotund face. His cheeks were red from running and sweat peppered his forehead. On entering the room, he found it hard to disguise his surprise.

"Cawd der hell, what's all this then?" He had a broad Suffolk accent.

"Oh, officer, we are conducting an art class."

"Bit late, hin it?"

"It's to do with the light." Mrs Wilbraham spoke as if it was the most natural thing in the world.

The other police officer was slight and sported short, cropped, ginger hair. Mel took an instant dislike to him. His manner was to the point and officious.

"Good evening. I am Sergeant Peters. We have reason to believe a person of interest is in the area."

"How awful. Are we safe?" Mrs Wilbraham looked genuinely alarmed.

Ignoring her question, he asked, "Mind if I look around?" It was more of a demand than a request.

"Oh, officer, we would be most grateful. Perhaps you could look in the kitchen that leads to the back and, oh, check the garden."

Before he left, he suddenly stopped and pointed at droplets of blood on the floor.

"What's that?" he said sharply.

Bright red and slightly congealed, there was no disguising what it was. It was from the gash on Eddie's head that was now thoroughly covered in green paint. There was an unbearable silence as the officer accusingly stared at them.

"More out here." There was a trail of blood patches along the corridor.

Mel piped up. She was surprised at how conversational her voice sounded. "Oh, that must have been me...cut my hand earlier thought I had cleaned it all up."

She pointed to her knuckle, which had been sliced on the door when Eddie had arrived. Mel was surprised at how deep the cut was and had forgotten all about it in the panic. Blood had run down her hand and had dried. The officers examined her hand, noticing a severed piece of skin above the cut flapped across the wound. They looked satisfied.

“Shame about my carpet,” said Mrs Wilbraham.

“Sorry.”

“It is an Axminster. Expensive in its day, a little faded now.”

“My wife mixes salt with water to make a paste. That’ll get it out,” offered the officer. The younger one glared.

“For Christ's sake. Hubbard, stay here. I’ll take a thorough look in the house and garden.” With that, he was gone, and they could hear his urgent footsteps opening and banging doors.

Despite the obvious age difference, Hubbard was clearly Peter’s junior.

As if picking up on their surprise, he said, “Been fast-tracked. He’s a graduate.”

Mrs Wilbraham pulled a face. “Can’t teach experience.”

The older man smiled but did not collude. Mel leant over and offered the man a Garibaldi. He took it gratefully and wolfed it down.

“Here, have another.”

The officer, sensing he was being buttered up, looked suspiciously at Eddie.

"So, you have been here all night." Eddie felt he might lose control of his bowels but managed a grunt. Mrs Wilbraham rushed in.

"Try not to speak...that paint will get in your mouth."

"So, what's with all the green paint?"

"It's art," Mrs Wilbraham replied weakly. He frowned and did not look convinced. Mel launched into an explanation that surprised everyone, including herself.

"Mrs Wilbraham, as you probably know, is a well-known national artist but wanted to do something local. She is exploring the interplay between the land and Suffolk folklore. The green paint symbolises the earth; the figure represents wooden men. They are depicted in churches across East Anglia. Often referred to as wild men, they are predominately depicted as naked."

"I plan to do an exhibition on the theme," Mrs Wilbraham added.

The officer nodded. "So why is he naked?"

"The wooden men of Suffolk are always without clothes. It represents their closeness to nature."

Eddie stood shivering in his blanket. The policeman leant over Tina's drawing. She had not even glanced at it and saw that it was a sketch predominately of a man's genitalia. He winked at Eddie.

"You're a lucky boy."

"Officer, we are the lucky ones. He is an exemplary model."

"Yeah, well, rather you than me."

Eddie managed a thin smile but felt it was more of a grimace. Tina felt unable to contribute and remained mute. Her mouth was dry, and she willed for it to be over. By now, Peters had returned.

"Did you know we were in the presence of a famous artist?"

Ignoring his colleague, he said simply, "All clear...he's probably long gone by now."

"Well, thank you, officers. We will all sleep better in our beds tonight."

His radio crackled, and a voice came over the radio with a possible sighting.

"Got to go...." The older man went to grab another biscuit. "Hubbard, now!"

Mel hurried them to the door. "We'll be sure to contact you if we see or hear anything." She pushed a squashed biscuit into the older man's hand.

"Thank ya."

Closing the heavy wooden door, she leant against it. She felt her legs go, and she stood there for several seconds before she felt able to walk the short distance back to the lounge.

Mrs Wilbraham pulled out one of Eddie's boots from under her skirt.

"Thought they were never going to go." She pulled out the other one. "Lucky they weren't stilettos."

Eddie stood in his blanket. His eyes were red. He was shivering uncontrollably and rocking back and forth. Mrs Wilbraham ordered some hot tea, and Mel rushed to get it for him. The older woman sat him down on the settee and put her hand around his shoulders. She gently brushed the hair out of his eyes and rubbed his back.

"It's ok," she cooed.

Mel came back with the tea and put four sugars into the cup. Eddie sipped it gently. He couldn't speak. Mrs Wilbraham looked at Tina and recognised the same shocked expressions. She had two traumatised children in her house. Mel had been magnificent, but she also looked to her for answers. She was still sitting on the pile of clothes and drugs. She needed time to think.

Eddie's eyes were wide, and he mouthed the words, "Vincent. Think he's dead." They all looked at Eddie. He was crying. "The car...."

"It's ok." Mrs Wilbraham put her arm around him and cuddled him. Mel and Tina looked on, feeling numb and useless.

At last, Eddie stopped crying and just stared at the floor. Tina, who had not said a word the whole time, suddenly spoke.

"We need to clean up that wound."

She went and fetched some hot water and a bowl. With gentle hands, she wiped away the green from around his eyes. The cut was sore, and Eddie winced. The paint was mixed with blood and looked like a shade of clay in the water. At last, Tina was satisfied and put on some antiseptic. Eddie winced again. The rhythmic wiping of the wound seemed to help Tina. She had felt so helpless and useless, but this gave her a feeling of control.

Mrs Wilbraham looked at the three urchins in her lounge. It seemed so surreal. Her mind was racing, and the responsibility she felt for them momentarily overwhelmed her. She looked at the bottle of brandy but decided she needed a clear head, she needed time, and everything would look better in the morning.

"Right, Eddie, you sleep here. Tina, you have the chaise lounge and Mel, take the cushions off this chair and just make a bed on the floor."

"I'll put a sheet on the settee to try and stop some of that paint," said Mel.

"Good idea. Tomorrow is a time for plans and talking."

They all nodded. "I'll take these." She picked up the clothes and boots and held them close to her chest. "They will be coming to bed with me in case we have any more visitors." They all looked at her, terrified. "It's a precaution. You can all say I went to bed, and you decided to stay. What with a dangerous criminal on the loose…ah Eddie?"

But he did not answer.

CHAPTER 28

Mrs Wilbraham stayed awake most of the night thinking. Eddie must be kept out of this, whatever this dreadful mess was. She was sure he would have been forced into it by his ghastly brother or that father of his. Whatever had happened, she knew it was terrible. Eddie's eyes, so normally full of light, were black. She had seen it before when his mother had died. He was only young and had hugged her as if his life depended on it. She had never forgotten the look on his face. That terrified boy was back.

She looked at his filthy, torn clothes. There was blood on the T-shirt, and his boots were caked in mud. They would have to be disposed of quickly. She turned over suddenly, feeling her arthritic hip and looked at the parcel of what she presumed was drugs. In all the drama, she had almost forgotten about it. Why had Eddie not just ditched it? He clearly was incriminating himself by carrying it. She resolved to ask him the next day.

Dragging herself up to the bathroom, she could not

help but peek into the lounge. The three youngsters were all quiet, but she doubted if any of them were asleep. Her suspicions were confirmed when Mel stirred and got up.

"Whisper. I don't want Eddie disturbed."

"What are we going to do?"

She again felt the weight of expectation but knew she must keep calm.

"First priority, get rid of the clothes and boots."

"How?"

"There is an old well in my garden in the Victorian greenhouse. It's all but fallen down. Bit of a job, but someone could throw them down it."

"Then put everything back like it's never been touched." Mel was a smart girl, and Mrs Wilbraham assumed that this duty would have to be done by her. "Going to need...."

"Yes, he can't walk around naked."

"Clothes at the caravan."

"Will they fit?"

"I'll find something."

"Go...." Mel nodded and hastily left the house.

By the clock tower, it was nearly six. The streets were deserted, and Mel made her way to the caravan park. The chaos and noise of the night before was replaced by silence. She strained in the distance to see if she could see anything. The coastal road, normally so busy with holidaymakers, was deserted. The sea had encroached right up to the wall adding to her feeling of claustrophobia.

Stealthily walking between the caravans, she scanned the site for washing. A man's pair of Levi's hung limply on a makeshift washing line. They were a little big for Eddie and slightly damp but would have to do. She quickly whipped them down and ran as fast as she could back to the caravan.

Once inside, she allowed herself to breathe. Tina's tidy room was surprisingly cosy. It was the first time she had been in there properly and found the heavy metal T-shirts with relative ease. Choosing the largest one she could, she saw that it had a smirking devil on the front with the words Iron Maiden. She grabbed a towel and rolled the jeans and T-shirt in it. Racing back to the cottage, she stole a pair of worn flip-flops.

Nearing the house, Sealtdock was beginning to come to life. A few people were leaving their homes for work. Their voices carried in the air, and she strained to hear.

"Terrible business."

"Out on the heath."

"Road's closed."

"Did he die?"

"Looks that way."

Mel's stomach ached. She was hot from running, but the words caused a cold sweat to suddenly descend on her. Her armpits were soaking and uncomfortable. *Don't think about it. Don't think about it.* Despite repeating her mantra, she knew that something horrendous had happened. It was no great surprise, given the state Eddie had been in. She tried to focus on the task ahead. She just needed to get back to Mrs Wilbraham and give Eddie the bundle. Disposing of his clothes would be the next useful task she could do.

Back at the house, Mrs Wilbraham had taken control. Tina had run a bath and Eddie was instructed to wash off the paint of yesterday. He lay in the water, unable to move. Mrs Wilbraham stood outside the door. She could not hear the splashing of water so bellowed through the door.

"Eddie, you must wash it all off. There is a bar of Lifebuoy on the side."

He felt numb and, unable to think, limply washed his body. The dirt from the heath mixed with the paint had turned the water a turgid grey. It repulsed him, and for a second, he saw the grotesque broken body of his brother. He tried to shake the memory from his mind by plunging his head under the water. He had not closed his nose and the filthy water went into his throat, momentarily choking him. He had to get out of the water and began to manically scrub his skin until there was no trace of the mud left. When he got out, the scum stuck to his body. In desperation, he grabbed the plastic shower attachment.

One end was perished with age and fell off the tap, dousing him in freezing water.

He grabbed a towel and tightly wrapped it around him. Mel threw a pile of clothes at him through the crack in the door. He slowly got dressed and tried to think about what he would say to Mrs Wilbraham.

When Mel got back from the garden, Tina was making tea and toast. Eddie appeared, his hair still soaking, drenching the back of his T-shirt. He was shivering and Mrs Wilbraham was unsure if this was just because he was cold. He looked like a little boy. The jeans were too big, and he constantly pulled them up.

"Come here." Mel grabbed the waist and rolled them over several times at the top. She stood back to admire her work. "Passable."

Mrs Wilbraham instructed them to eat. The toast, now cold, proved difficult to swallow.

"Soak it in tea, but you must eat."

Eddie did as he was told but choked. Mel passed him some tea and he forced down the lump stuck in his throat. When Mrs Wilbraham was satisfied everyone had eaten something, she told Tina and Mel to leave the room.

Eddie looked at the older woman and burst into tears. Holding his hand, she waited until he was able to talk. Slowly he poured out the details of what he had done with Vincent.

"I never wanted...."

"I know you're a good boy."

Eddie told her about the drugs being loaded on the beach and how Vincent had sped away like he was possessed. He relived the crash, sat back and looked at her, his eyes bright red.

"Vince…I think...."

He couldn't say the word, and Mel had already told him of the conversations she had overheard on the street. She hugged him as he shook with crying. After he had stopped, she asked simply about the packet of drugs.

"He gave me instructions...I wasn't thinking...should have."

"What did he tell you to do?"

"Give it to the Ellis boys…we owe them money."

Even Mrs Wilbraham had heard about the notorious Ellis family. They had intrigued her, but she also knew they could be vicious. There was a story of an arson attack, where people had died, and rumours of violence over the years.

"I need to give it to them, or they will hurt me and my dad."

"Then that is what you must do...."

"But...."

"I'll keep it here. You need to go on as if nothing has happened."

"I can't."

"Must...this isn't over yet." Eddie looked at the older woman. She was speaking the truth, and painful as it was, he knew he would have to face his father. He had no idea if he would know about Vincent. "Go out and sell ice cream. Mel can come with you."

Once they had left the house, she took the packet of drugs and walked to the art room. She wrapped it in plastic and placed it in an empty paint pot. She then placed that in another pot of green emulsion. Doug had bought it years ago when they were going to refurbish. It had been a bold choice and they had laughed how it would outrage the neighbours. It had lain there for ten years and was rusted around the lid. She struggled with the top, but eventually, it prised off. It just fitted inside and would mask any smell if the police came back.

She walked past the bathroom. Tina was on her knees scrubbing the bath. There was a heavy tide mark not helped by the resistance of the paint.

"Be ok, won't it?" She looked at Mrs Wilbraham with wide eyes.

"We'll get there."

"Vincent?"

The word hung in the air and Mrs Wilbraham was unsure how to answer. She knew he had wounded Tina but telling her that she thought he was dead might frighten her more. Fragile as she was, she would eventually hear the rumours. No, it was best if it came from her.

"Tina, I could do with a cup of tea. Let's have a chat."

CHAPTER 29

Eddie's father stood awkwardly against the crematorium wall. He wore a dated blue suit from his younger days and puffed relentlessly on a cigarette. It was hot, and he was uncomfortable. The jacket swamped him, accentuating his bony frame.

Eddie stood an awkward distance away, clutching Mel's hand. He just wanted this day to be over. He had hardly spoken to his father since that night. He knew his father blamed him for Vince's death. He had camped out at Mrs Wilbraham's and had let her help him arrange the funeral. His father had been incapable, but the funeral home had been fantastic. He looked at his dad, his throat felt tight, and he wanted to run.

A group of Vince's friends sat on their bikes at a distance, waiting to be let in. He recognised a few of them. They all wore black bandanas as a mark of respect. At last, the people in the previous service began to file out. It was their turn. Mel squeezed his hand.

"All be over soon."

There had been no money for a service, but the Amhurst's Funeral Parlour had arranged it as a favour. It was very basic, as no one had volunteered to speak, but at least it was something. Eddie remembered his mother's cremation and how he had cried for days. Not once had his father put his arm around him, and his brother had just stared straight ahead. He missed her so badly.

Caroline Amhurst had gone to school with Eddie's mother, and her son Tommy sometimes rode out with Vince. He was a bit younger than Vincent and looked up to him. He was, however, very much on the periphery of the group. Out of all the bikers, he was the only one that made the effort to speak to Eddie.

"How you holding up?"

"Yeah, all right."

Eddie went over to thank Tommy's mother, and she patted his arm and asked what they planned to do with the ashes.

"Hint given it much thought."

"Well, you come and pick them up when you are ready. You know where we are."

He thanked her again and looked around for Mel. Normal families would have a wake of some sort, but everyone just filtered away. It had been like a dream. A few of the bikers had nodded, but no one had stopped to chat.

Eddie was desperate for it to end. He looked around for his father, but he was already picking his way through the grounds of the crematorium. They watched as he pulled a flask out of his pocket and took a long swig from it. Mel could not think of anything to say. She had never been to a cremation or funeral but was acutely aware that this was far from normal.

"Come on, let's get some chips."

Eddie watched his father disappear. "Yeah...let's."

Out of the corner of his eye, he saw one of the Ellis twins. Although standing a long distance away, Eddie was sure he recognised him. Acid flooded his stomach, and for a moment, he thought he might faint.

"You ok?"

"Yeah, just need to go." Eddie sat in the van and started the engine. Their presence at his brother's funeral was no coincidence. They wanted what had been promised. "Mel, do you mind if we just go back? I need a lie-down."

The next day Eddie pulled up outside his father's house. He needed to get his stuff. Mrs Wilbraham had insisted on coming with him. He had told her he could do it on his own, but he was grateful for the moral support.

"It's ok. You don't need to come."

Mrs Wilbraham looked at the boy in front of her. He had been through enough. This time she would come with him. God only knew the violence he had suffered at the hand of that dreadful man. She always suspected he had hit Eddie's mum, but she never realised what a beast he was.

"I warn you. It's a mess."

Mrs Wilbraham picked her way through the rubbish in the front yard and recoiled at the endless dog mess. Eddie's dad let the animals roam and do as they wished. Judging by the rancid dog faeces, flecked with a stale white powder and flies, he left disposing of the filth to nature. The backdoor had a large crack in the glass, and ancient white paint flaked into the air. She pushed it and two snarling dogs jumped up at the glass. Shocked, she almost fell. An aggressive male voice shouted.

"Whoever you are...fuck off!"

Eddie caught her arm. "It's ok. I'll do it."

While he had years of managing the dogs, he still found them unpredictable. He tried to pat one on the head. "All right, girl." One jumped up at him. He could smell its rancid breath, and its slobber turned his stomach. "Get down," he commanded. Relieved, the dog did as it was told.

Eddie's dad was slumped in his chair, clutching an empty bottle of cider. When Eddie tried to walk past him, he painfully clasped his arm. The old man, despite his size, was still strong. Eddie had to peel back every finger to release the grip. Between each finger, there was a green-yellow fungus that he had not noticed before. He stared at his hand, fascinated. At last, he was free and pushed his father away.

"Boy," he gesticulated to the fridge, "get me a can." Eddie ignored him. Walking up to his bedroom, he could hear the old man shouting and clattering around. "A can!"

He grabbed his old army bag that he used for school. It still had childish writing on it of bands he used to follow and a 'save the whale' badge. His mum had bought it for him. He remembered being slightly disappointed she had not chosen AC/DC. He rubbed it affectionally, trying to remember her face. He took a last look at the crumbling dinosaur wallpaper and his battered bed. The carpet was filthy and so worn that the boards were nearly coming through. Grabbing a couple of T-shirts and a pair of jeans, he stuffed them in his bag. He then carefully placed on the top the crumpled picture of Mel.

He made his way back to the kitchen, where his father was still ranting and stood aggressively in his way. Eddie shoved him away and shouted in his face.

"Going! Hint coming back!"

He doubted if his father had even registered what he said. He merely sat down and patted his dog, glaring at his son. Eddie picked his way through the beer cans and dog food tins littering the floor. He thought about slamming the door, but what would be the point?

When he got back in the van, Mrs Wilbraham rubbed his knee. "All done?"

Glancing at his paltry belongings, she felt suddenly appalled at herself. She had no idea he was living in such squalor. If the outside of the house was anything to go by, the inside must be equally atrocious. She patted his knee again.

"You ok?"

He had expected a confrontation, but his father did not care. There was no relationship to save, and that hurt more.

"I didn't tell him we are going to pay off the Ellises. Too drunk."

"Let the bastard sweat."

They drove in silence past the barn, where Vince had kicked the dog to death, and they had stored the car before that fateful night. It looked as if it might fall down at any second. He took one last look at the house and vowed he would never set foot in this road again.

***

The next day, Eddie drove past the Amhurst Funeral Services building. It had flowers outside and a tasteful cross above the door. He had never really looked at it in detail before. For years he had avoided it as it reminded him of his mother. It felt wrong that Vince was still in there—he just needed it over. His father would not pick the ashes up and they could not stay there forever.

Opening the door, he walked in. Tommy was sitting at the desk, smartly dressed in a suit, and he almost did not recognise him. He greeted Eddie warmly.

"Come for Vince?" Eddie nodded. "What you going to do?"

"Don't know...might scatter them."

Tommy held his arm. "Might be good down the old sea road."

"Reckon?"

"He'd drive down there like a bat out of hell." It was true. It was one of the few places in Sealtdock that was a long uninterrupted road. "Hint really seen him the last couple of years. Been working for my dad. Had to get my hair cut and everything. To be honest, he didn't really like me being a biker." Eddie stared vacantly at the smiling boy. He wondered what his life would have been like with a father like Tommy's. "But I still got the bike. I go out still but got to work. That'll be worst in the winter. It's our busiest time."

Eddie felt unable to speak. He was aware Tommy's inane chatter was him overcompensating for the silence. Tommy told Eddie to take a seat and returned with an urn holding Vincent's remains.

"Here you go."

"Thanks." Eddie walked away carrying the urn. It was surprisingly heavy. But then he reasoned that Vince was a big bloke. The thought of it made him feel strange.

It did not feel right to keep it in the van, but he did not want it in Mrs Wilbraham's house. He placed it underneath the ice cream counter. It seemed like a ridiculous place to keep it, but he did not want it in the front with him. He wondered how many hygiene regulations he was breaking.

***

Eddie stood looking out to sea, Vincent's ashes between his feet. He had told his father what he wanted to do but doubted he would come. There was a breeze, and the sea was choppy. He noticed the salt in the air.

Straining his neck, he looked at the town clock just visible from where he was standing. It was nearly six, but he still did not show. Anger swelled in his chest, and he was surprised. He had not expected his dad to make the effort even if Vincent was his favourite son. He had been in two minds about whether to scatter the ashes. Part of him was relieved he no longer had to keep them. He was furious with Vincent for what he had done to Tina. Bullied by him for as long as he could remember, he was not sure how he should feel. No, it would be good, he told himself. Mrs Wilbraham and Mel had both offered to come with him. He had looked at their concerned faces, but he had wanted to do it alone.

Out of nowhere, he heard the unmistakable sound of motorbikes revving. Turning around, Tommy and a group of riders were heading towards him. They pulled alongside.

"Tell us to fuck off, but I wondered if you wanted to take the last ride with him."

Tommy gestured for Eddie to get on the back of the bike. Like Vincent's, it was a black Norton. Eddie, clutching the urn, clambered on, and they sped off. The bikers followed behind. They screamed along the long coastal road, and several times, he felt he might lose the urn or fall off. He felt the wind rushing against his face. The urn danced in his arm, and he desperately clung on. At last, they came to a standstill, and a relieved Eddie got off. He went to lift the lid, and Tommy held his arm.

"Do you think Vince would prefer it…if we were riding? Fast?" The other bikers nodded their approval. "Like shit off a shovel."

Eddie smiled. "Not quite sure how we would manage that…I only just held on."

"Got some duct tape. We could stick it to the back."

"That hold?"

"That's strong old stuff."

Eddie stood, still amused at the banality of the best way to scatter Vince's ashes while riding.

"We'd ride behind," said one of the bikers.

"Not if you don't want that in your face." Tommy pointed at the urn. "No disrespect, Eddie."

"Look, I'll just hold it and hang onto Tommy with one hand. If I think I might fall, I'll have to drop it."

The other bikers went on ahead at a slow speed and Eddie clambered back on. He gently prised the lid up.

"Ready?"

The bike roared down the road and Eddie watched as the ashes flowed in a stream behind them. Tommy revved the engine and went faster. The ashes rose like a cloud of starlings swirling in a mass like a dark mist. Back and forward, they swayed, almost forming a shape before changing direction and rising into the sky. The ashes hung in the air, circled around again and then were gone.

Tommy stopped and shouted over his shoulder. "Cawd der hell. Vince would have liked that."

"Reckon he did."

The other bikers gathered around.

"Going to the Bull."

"Gonna give him a good send-off."

Eddie declined their offer and a lift. He watched as they drove away, and he slowly started to walk back to Mrs Wilbraham's house. It had been a good day. Despite his fury with Vince, he had needed a send-off, and Tommy had helped enormously.

He climbed down to the beach, where the tide was beginning to go out. Although the sand was wet, he sat down. Rolling a cigarette, he noticed patches of grey ash on his jacket. It shocked him how vehemently it horrified him. Parts of Vince were all over him. He stood up, trying desperately to flick the dust away. The jacket was old, and where the leather was worn, the ash had got into the gaps.

Violently shaking it, he was not convinced it had all gone.

"Get off…Off!"

He frantically shook it and then walked down to the crashing waves and hurled the jacket into the sea. It bobbed in the water and kept coming back. The sleeve rose and fell in the swell. Eddie, transfixed by the jacket, found himself waving. He checked himself and looked around to make sure no one had seen him. Eventually, it was claimed by the sea, and he just saw the cuff before it disappeared forever.

Eddie suddenly felt very tired. The seafront was deserted, and he began the long walk back to Mrs Wilbraham's house.

CHAPTER 30

They drove to the north beach. It was the posher part of town favoured by families. A large sign welcomed people and boasted a free car park and toilets. Despite it being nearly six o'clock, it was still warm, and children were running on the sand dunes in their swimsuits. Eddie pulled in and looked at Mrs Wilbraham. She seemed uncharacteristically quiet, but she grabbed his knee.

"Last hurdle."

Eddie got out, clutching the string shopping bag. He made his way over to the Victorian toilets. They had once been a salt-house bath and had been converted by the local council. He pushed open the white-painted door and stepped inside. Despite the hot day, the toilets were cold, and water dripped on the floor from lurid green corroded pipes. It seemed dark after the bright sunshine. The acrid stench of ammonia was overwhelming.

Eddie realised he was not alone. Out of the stall came

the shiny, bald head of one of the Ellis boys. Up close, Eddie could see he was pure muscle. He reminded him of a butcher's dog. His brother had watched Eddie come in and stood by the door. He placed his boot across the threshold to prevent any interruptions. Up close, Eddie could see he was quite slight. His face was long with tuffs of gingery stubble, and his Adam's apple protruded unnaturally. It struck Eddie how different they were.

The taller one moved a pile of sand with his foot.

"Don't know why they don't piss in the sea." His voice was much deeper than his thin frame suggested. He had a strong accent, and he looked at Eddie.

"Hey, you got it?" Eddie nodded and pulled out the packet.

Flecks of green paint stuck to the plastic covering. The smaller one reached in his pocket and pulled out a red Swiss army knife. He cut the corner and scooped out the resin inside, and the brothers smelt it. Eddie stood completely still. He noticed a cigarette butt in the urinal and concentrated on it. Finally, the taller one spoke.

"Ok."

He flicked his head to indicate he could leave. Eddie physically felt his shoulders relax, and he turned to walk out when a powerful hand suddenly grasped his arm. He slowly turned, expecting to be hit with a fist, but instead, the taller one spoke.

"Sorry for your loss, bah. Debt paid in full."

Eddie stood there, unable to move. It took a second to fully grasp the words. He caught a look at himself in the filthy, cracked mirror on the wall. His eyes were black, and his skin seemed an unnatural white. He nodded and walked out into the sunshine. Shielding his eyes from the glare, he made his way towards Mrs Wilbraham.

She had been watching from the van, and at last, he had come out, squinting in the bright light. Children with buckets and spades ran around his feet. Eddie climbed into the van.

"It's done," he said simply. He felt drained. A small child banged on the window and made him jump.

"Mister, can I have an ice cream?"

Mrs Wilbraham shooed him away, but Eddie jumped out, smiling.

"What's your name?"

"Peter."

"Well, Peter, as you are my first customer today, you can have whatever you want on the house." The boy looked confused. "For free."

He rolled the word around in his mouth while Eddie piled the ice cream high with every topping and gave it to him.

CHAPTER 31

Rounding the corner past the toilet blocks, they felt slightly nervous. It was the first time they had been back since everything had happened. Out of the corner of her eye, Tina suddenly spotted the police car. Ducking behind the side of the nearest caravan, she hissed to Mel.

"Why did you tell?"

"I never."

"Liar!" Panicking, Tina ran. Mel stood firmly to the spot, not knowing what to do.

***

Pauline had watched the police circling the car. She scanned the park for any clue to her niece's whereabouts. Then she saw her. Mel was just standing staring blankly at her. She found herself running.

"You're skin and bones. Come here." She threw her arms around Mel. "Thank you, God! Thank you." Mel found herself hugging her back, and she realised she was crying.

Clive was suddenly beside them. "Oh, Mel, we've been so worried...."

Mel lifted her head. Tears were in her eyes and obscured her vision. The figure walking towards her was her mother. She was wearing a bright pink top and was smiling. Overwhelmed, she could hardly speak.

"Mum," she blurted out.

"It's me, darling." Her arms were soon around her. She felt warm. She felt solid. Alice gently whispered in her ear. "I'm back."

It took Mel a moment to realise they were not alone. Two police officers were looking at the stolen Mini and taking notes. Pauline rubbed her hands, her face full of concern.

"Don't worry. You're not in trouble." Mel looked up. It was a policewoman, but all she could see was the uniform. "Where's Tina?"

A rough-looking man almost barged the woman aside and shouted at Mel. "You had better bloody tell us."

Pauline waded in. "Hold yew hard! You watch how you talk."

The officer also told the man to wait and continued to try and coax information out of the frightened girl. Mel was aware of the expectant faces around her.

"I don't know."

***

Tina wiped the back of her neck. It was wet and cold. She was not sure where to go. The road to the coast was exposed. Feeling in her pocket, she still had the key to one of the vacant caravans. She ran in-between the occupied caravans avoiding any contact.

"Come on…come on." Trying the lock, she dropped the keys twice and scrambled inside.

The room had not been cleaned yet, and she sank to her hands and knees. Bizarrely, the duvet was in the sitting room. Wrapping it around herself, she lay on the floor. Her mind raced. They had found her, and she would have to go back.

The talking outside carried through the air. She could not quite make out the words. Not daring to breathe, she noticed the door was slightly ajar. Dragging herself along the floor, she stared through the crack. She could see the stripes of the police car. Her mother was leaning against their caravan, dwarfed by Aidy. He was manically walking up and down, shouting. Pauline was arguing with him while her mother passively looked on.

Tina hugged her knees and rocked backwards and forwards. If she tried to leave now, they would see her. She tried to think of a plan. There might be food in the fridge which would keep her going. She could slip out at night. She lay back down and tried not to move, frightened that the very act of drawing breath might alert them to her.

Norman had watched from a distance. He had seen Tina bolt away and was sure she had hidden in one of the caravans still waiting to be cleaned. Walking around the Mini, the police were making calls on their radio. Families were staring out of their caravan windows, and quite a crowd had gathered outside.

Snatching his keys and keen not to catch anyone's eye, he walked toward caravan number eight. Hesitating at the door, he called.

"Tina...that's all right, it's Norm."

Jamming the key into the lock, he realised the door was already open. Slowly pushing it open, he saw Tina hunched in the corner. Black kohl pencil streamed in lines down her face, and she was shaking. He sat on the settee and took a crumbled bourbon out of his top pocket.

"Bin saving this...reckon you need it more than me." Tina looked up. "Not sure what trouble you're in, girl, but ole Norman will stay with ya." She took the biscuit and held it in her fist.

"Thank you," she whispered.

They sat in silence. Norman did not have a plan, but he knew he had to be there. He looked around the room.

"Cawd der hell. They'd left this in a right ole mess."

One of the holidaymakers had seen Tina dash into the caravan. They had been excited by their own importance and had enthusiastically pointed the way. Aidy rushed on ahead. Flinging the door open, he shouted.

"Git your stuff...you're coming home." Tina did not move, and Norman stood in front of her blocking his way. "Get up, gal, now!"

The policewoman intervened. "I think it's better if you wait outside." More forcibly, she added, "It's not a request."

Tina's mother stood beside him and pulled at his sleeve. He shook her arm away and they reluctantly left.

"We're only outside. We hint going nowhere."

Norman looked at Tina. Although an old man, he had been a champion boxer in the army and wanted to hit Aidy.

"It's ok, gal. We'll sort this out."

Tina remained hunched against the side of the caravan, unable to move. He looked at the policewoman who crouched down and gently asked.

"Want to talk?"

Aidy was still ranting outside and trying to see in the window. Norman stood up, drew the curtain, and placed his foot against the door.

"Hint no one coming in here. They'll have to break my bluudy foot."

Mel heard the commotion at the caravan and had seen the couple and the police striding purposefully towards it. She guessed the woman and man were Tina's mum and stepdad.

"Mum. I'm not going anywhere, but I have to check Tina is all right."

Stroking Mel's hair, she said quietly, "Ok."

Alice, still weak from withdrawing from such strong drugs, looked pleadingly at Pauline.

"I'm coming with you, girl." Mel felt better with the older woman by her side.

When they reached the caravan, Tina's mother was sitting on the step and Aidy was prowling in circles. Pauline pushed past him and sat next to Tracey. She was incredibly thin and looked exhausted. Her eyes were hollow, and she looked lost. Taking her hand, she whispered.

"Right old mess, hin it?"

Tracey just managed a nod.

Mel banged on the door. "Tina, it's me...it's me."

The policewoman checked with Tina. Mel was let in by Norman and the door was slammed in Aidy's face. Mel rushed over to Tina and sat beside her.

"My Aunty Pauline's out there, and no one will get past her." And Tina believed it.

***

Mrs Wilbraham had decided to join Eddie on his ice cream rounds that day. He seemed out of sorts and unusually quiet. She had hoped that Eddie would confide in her about what was troubling him. He had been through so much lately, and she was worried there was unfinished business.

As she and Eddie bumped along the coastal road, they saw the police car driving into the caravan park. Eddie looked at Mrs Wilbraham and had the feeling something was wrong. He violently swung the van into the site and followed the bumpy road. They could see the police beside the Mini and a mass of people were gathered around.

By the time they arrived, Tina was being led out, followed by Norman and Mel. Mrs Wilbraham pushed past the holidaymakers who had surrounded the caravan, and she jostled them out of her way.

"Coming through."

Aidy shouted at Tina. "About bluudy time. Get out." He went to pull her sleeve, but Pauline grabbed his arm. He threw her away aggressively. "Get off!" Pauline stood in front of him. They glared at each other.

Mrs Wilbraham, closely followed by Eddie, made a beeline for Tina. She embraced her and put a protective arm around her.

"This child is not going…with that brute. She can stay with me."

"She'll do as she is bluudy well told. That's her mum." Tracey had not made a sound and was still sitting on the steps. She was pulling at the frayed cloth on her jeans.

Spinning around, Mrs Wilbraham charged at him. He was completely taken by surprise by the elderly woman. Ramming the tip of her walking stick into his foot, she twisted it around and pushed it in with all her might. He yelped in pain. Leaning close to his ear, she hissed.

"I know about your filthy little secret." For a moment, he went white, the colour draining from his face. "Want to explain to the police, do you?"

Tina looked terrified. She was still shaking, and snot ran into her mouth. Aidy stared her straight in the face. He flicked his head towards Tina.

"She wouldn't dare."

"No, but I would."

Pauline walked up to the second police officer. "That child is clearly terrified. We need to sort this, but you get him away from the mother. He's a bully...he hint a blood relative. Tracey won't do anything while he's there." The policeman looked at the older woman.

"If we ask him to leave, she'll go with him." He pointed to Tracey. "And we need the mother's permission to sort this out."

"Arrest him or something."

"Can't. He needs to do something."

"Righto." Striding up to Aidy, she pushed her face right into his. "Bully...bastard," she goaded.

Fresh from the humiliation of Mrs Wilbraham, he was holding his foot. Pauline barged him with her hip. While only five feet, she was solid, and he fell to the ground. He quickly recovered and went to slap her. Clive dashed forward. Aidy lowered his arm and screwed up his face.

"I know what you're trying to do...I hint that stupid."

He towered over them triumphantly. Pauline glared back at him but felt deflated. She had never realised things were so bad and could only imagine what brutality Tina had suffered, or worse.

Pauline laid an arm around Tina's convulsing shoulders. "That's all right, girl."

"I can't go back."

"Not sure you can stay here. But we will sort something out."

Mrs Wilbraham leaned forward. "She can stay with me."

Tracey shook her head. When she spoke, her voice was so thick that they had to lean in to hear her. "Aidy will go mad…lose his benefits."

Pauline took her aside, knowing the volume of people was too much for her. She held her bony hand.

"Tina needs to be where she's safe. You do too. Is he knocking you about?"

She did not answer, but Pauline had already seen the marks on her arms. They were more than the bruises of a drunk.

"Don't want no police."

"Oh, Tracey, you can talk to the police. Get him removed." Tracey shook her head. Pauline took her by the shoulders. "If you won't get rid of him, then let your little bird be free." Tracey merely looked down.

Pauline sat with her for a while, quietly talking while the others huddled around Tina. She had stopped shaking and calmed down considerably. The policewoman, keen not to show approval, had been quietly impressed with Pauline. She glanced over to the slightly dumpy woman, grateful she had taken control of the situation. Pauline pulled the social worker aside.

"She can't go back to that house. You saw that man."

"Poor kid," the social worker sighed.

"About bluudy time you lot got involved. That child's been fending for herself since she was a tot. I made phone calls. Nothing ever was done."

"Not the only one who fell through the net." The social worker looked tired.

It was a similar story everywhere. Lack of funding had meant children like Tina, not in immediate danger of harm, were overlooked.

"The family is known to us, but she's not on a care order."

"Well, she bluudy well should be."

The social worker remembered her professional confidentiality. "Shouldn't really be discussing this with you." They glanced over to Tina's mother. "If her mum agrees, she can go and stay with Mrs Wilbraham. I'll have to make an assessment, but we could put her on a section 21." Pauline looked perplexed. "It's not a full care order, and to be honest, she's nearly eighteen." Pauline pulled a face. "It's a broken system. We have to work with families, but those in the care system don't fare any better, believe me."

Pauline looked at Tina. She looked brighter, but still very vulnerable. "Please just do the best you can. That child needs a chance."

The social worker smiled apologetically and made her way over to Tracey. She was standing a few feet away and rubbing her bare arms.

"I hint talking to no bluudy social worker. Get away!"

The social worker stepped back. She had seen this a

thousand times and knew that if she wanted her collaboration, she would have to calm things down.

Tina took a step forward, and Pauline stood by her side.

"Go on," said Pauline, pushing her gently. "Speak to your mum. Tell her what you want."

Tracey looked at her daughter. Her face was a strange grey as her makeup had run down and was rubbed into her skin. Snot ran down her face and she wiped it with her arm.

"Ok," said Tina.

Tracey was aware of the faces watching her. She awkwardly hugged her daughter but did not speak. Reaching into her back pocket, she handed Tina a gift. It was a screwed up five-pound note.

"Aidy gave it to me for fags." Tina looked at the crumpled note. "Take it." Tina did not move. "Got some tobacco...have that too." Tina stood on the spot, and she looked her mum straight in the eye. "I want to stay here." Tracey thrust the tobacco at her again. "Old Holborn... that hint stale."

"Mum?" she looked at her. "Mum, please?"

Her mother followed her with her eyes as she walked away, intently aware that everyone was watching her. She felt wretched and small. Aidy grabbed her arm and smiled. He made a beeline for Pauline, and they circled each other like snarling dogs.

"Keep your snout out."

Clive tried to interject but was shouted down. Pauline pulled him away.

"He hint worth it."

Eddie and Mel sat down on the steps and watched Aidy, his face taut with venom. Suddenly, Tina bolted across the campsite. She fell twice in her haste to leave. Mel and Eddie charged after her, shouting for her to come back. Quite a few people were watching the drama with the police, and Eddie found it hard to circumvent them. Twice he lost sight of Tina, only to see her head bob out from behind a tent.

At last, he made it to the coastal road, convinced he would be able to match her for speed on the tarmac. Horrified, he watched as Tina scrambled into a white waiting van. The thin ginger Ellis twin leered at him from the passenger seat and waved before screeching off along the road. By the time Mel had caught up with Eddie, he was white and could hardly speak.

"Jesus Christ, Mel. They've got Tina."

"But why? I thought they said the debt was paid!"

"They paid me a visit. They said some of the drugs were ruined because of the green paint. I don't think it was, but this is the Ellises we are dealing with. They've said I still owe money. I don't know what I'm going to do, but I've got to get her back. She's not safe with them."

CHAPTER 32

Eddie and Mel watched as the van screeched away.

Pulling at his sleeve, she shouted, "Quick, the police are just there."

Eddie's face darkened. "You can't tell. She got in that van. They didn't force her."

"But we have to find her."

"You don't know about the Ellis family," he almost whispered. "They've killed people. If we involve the police, they'll go after me, your family or…," he looked at Mel, "you."

"I'll be in Trotham."

"Don't matter…they're a massive family. They'll find you." The look in Eddie's eyes convinced her he was not exaggerating.

Pauline had seen them first and realised something was wrong. Mel was white, and between gasping breaths, she simply told her that Tina had run away. Pauline squeezed her hand.

"Hint going nowhere till we find her."

Mel watched as the news of Tina's escape permeated the group. The social worker and police went into a flurry of hushed conversations with lots of pointing and planning. Mel felt numb. Tina's mum just sat on the steps of a nearby caravan like a corpse. Aidy roared at the police and blamed Pauline.

"All that fucking about…should have just let me take her." Slowly the group dissipated. Mel got in the car with her mother, Pauline, and Clive.

"We'll find a guest house. There's got to be loads around here. We'll stay here, Mel, until this mess is sorted, don't you worry." Alice patted her knee, but Mel could only stare out the window. Eddie caught her eye, and they held each other's gaze.

They were soon bumping along the coastal road. The first two guest houses were full, but they soon found one that could accommodate them. Alice and Mel had to share, and the room reminded her of Aunty Pauline's with its oppressive dark furniture and draylon bed covers. She mumbled something about needing a shower.

"Oh yes, darling, I bet you do."

The shower was shared with two other rooms, but it

still felt like a luxury, especially with the frayed blue towels folded on the bed. She stood under the water flow for a long time. She felt the layers of grime and salt lift from her skin. Her mind crowded with fear, and she realised she had been squeezing the soap so hard it had spilt in two and clogged the drain. Soapy water soon collected around her feet and threatened to go over the edge of the tray.

Alice was banging on the door. "You all right, darling?"

Mel shook herself and cleared the drain. Disgusting hair and scum came out in her hand, and she manically scrubbed he fingers until they were raw. Reluctantly she got out and towelled herself dry. She tentatively touched the scabs on her stomach and thigh. Softened by the water, they had virtually healed but were still tender. She pushed at them and winced but enjoyed the sharp pain. Appalled at herself, she quickly dressed. Pauline and Clive were waiting in the corridor. Pauline apologised.

"Should have brought you some of your clothes. But we just dropped everything and came."

She looked at their expectant faces and felt hemmed in. "Just need to see Eddie...we can look for Tina." Alice glanced at Pauline.

"Darling, everyone wants to find her. But if you need to go, I understand." Pauline and Clive exchanged worried looks. "We waited to find you, reckon we can wait a bit longer. Just keep safe."

Running to Mrs Wilbraham's house, she saw Eddie leaving.

"Eddie...Eddie!" He continued to walk purposefully.

"No, Mel, you can't come with me." He saw the look of hurt on her face. "It's too...." He never finished his sentence as she snatched the keys out of his hand.

"Whatever this is, we do it together."

Eddie did not have the energy to argue. A plan had formed in his mind, and it was all he could do to carry it out. He longed for Mel's company, but he couldn't involve her anymore. He lurched for the keys, but she was ahead of him and had already clambered into the van. He pleaded with her again, but she wouldn't budge.

On the drive to the campsite, he told her he planned to steal Vince's bike and give it to the Ellises. He secretly prayed that his father hadn't already sold it, but as he could hardly dress himself, he doubted if he had done anything with it.

They parked at the side of the campsite and walked along the coastal road. Although it was getting dark, Eddie knew the road well and navigated the various bends. Mel gripped his hand, unsettled by the shining black tributaries. Startled birds flew out in front of them, making her jump.

"You go. I'll do this on my own." Mel shook her head.

When they reached the barn, they could smell the decomposing dog. Most of its bones picked white, but pockets of rancid flesh remained. For a moment, Eddie felt he might be sick. It wasn't just the sight, but the memory of Tina recalling the unspeakable cruelty she had witnessed from his brother.

Eddie squatted down against the wall of the barn. "The bike's in that shed. But the key, that's at the house. Vincent used to hang it by the fridge. The only thing he did put away in that kitchen," he added bitterly. "My dad will be drunk and hopefully asleep, but the dogs will be there." Eddie commanded her to stay at the barn.

"No, I'm coming."

"The dogs don't know you. They might be quiet with me, but you're a stranger. Whatever happens, wait here."

Mel knew what he was saying was true. She crouched behind the wooded slats and watched Eddie as he silently shot across the road. She could just make out the top of his head as he faltered at the door, and then he was gone.

Eddie pushed open the door of the kitchen. Almost off its hinges, it opened easily. His father was stretched out in the chair, a bottle of White Lightning clutched between his legs. The dogs were asleep around his feet. Little by little, he edged toward the fridge. In the dark, he couldn't quite make out the key, but he knew where it usually was. His father uttered some nonsense, and the dogs bristled but did not wake up.

At last, he made it to the fridge and realised, in horror, that the key was not there. It was so dark that he ran his hand along the kitchen bench, thinking it may have fallen.

Come on...come on."

His hand felt the unmistakable shape of Vincent's zippo lighter. He lit it, and the smell of petrol reminded him of his brother as he stared at the flame, transfixed. Sweeping the lighter along the side, he searched frantically for the key. At last, he saw it nestled between a can of dog food and an ashtray. He grabbed it a little too quickly and knocked the tin onto the floor. It crashed with a solid thud and rolled towards the sleeping dogs. Without looking, he ran out of the kitchen and slammed the door behind him. By now, the dogs were howling and jumping up against the door. He could hear his father shouting.

"Who's that? I'll get you!"

Eddie could hardly breathe. He dashed across to the garage and hurled open the door. Vincent's bike loomed in front of him. He had forgotten how large and magnificent it was. His hands were shaking so much that he could hardly put in the key. All the time, he could hear his dad shouting and the dogs barking furiously. He kicked the starter pedal, and nothing happened.

"Jesus Christ...please." Again, the engine clattered only to die with each attempt. Suddenly, his father was at the door.

"You leave that, boy."

Eddie tried again, and this time the engine jumped to life. He felt the power of the machine under him. It was all he could do to control it as he sped away. His father grabbed him and knocked him sideways. He just managed to regain his balance and drove up the path. The dogs charged after him, jumping and snarling at his heels. He could hear them panting and could smell their foul breath. Eddie was too quick. Mel watched as he hurtled past her, followed by his shouting father. She couldn't understand what he was saying, but his voice was thick with hatred.

He stood for a good ten minutes staring up the road. For a moment, she thought he had seen her, and she dared not move. At last, he went back to the house. One of the dogs made a beeline for her, and cold sweat poured down her back.

"Betsie, here now. Now!" The dog obediently turned around, and Mel dared to breathe. She stayed where she was, unable to move.

Eddie hid the bike in a hedge and went back for Mel. It had snagged on a branch and nearly fallen on top of him. The exhaust slammed against his leg, scalding him, and he cried out in pain. The leather seats reeked of Vincent, and he could almost hear him laughing at him. His arms hurt from trying to control the bike. The burn throbbed as he hobbled away.

Eddie didn't speak as he led Mel to the bike. She had seen the chase and could only guess at how close he had been to getting caught. It was a long walk, and at last, he pulled into a lane walled in by bramble.

"In there," Eddie mumbled.

He gestured with his head and uncovered the branches he had used to conceal it. Shining in the moonlight, the bike looked almost defiant. Mel helped him pull it out to the road.

"I can do this on my own."

Again, she grabbed his arm. "Let's get it done."

CHAPTER 33

Clambering on the back, she could feel the malevolent power of the bike. It tossed them both sideways as they careered down the road. Eddie had told her to hold on to the handles underneath, but it felt unsafe. The bike was too big for Eddie, and he was inexperienced. Several times, they nearly fell, but they carried on. At last, they were almost at the Ellis family home.

Neither spoke as they walked up the path and knocked on the bungalow door. After what seemed like an hour, there was rustling inside, and a voice called out.

"Yit...what you want?" A small compact woman opened the door. Her face, lined and darkened by the sun, was framed by a severe grey ponytail. Eddie looked behind her for the twins. "What you want?" Her voice cold and accusing.

Eddie managed to croak, "Tina."

Shouting for her sons, Thomas and Jim, she opened the door and gestured for Eddie and Mel to come in, instructing them to stand.

In the light, her skin took on a granite colour, and ancient acne scars weathered her face. Mel was reminded of a piece of lava, a souvenir from a school trip to Mount Etna. Forgotten, it had lain on her windowsill craggy, hard and pocketed with holes. Mel jolted herself back to the present. Eddie was unbearably white, the silence overwhelming.

Eventually, the boys arrived. The thinner one looked them up and down.

"Tina?" asked Eddie.

"She's all right."

"How do I know?"

The snarling lava spoke. "My boy told you, she hint come to no harm."

Jim spoke again. "Got my money?"

Eddie pulled out the bike keyring, with its grotesque skull design, and waved it in the air.

"That's Vince's bike. He always had the best one. That's a Norton...kept it good." Jim snatched the keys from his hand.

"That's a start, boy."

"But it's worth…."

"Loads of them drugs were ruined, so this is just a dent. We need more money. Two grand should settle it."

The silent twin pushed them towards the door. He was muscular and dwarfed Eddie.

"I want to see Tina...." Eddie was pleading.

Old Mrs Ellis laughed. "When my boys git what's owed, then you get to see her."

Mel tried to plead with them but was told in no uncertain terms.

"Fuck off!"

They found themselves outside the door. Eddie looked at Mel, and he looked tired.

"I don't know what to do," he said simply.

Exhausted, they began the slow walk home. It took them a good half an hour, and when they got back to the guesthouse, Pauline and Clive were waiting outside.

"I know you're worried about Tina. Please don't come back so late."

Eddie mumbled an apology, and then he was gone. Pauline put her shawl around Mel's shoulders.

"Let's git you home."

Mel was so tired she merely followed.

***

Tina wasn't sure when she realised she wasn't allowed to leave.

She had been running from Eddie and Mel when she heard a beep and a voice shout, "Need a lift?"

Grateful, she had climbed into the van without thinking and, as they drove away, the distance made her anxiety begin to slip away. She had welcomed the numbness. One of the boys had spoken.

"Got some pear drops in there."

She caught sight of her eyes in the chrome around the glove compartment. Her face was streaked with dark kohl, her eyes raw from crying. Trying to wipe her face with her sleeve, she realised it was useless. She found a crumpled paper bag and offered her rescuers a sweet. They each took one, and then no one spoke. Looking out the window, they bumped their way out of Sealtdock along the barren roads flanked by snaking tributaries. Tina shut her eyes and helped herself to another sweet. The sugar cut her tongue, but it gave her a shot of energy.

Later, she was led to an immaculate caravan with a beautifully made bed. She had dropped into it. The crisp white sheet felt delicious against her clammy body. She couldn't take in her surroundings. There was no room for thought. She just needed to sleep.

***

She was woken by a knock on the door. The short, stocky one had brought her breakfast on a flowery 1960s tray. His rough fingers looked bizarre against the delicate pink roses, and he had almost blushed.

"Got you cornflakes. Put some Frosties on them, too. That's my favourite."

The milk was in a little white jug, and he placed the tray down and left. Tina greedily ate the cereal and sat back on the bed. The caravan was nothing like the one she and Mel had lived in. It had clean, blue curtains adorning each window with proper tiebacks. There was a little kitchenette area, a television, and another room she assumed was a toilet. The cupboards housed various jeans and T-shirts and a large winter coat. She guessed it belonged to one of the boys. A music player sat on the side, and piled neatly, on either side, were numerous tapes. Each one had a beautiful handwritten label. She knew they would be heavy metal without even looking at them. It struck her that there were no knickknacks. After Mrs Wilbraham's house, she had got used to disorder, everything crammed together, every space filled. The caravan was also incredibly clean.

The door to the caravan had been kept locked. Thomas had almost apologised, but Jim had enjoyed telling her who they were and what they would do.

"You don't leave. If you do, you'll find out."

Numbed by everything that happened, she just lay down and watched the sky out of the window. Where would she run to? At least here, she was fed. If any anxious thoughts entered her head, she merely pushed them down. Strangely she felt safe.

CHAPTER 34

When Eddie had sat Mrs Wilbraham down in the lounge, she had sensed something was wrong. He had the same eyes as he had when Vincent died. She wanted to hold him and tell him everything would be fine, but panic had seared through her. It was all she could do to listen.

His face had an identical frantic expression as that night. She had chastised herself that they had all looked to her for answers, and she had enjoyed it. Since Doug had died, she had existed in a mist of anger that had eventually turned to aching grief. The rest of the world had not mattered, and she had blocked it out with alcohol and marijuana. The three children had forced her to make decisions, and she had felt exhilarated by the adventure. Again, she was struck by how selfish that sounded, but it was the truth. It had been so unexpected: the knock on the door, the petrified boy, unable to plan, acting on the spur of the moment. Now she was faced with real danger, something she could not fix in a moment of inspiration.

He blurted out how they said some of the drugs had been ruined with the paint and they were demanding another two thousand pounds. He went on to tell her that he had tried to settle the debt with Vince's bike.

"But they said it weren't enough. How can I ever pay them off?"

"Eddie, we need to tell the police." She hoped her voice sounded reassuring and calm, but she knew it betrayed her.

"No!" He had almost screamed. "They know so many people. If they go to prison, they will just get one of their family to sort us out. Tina won't be safe. Ever!"

Mrs Wilbraham thought of the hysterical girl cowering in the caravan. She had seemed so young, so vulnerable, and much as she wanted to pass the responsibility to the police, she was no fool. Black rings framed Eddie's eyes, and he looked like he might faint. She felt an overwhelming tenderness towards him. Grabbing his shoulders, she looked him straight in the face.

"We will sort this mess out. Have faith." She wasn't sure where that word had come from, but it seemed to appease the frightened boy. He nodded and walked slowly away. Lying down on the sofa, he was asleep within seconds.

Mrs Wilbraham paced the house, trying to think. The Ellis family were notorious around this part of the world. She had never been frightened by people—had sent complaining neighbours away and told numerous carers to fuck off. This was different now. There were other people involved. People she realised she cared about. In a sudden moment of clarity, she knew what she must do. Taking the old key from its velvet nest, she walked up the stairs towards the forbidden door, and with trembling hands, she turned the lock.

The door dislodged a pile of dust as it creaked open, which flew from the mantle and into her eyes. Cobwebs shrouded her face and hair as she ventured inside. The ancient bulb no longer worked, and the only light was from a small triangular gap at the top of the curtains. Doug's artwork stood draped in cloths resembling tombstones. Despite the protective canvas, the curtains were drawn and layered with grime. Dust filled her throat, but that was not the reason she couldn't breathe. She tentatively pulled back one of the corners of the covering. A nude figure lay stretched out on a chaise longue. It was her. She traced the confident brush stroke with her hand. She could almost feel him. The memory of him playfully flicking paint at her took her by surprise. Slowly, she uncovered the rest of the painting and stood back to admire it. Blinking, she drew back the curtain letting in the last of the evening's light. It still felt dark, and the figure took on an almost ghostly pallor. It unnerved her. She felt like she was trespassing.

She pulled more and more of the cloths away, revealing painting after painting. She had forgotten just how talented Doug was. Each picture took her back to another time. Many of the pictures were of her brushing her hair or simply laughing. She found herself smiling with the young woman before her. They had played and painted and loved all in these canvases. Pulling the blackened material away, she suddenly stopped. There, nestled among the pictures, a self-portrait, unfinished, rough, but unmistakably him. She wasn't sure how long she had stared at the picture.

Almost lifelike, it was as if he was in the room with her. The light continued to dim, and with it, Doug's features. It reminded her of that night when she had found him on the bed. They said it was quick, a brain aneurism. Meaningless words from doctors. She didn't care what caused it—he was dead.

At first, she had kept his pictures around the house. But they were too painful. Slowly each one had been placed in this room, lovingly draped in cloths, to protect them. She had taken particular care of the self-portrait as if she was tucking him up in bed.

"Old fool."

She berated herself with the memory. On that day, she vowed she would never sell them. Apart from the leak, when Eddie's mother had helped her look to see the potential damage, she had never set foot in this room. A designated shrine, it had just proved to be a point of pain. Until this day, she had never looked at them. Again, she felt the need to look away. Tiptoeing around each one, the room reminded her of a morgue, and it was no fitting epitaph. Tears ran down her face as she circled the pictures, each one piercing her with memories: he was holding her hand, pouring her another glass of Vermouth, laughing about upsetting the neighbours.

She wasn't sure how long she stood there, but at last, it was pitch black. She sank to the floor, breathing him in, but the dust was too much, and she needed water. She laughed at herself. Doug would have poured a real drink. Strangely, she didn't want one. Looking in the hall mirror, she picked the cobwebs from her hair. She realised how old she had become. Dust peppered her hair and clothes, but her eyes were bright. Straightening her dress and brushing it down the best she could, she knew what she had to do.

Eddie was asleep on the sofa while 'It's a Knockout' blared on the television in the background. Careful not to wake him, she gently lifted the key to his van and walked outside.

CHAPTER 35

Pain seared through her arthritic hip as she pulled herself up into the driver's seat. It seemed so enormous. Fiddling with the levers, she eventually managed to reach the pedals. The handles were heavy and stiff, but eventually, she was satisfied. She had stridden out with such conviction, but each delay chipped away at her confidence. With both hands, she grabbed the gear stick and forced it into first gear.

At last, she was ready to start driving. The steering wheel pulled at her arms, and it was all she could do to manoeuvre it off the kerb. She hoped the over-revving did not wake Eddie. Switching on the lights, the van jolted up the road, narrowly missing a parked car.

When she got out of Sealtdock onto the open road, driving seemed easier. She hadn't got out of third gear as fourth was so impossibly stiff, and even though the roads were so bendy, she didn't care. Eddie had said they were out on the Ipswich road. It had been a long time since she had even left her house, and in the dark, everything seemed unfamiliar. At last, she came across a bungalow set back from the road with various vehicles surrounding it. Two white caravans loomed in the background. For a moment, she lost her nerve and then, remembering Eddie's face, she swung the door out and climbed out. Clutching the keys in her palm until it almost bled, she walked up to the door.

The door swung open by a small, wizened woman. Expecting the Ellis twins, she was momentarily knocked off-kilter. When she spoke, she knew she was in the right place.

"Two visitors in one night. What you want?" She smirked coldly.

The twins were instantly behind her, and she suddenly questioned her decision to come. Bravely Mrs Wilbraham ploughed on.

"I think you'll be interested in what I have to say."

The thin twin leant forward. "Hey, you got my money?"

Mrs Wilbraham looked at the boy before her. Wiry, without an inch of fat or muscle, with thinned hair and teenage-whispery stubble, it was hard to imagine he had terrorised Eddie. But it was his eyes that frightened her.

"I can get it." The room fell silent, and she realised this was her chance. "I have in my possession several valuable paintings. To the right dealer, they would be worth many thousands of pounds."

"Pictures hint worth nothing to us…difficult to shift." Mrs Wilbraham looked at the boy; he was laughing at her.

"They...."

But he didn't let her finish. "Get out. We don't need some crap pictures...that's nothing." He grabbed her arm with his bony fingers and began to push her toward the door. She threw off his hand and shouted into his face.

"Nothing! Nothing! You, boy, have no idea." The other twin, silent until now, sensed trouble and stood next to his brother, bristling in the charged atmosphere. Mrs Wilbraham continued to shout. "Doug was the most talented artist you have ever seen. They are not trinkets. Each one is a treasured possession." Jim went to speak but was shouted down. "This is not some poor stolen dog or a load of knock-off tellies. This is art, and it means everything to me."

She had momentarily forgotten where she was. The boys were unsure how to tackle this feisty, ancient woman. They were used to people cowering and pleading, but she was defiant. A frail, tiny woman in their own home, insulting them. They looked to their mother for help.

"You think you can take what you want. It's all I have left." Then just as unexpectedly, she began to cry.

Mrs Ellis looked at the boys and waved them away. "Git her a glass of water." She watched as the older woman gulped it down. Her eyes were red and defiant.

"Don't think I offer these lightly."

Mrs Ellis took down a photo of a man from the mantelpiece. He had black hair smoothed down with Brylcreem, and he was smiling at the camera.

"That's my Tommy…married over fifty years. Got my boys, even named one after him, but it hint the same."

Mrs Wilbraham looked at the man in the photograph. The silver frame had been lovingly polished and preserved. He was a handsome man. With a strong jawbone, his crooked nose gave a hint of the life he had led.

"Only photo I got of him." Mrs Ellis smiled. "When you're young, you don't think, do you? Too busy living." Mrs Wilbraham nodded. "He was a boxer in his day. A good one too. Could kill a man with his hands, never did. He knew when to stop." She shot a pointed look at her sons and then at the posh woman before her. "Not the life you would recognise, but in his way, he was a good man."

Mrs Wilbraham looked around the room and realised how ridiculous she had been. She had come here with a plan. They would understand the value of the painting and be prepared to wait for her to sell them. What was she thinking? They would sell them at a car boot sale for peanuts, and the debt would never be paid. Mrs Wilbraham launched into a last-ditch effort to convince them.

"If I sold the paintings, I could get a much better price. I could prove provenance. Where they come from. They would command a much higher price."

The old woman wasn't listening. She was looking at the photograph. "All I got."

Mrs Wilbraham studied her. In many ways, she wasn't that different to herself. "I could paint him," she mumbled. The other woman looked up. "I was considered a good artist in my time. I could paint him...a large canvas." Mrs Ellis looked up and smiled. She gestured to the area over the fireplace.

"How big?" It seemed such a ridiculous question.

"As you want." The twins came into the room and flanked their mother. She waved them away. "We got business to conclude."

"I can start straight away. But I need…."

"Just tell my boys what. They'll get it."

Mrs Wilbraham began to reel off a list. "Paint, brushes, canvases and…" she looked straight at the scowling boy, "a bloody big bottle of Vermouth."

Within minutes she was sat bouncing down the road in a white van. The silent twin was driving and stared straight ahead. Strangely, she didn't mind him. It was the weedy one that frightened her.

"I'll give you directions...."

"We know where you live." The words shocked her. Of course, they did. Eddie had been terrified and no wonder. She stared out of the window until they reached her house.

Eddie stood in front of her as the Ellis boys accompanied Mrs Wilbraham into her house.

“It’s ok. I’ll explain later.”

Eddie did not look convinced, but there was nothing he could do. Mrs Wilbraham held his hand as she barked instructions at the pair. It all seemed so surreal, but she had seen a path out of this disaster, and she was going to take it. Eddie squeezed her hand.

“I’m coming with you.”

“No, you hint,” Jim snarled.

“Don’t worry, Eddie. I’ll be back.”

With that, the provisions were dumped in the van, and they bolted back up the road to the bungalow. Eddie watched from the window as they disappeared. Not sure whether to follow, he realised his van had gone.

Once back, Mrs Wilbraham sank into a dusty armchair. She momentarily felt scared. What if she didn’t like her work? What if it was all for nothing? She hadn’t even agreed to let her sell Doug’s work. It was nearly morning, and she was tired. She stood up. No, this was going to work. It had to.

Mrs Ellis came in with a bottle of brandy. She took out two beautiful Waterford crystal glasses and poured them both a drink.

“Reckon if you’re to paint Tommy…I want you to know what he was like.”

Mrs Wilbraham was touched by the hard woman in

front of her. Her loss was as raw as her own. She was also surprised. A painting was so much more than a physical resemblance. She needed to get the essence of the man on the canvas. Strangely this tough woman had understood that.

The light began to seep through the curtains and the two women talked into the night. She learnt about how they had met. How dangerous Tommy had seemed and how he had been so tender with her. His deep laugh and quick wit.

Mrs Wilbraham found herself sharing memories of Doug. "Brought out the devil in each other. Anything seemed possible."

She made Mrs Ellis laugh with tales of their drunken antics. The boys lurked in the background but being excluded, they melted away. The brandy fired her stomach and Mrs Wilbraham found she was talking more freely than she had for years.

After a couple of hours, Mrs Ellis spoke about the day Tommy had died, a road accident.

"He was rushing to get home," her voice broke, "hint seen him for a few days."

She recognised the aching, the pain, and saw that she was crying. Mrs Wilbraham told her about the day she had found Doug.

"Never told anyone that. Can't believe it was ten years ago."

They sat in silence for several minutes. The bottle was all but empty and they were both exhausted.

"Reckon I'm knackered. You could start on the picture ammorra." Mrs Wilbraham nodded. "Lie on the settee...I'll git you a blanket."

Mrs Wilbraham rested her head on the cushion and was immediately asleep. Mrs Ellis watched her from the door. It has been a long and unexpected night.

***

As the last light in the house switched off, Aidy got out of his car. He had been driving around trying to find Tina and had noticed the ice cream van on the kerb. He had watched from afar as the boys had taken the old woman back to the house and followed them back. Convinced Tina was there, he climbed over the fence. Hiding in the shadows, he eventually reached the caravans.

CHAPTER 36

Tina watched Mrs Wilbraham appear. She had wanted to bang on the window but was scared of Jim. He had told her what would happen if she tried to run. Anxiously, she had heard Mrs Wilbraham shouting, unable to make out the words. Her mind raced. She was even more confused when they brought Mrs Wilbraham back. She lay on the bed clutching the pillow. Despite the quiet, she couldn't sleep.

There was a scratch at the window. Immediately she thought that Eddie had come to find her. She dashed over and pulled back the curtain only to see Aidy standing in the morning light. He looked almost demonic.

"You git out here now, gal." Tina threw herself on her bed. He continued to rage outside when Jim was suddenly beside him. They were circling each other.

"Who the fuck are you, boy?"

He looked Jim up and down. Aidy was so much larger and muscular; he wasn't a threat.

"Never mind that, you get that gal...she's mine. I'm taking her home."

"No, that hint going to happen."

"You and whose pikey army?"

Aidy laughed and stepped closer, towering over the younger man. Suddenly, he felt the air leave his lungs as he was grabbed from behind and hurled onto the ground. Dazed, he tried to stand up, but Jim booted him in the side, and he fell back down. Thomas stood over Aidy and gestured towards Tina.

"She don't belong to you."

Aidy stood up. He was physically shaken. "I'll leave."

Jim smiled at his brother. "I don't think we can allow that."

They grabbed him by his arms and hauled him away. Tina stared after them, and Thomas caught her eye and nodded. She hoped they would just beat him up and then let him go. Part of her felt ashamed that she had wanted him hurt. For so long, he had terrorised her, but it hadn't felt pleasurable. She just felt numb. Lying back down on the bed, she clutched the pillow and prayed that Mrs Wilbraham was ok.

***

For two solid days, Mrs Wilbraham worked on the painting. The boys had brought her food, but she had only nibbled at it. At first, she had faltered, unsure of her skills, but, with time, she relaxed into the picture. She felt the power in her arthritic fingers as she sketched the man before her. Mrs Ellis had asked if she could peek but then changed her mind.

"I know you artistic types don't like to be disturbed."

Mrs Wilbraham had been grateful for the quiet. She agonised whether she should draw just a conventional picture, but she wasn't a seaside portrait painter. This had to be special. She wanted to express the power of the man, and she found herself using strong brush strokes. Despite being lined with age, his face had mischief to it, and she tried to capture it the best she could. The eyes she found the hardest. Studying the picture, they appeared warm and amused. Yes, whatever those Ellis boys had done, their mother deserved her all. For hours she worked without a break. The paint almost came alive on the canvas, and she wondered why she had stayed away for so long.

At last, it was done. She fiddled with the hair and background but instinctively knew when to stop. Doug had always said that was the sign of a good artist. She smiled at the memory.

Sinking into the chair, she poured herself a drink. It burnt her stomach and she realised she was ravenous. Silently she studied the painting and began to panic. Mrs Ellis was no art critic, and she might not appreciate it. It was too late to worry. She was too exhausted to do any more.

The twins came into the room and sat looking at her. "Done it yet?"

She nodded that she had. "Can you get your mother?"

Fear suddenly surged in her chest. Tom went off to find her and Jim continued to glare at Mrs Wilbraham. His mouth twisted into a grin.

"Hope she likes it." He smirked, as if reading her mind.

Mrs Ellis walked slowly into the room. She waved the boys away, took a deep breath, and walked toward the painting.

She spent an age studying the picture and said nothing. Mrs Wilbraham watched her, convinced that she hated it. Finally, she spoke.

"Reckon you got 'im good." The words took a moment to sink in. "Yit, you got him." The relief nearly floored her, and she had to steady herself against the chair arm. "That's like he's here in the room with me…I hint no art expert, but I can see him." She went to touch his arm, but Mrs Wilbraham stopped her.

"Paint isn't dry."

"Oh, no...he just looks so real."

Over a mug of tea and another brandy, Mrs Wilbraham brought up the matter of the paintings. She explained that, even if it took six months, she would get a high price.

"I know you're a businesswoman...."

Mrs Ellis seemed to understand, and they shook hands on two thousand pounds. Mrs Wilbraham looked at the stocky woman. They weren't friends, but there was a strange bond between them. She took a deep breath.

"Got a favour to ask. Aidy…Tina's stepfather, terrible man. If I give you another £1000, could you scare him off? I know Jim roughed him up a bit but maybe this time break a rib or something. If he was out of the picture Tina...."

Mrs Ellis smiled. "You hint that different to us, you know." She patted Mrs Wilbraham's hand and cast a quick look at her sons. "That's one you can have for free."

CHAPTER 37

The twins had driven Mrs Wilbraham and Tina back to her house. Eddie and Mel had almost cried with relief. The next few hours had shot by, as the police were informed, and various professionals had come to the house.

Pauline and Clive held hands and leaned against the wall. Alice watched as her daughter said her goodbyes.

Mel grabbed Tina's arm. "You ok?" Tina nodded. She glanced back and saw that her mother was talking to the social worker.

"Guess I'm about ready to go," said Mel. Tina suddenly hugged her. "You take care."

"You too," said Tina.

"Not going to London, going to stay with my aunty and uncle. Reckon you were right all along...and my mum."

Tina smiled. “Had some fun.”

“Well, some....” They laughed. Mel hugged her again.

Mrs Wilbraham came bounding over and enveloped Mel in her large black cardigan. It was the first time she had shown any physical affection and Mel was slightly taken aback. Suddenly Mrs Wilbraham grabbed her by the shoulders and said solemnly.

“You go, Mel, leave Sealtdock and don’t you dare come back. Don’t you look back.” Mel nodded. She felt she understood what the older woman was trying to say. “I’ll look after Eddie and Tina. Got your whole life to live, and that’s an order.”

“I will.” They both knew it was time for her to go. “I’ll miss you.”

Mrs Wilbraham smiled. She held her hand and then let it drop. “Don’t you look back.” With that, she turned and walked away.

Mel found herself staring at Eddie. He was leaning against the wall, watching. She grabbed his arm.

“It’s ok, Mel. I know you have to go.”

“But….”

“It’s ok.”

“I’ll miss you...write to me.” They promised but knew it was goodbye. Eddie brushed the hair out of her eyes.

"You going back to school?" Eddie asked.

"Not my old one. Going to go to the local comprehensive, Tina's old school. Not that she ever went."

"Be ok?"

"Yeah, I'll be fine." She said the words with conviction and meant it.

The door of the old Morris Minor clicked shut. It smelt of white bread and tea. Mel suddenly felt starving. As if reading her mind, Pauline passed her a fish paste sandwich. Gobbling it down reminded her of the first time they had broken into the caravan and eaten the food they had found in the boot.

"Can we just go and look at the caravan site? Don't know why, just want to see it one last time."

The old caravan looked forlorn and surprisingly small. The door was almost hanging off its hinges, and despite their gallant effort to scrub it clean, it still retained much of the green algae around the windows and roof seal.

Clive looked over his shoulder. "Ready?"

Mel managed a smile. "As I'll ever be."

Her mother sat in the back with her and patted her knee. Pauline had devised some ingenious bag over the back of the seat and whatever was inside rubbed her leg. She fumbled within and found an old book—an encyclopaedia. Inside was filled with the most beautiful pictures of wild birds. Mel ran her hand over it.

"Can I give this to Eddie…he loves birds?"

"Ask your aunty. It's hers."

"If he loves birds, then he is a kindred soul. He must have it."

"Wait!" Clive rummaged in the glove compartment and pulled out an old pair of binoculars in a brown leather case. "Give him these too."

They drove back to Mrs Wilbraham's house. Tina and Eddie were about to head out in the old van when Mel jumped out of the car and ran towards Eddie.

"Hold up." She had only just caught him. "Got this for you." He opened the book and leafed through the pages running his hands over the artwork. He looked like he might cry.

"Oh, Mel...it's beautiful."

She placed the binoculars around his neck. "Now you can catch that boom boom one."

He laughed and held her hands. "Mrs W's going to teach me to paint. I'm going to art college."

"Brilliant!"

"Might need to get some qualifications, but she's looked into that. I can go to the local tech, then apply to the art college."

"Might need to cut your hair and become a New Romantic." He pulled a face. "And get a braid." She flicked her plaited tail at him.

"Don't want to go that bloody bad." She playfully slapped him. They embraced for the last time. "Bye." He let go of her hand, and she walked away. "Wait." Eddie pulled out the crumbled picture of Mel he had in his back pocket.

She took it and handed it back. "Don't forget me." She walked towards the car. Passing the ice cream van, Tina was getting ready to jump in the back.

"Get any trouble off those girls at school, tell them to fuck off," Tina shouted.

"Or twat them?" Mel shouted back.

"That too."

Mel got back in the car, and they drove away.

Alice reached over and clasped her fingers. Her hand was small and slim, but her grasp was strong. They looked at each other and smiled. Mel took a deep breath as the car began the descent along the sea road and out of Sealtdock. They sat in a comfortable silence past the clock tower, the pet shop and Fatty Arbuckle's. The coastal road stretched before them and Mel stared straight ahead, remembering

Mrs Wilbraham's words. She felt a strange superstition about turning around and needed to be far away.

Suddenly they all fell forward as Clive sharply braked. "Goodness, that was a sharp bend."

Mel looked at the corner. It was unmistakably where the crash had been. The earth was rucked where the car had sped off the road and there was a makeshift shrine. A pile of denim jackets hung on a piece of wood. They were covered in a thin layer of dust which blew relentlessly, muting the colourful heavy metal sewn-on badges. The shrine looked like it had been there for years. A small dust devil moved across the landscape before disappearing into the earth.

CHAPTER 38

Mel happily accompanied her aunt to the summer fete. Usually, she would have scoffed at how parochial it was, but she was enjoying herself. Emma sat proudly on the tombola stand, smiling and loudly greeting everyone that passed. The prizes were more extravagant than normal—expensive jams and chutneys bought from a little boutique in Cambridge. Pauline noticed that the two bottles of quince wine she had contributed were hidden at the back, with the rest of the local wares.

Emma had been planning the fete for months. It was bigger and more professional than anything Trotham had seen before. She had sent the children to her mother's so she could give it her full attention. Her posse of followers surrounded her, cooing at how marvellous everything looked. Pauline nodded hello and made a beeline for Betty's table.

She was manning the crocheted lady toilet roll holder stand. Mel smiled at her mother as they viewed the rows of pink and white ladies. Pauline tapped Mel's arm.

"Think it's time we replaced Lady Grey. Cawd der hell, I reckon I got her before you were even born."

The old doll in the bathroom was frayed and bedraggled. Mel nodded and was given the job of choosing the replacement. She studied the rows of dolls dressed in pink, white and the occasional powder blue. The doll at the back had a broken eye which reminded her of the landlady in the pub that first night in Sealtdock. Betty leant over.

"That one's a bit bashed up, gal...choose another."

Mel had set her heart on it. Whoever had made it had also run out of pink wool and had used another colour to finish it off.

"She looks like she needs a home," said Mel.

Pauline smiled and paid Betty twenty pence. Mel was now enjoying herself. Clive winked at her as Pauline spotted a line of her homemade wine at the next stall. Alice ate a toffee apple and watched the locals play Kick the Bucket in the pub's beer garden. Over the noisy crowd, Clive explained it was an ancient Suffolk game, but there were variations of it worldwide.

Maureen ran over to Pauline and embraced her. She looked taller somehow and squeezed her hand.

"Weren't sure you was going to come...you know Alan

will be here," Pauline whispered. "Emma will make sure of that."

They glanced over at the tombola. Emma was surrounded by her cronies, all dressed identically in their polka dot shirts and immaculate hairdos. Alan stood behind them, looking bored. He ran his fingers through his hair, flicking it into place. Maureen grasped Pauline's hand. She felt an overwhelming wave of revulsion.

"Such a fool, Paul."

Pauline looked at Emma, rearranging her prizes. "Poor cow, stuck with that."

Maureen tried to smile but felt ground down. Suddenly a hand was on her shoulder and made her jump.

"Did those old cucumbers do the trick?" She looked up to see Eric Cracknel smiling before her. He had shaved, and as he lifted his cap, his head shone like a conker.

Maureen smiled. "Yes, that done a good job. Thank you."

"Good, good, grew them on my allotment." He took a deep breath. "Perhaps you're like to come up and see them." A flush of colour ran up his face and sweat ran into his eyes.

"Do you always invite ladies to look at your cucumbers?" He felt his neck tighten in embarrassment. Maureen smiled. "Love to see your allotment, and then, maybe, we could go to the pub for a drink?"

Eric managed to stutter some words about calling her and looking forward to it. He bounded away, grinning. Maureen waved at Pauline and, taking a deep breath, strode up to the tombola.

Mel wasn't sure what happened next. Maureen had bought a ticket for the tombola and won a rather pathetic packet of Bassett Wine Gums.

Passing her the sweets, Alan had leant over, with his oily smile, and whispered. "Cake and the tarts are over there. I suggest you go and join them."

When she spoke about it later, Maureen said she just snapped. She slapped him so hard he fell on the revolving tombola barrel, smashing the expensive glass jars of pickled fruits and jams. Their contents spewed over his expensive chino slacks, and he fell awkwardly on the glass shards littering the grass.

"You bitch...I'm bleeding."

Watching from the side, Eric thought for a moment that Alan might hit Maureen and dashed across to stand between them. Emma, stunned, turned toward her husband. Maureen stood magnificently above him, legs apart, hands on her hips.

"You, Alan Lucas, are a nasty piece of work."

Emma leant over her husband. She knew that it must be something momentous to make the woman react so violently. Unsure what to think, she began clucking over his bleeding hands, glaring at Maureen.

"What the fu...."

"Had so many women, I bet he's diseased," Maureen spat.

Emma let the words drop. She had always suspected—the late nights, endless overtime and receipts for dinners. On the one occasion she had questioned him, he had insisted it was a council function. He had punished her by ignoring her for a day, as 'trust' was so important in a marriage. He had lied, almost convincingly, and she had learnt to bury the doubt. Unsure what to do, Emma ran, followed by her entourage, while Alan scurried behind her.

"Emma, wait! Emma, please."

Later he would return home to find his clothes ripped and strewn along the road, and the word 'Fucker' scrawled along the side of his expensive car.

Back at the fete, Maureen almost buckled with adrenaline. She turned to Eric.

"S'pose you don't want to see me now?" He merely smiled and took her hand.

"Let's give that ole allotment a miss. Reckon you could do with that drink now."

Mel marvelled at how quickly the fete returned to normal. Slowly the silence was broken by nervous grins and then conversations. Alice smiled at Mel. She had known about the affair and said nothing. She was a good girl. Children ran around, and the game of Kick the Bucket continued uproariously. Pauline busied herself cleaning up the broken pots and managed to salvage some jars. She wiped the chutney and jam off them with her sleeve. To her delight, they were intact. Stoically lifting the tombola, she stood behind it and declared.

"Open for business."

Clive smiled at his wife. "Your rightful place."

Clutching her wonky doll, Mel wandered around the fete. Her mother bought her some lemonade, and they rummaged on the white elephant stand. She was struck by how happy she was.

CHAPTER 39

Despite the soaring temperatures, Pauline was in the kitchen, making a bread-and-butter pudding.

"Mel gal, can you get some ole milk? Money's on the side."

On the way to the shops, Mel passed the gang of bikers. In the heat, they had lost their leather jackets but were still sweltering in their black heavy metal T-shirts. One of them gestured to Mel.

"You're that girl what run away. Hint ya?"

Mel slowly nodded. "Yes."

"Going back to London, are ya?"

"No, local comprehensive."

A new leader had filled the abyss left by Tina. She thrust her face close to Mel.

"Watch it," she hissed, "new girl."

Mel pushed her hard in the chest and shouted, "No, you fucking watch it."

The new top dog fell backwards and looked to her pack for help. They merely parted, letting Mel walk through the middle of them.

"You'd better watch it, new girl...."

The words bounced off her making her laugh. Tina would be proud of her. She repeated the words to herself, '*new girl*'.

ACKNOWLEDGEMENTS

Thanks to everyone on the TAUK Publishing team, especially Estelle. Her support, encouragement and hilarious sense of humour made this book possible. Thanks also to the talented Michelle, who took the time to understand the cover I wanted.

Aside from my family, a special thank you must go to Monica, who made me dust off the draft and gave me the kick I needed. Astrid, you took the time to read my manuscript and gave me the confidence to realise it resonated with a younger age group.

Ann, you deserve an acknowledgement for not being a yes person, I didn't like it at the time, but you made me change the ending for the better.

Wayne and Jennifer also helped me greatly by reading the book and giving me the push I needed to get it published. I must also thank the local Loughborough McDonalds who filled me with coffee while I sat ridiculously early in the morning tapping away.

ABOUT THE AUTHOR

Having grown up in rural Suffolk, Andrea has a real affinity with the area's people, accent, history and extraordinary scenery.

Andrea has a strong sense of social justice. Having worked as both a social worker and probation officer, she is uniquely placed to capture the people who, in other circumstances, would have thrived.

Nostalgic for the 1980s, Andrea is intrigued by the last generation whose curfew was dictated by streetlights and smoking was allowed in pubs. She enjoys bringing this alive throughout her book.

Andrea, who has since moved away from Suffolk, now lives happily with her partner and children. Having published this debut novel, she hopes to continue writing books with inspiring stories and resonating characters.

Follow Andrea:

Facebook: @throwingsaltatthedevilauthor
Twitter: @BooksMoulding

Printed in Great Britain
by Amazon

87392964R00214